A Season of Change

Other Books by Lynette Sowell

Quilts of Love Series
Tempest's Course

Seasons in Pinecraft Series
A Season of Change
A Path Made Plain (Fall 2014)
A Promise of Grace (Spring 2015)

A Season of Change

Seasons in Pinecraft Series, Book 1

Lynette Sowell

A Season of Change

ISBN-13: 978-1-4267-5355-8

Published by Abingdon Press, P.O. Box 801, Nashville, TN 37202

www.abingdonpress.com

Published in association with the MacGregor Literary Agency.

The persons and events portrayed in this work of fiction are the creations of the author, and any resemblance to persons living or dead is purely coincidental.

Library of Congress Cataloging-in-Publication Data

Sowell, Lynette.
A Season of Change / Lynette Sowell.
pages cm. — (Seasons in Pinecraft Series ; 1)
ISBN 978-1-4267-5355-8 (trade pbk., adhesive : alk. paper)
1. Amish—Fiction. 2. Christian fiction. 3. Love stories. I. Title.
PS3619.O965S43 2014
813'.6—dc23

2014009990

Printed in the United States of America

1 2 3 4 5 6 7 8 9 10 / 19 18 17 16 15 14

For C.J. with love,
because you always make me feel
like I've just come home.

Acknowledgments

With many, many thanks to my friends, Sherry Gore and Katie Troyer, for answering my many questions and welcoming me into your village and your worlds. If I get anything "wrong" about Pinecraft and its Plain people, the error is unintentional, my own, and not yours. Pinecraft felt like a home away from home as I walked and bicycled its sunny streets, and I think of the village fondly and often.

There's a season for everything
and a time for every matter under the heavens.
Ecclesiastes 3:1 CEB

1

"We're having ice cream at Christmas time, *Daed*?" Zeke Miller trotted alongside his father on the pavement, trying to keep up with Jacob's pace. The boy would definitely sleep well tonight; he'd barely stopped since he'd gotten off the Pioneer Trails bus and tumbled into the Florida sunshine.

"Yes, we are. It's hard to imagine, isn't it? We're definitely a long way from home." Jacob rubbed the top of his son's head. At only five, Zeke didn't comprehend the idea of ice cream in winter. His sister, Rebecca, a dozen paces ahead of them, pranced alongside her cousins. The sound of the children's giggles drifted on the air.

Jacob slowed his steps to match Zeke's five-year-old stride. Their figures made long shadows as they strode toward Big Olaf's Ice Cream Parlor. The December twilight came early, even in Sarasota.

To Jacob, the words "Christmas" and "ice cream" didn't belong in the same sentence. And he certainly never thought he would be entertaining the children's eager pleas to ride the bus to the *beach* on Christmas day. But, here they were, nestled in Sarasota's winter haven called Pinecraft.

"We're here, we're here!" Rebecca giggled, and stumbled. "*Ach.*" She stopped long enough to stick her foot back into the pink plastic flip-flops, a gift from her cousin Maybelle.

Jacob shook his head over his daughter wearing the sandals, but a smile tugged at the corners of his mouth anyway. As soon as they'd all climbed off the immense travel bus and stepped onto the parking lot of Pinecraft's Mennonite Tourist Church, the surroundings seemed to draw them in. The children burst with energy after being stuck on a bus for two days, save for a stop here and there to stretch their legs or pick up more passengers. The more distance between Ohio, the more passengers on the bus.

At first the novelty of riding on a mechanized vehicle had the children enthralled with the speed they traveled and the levers that brought the seats forward and backward, but eventually even Rebecca fidgeted and squirmed in her seat. Bored, as all the children soon became.

Jacob sympathized, but instead of running like a child would, he stared at his surroundings, the rows of homes both large and small, the orange and grapefruit trees in front yards. And the palm trees, of course.

He'd never had the opportunity to visit Florida, even after his grandparents bought a home here in Pinecraft. He hadn't seen the practicality of cramming himself on a bus and traveling hundreds of miles only to do the same two weeks later. Finally, however, desperation had won out over practicality.

He'd only seen photos of palm trees, only heard about members of his Order using tricycles for transportation instead of horse and buggy. No room for horses in a city. His own grandfather rode an adult-size tricycle with a large basket, peddling fruit for sale to tourists.

Zeke's grin lit his face and he pulled his hand from Jacob's grasp, trotted ahead to catch up with his sister and cousins.

Here, hundreds of miles from Ohio's fields and the cabinet factory where Jacob worked, his children laughed like they hadn't in six months. This made him smile, too, though his heart still hurt.

Hannah, gone so soon. When they were younger, they'd exchanged glances across the room on Sundays until he found the nerve to talk to her at a singing. Then they married when he was but twenty-three and she eighteen. They'd both vowed to embrace their Order and planned to be married as long as the Lord allowed. Which had turned out to be a mere eight years.

Hannah's third pregnancy had been much harder than the first two, and even modern technology hadn't saved her when the midwife urged him to allow the *Englisch* physicians to stabilize her at an *Englisch* hospital. The *boppli*, another son they'd named Samuel, had come too early. No one could have warned Jacob how difficult it was to carry a double load of grief. Their days together were finished on this earth, but Jacob found himself asking, *Why?*

He caught sight of his brother waiting for him at the sidewalk's edge. "The Yoders are arriving on the last bus before Christmas," Ephraim said.

The loaded statement snapped Jacob out of his pondering. A good thing. He was moving on, as he should. But he could still feel the emptiness in his bed every night Hannah wasn't there. Even though *Mammi* had given him the twin air mattress to sleep on while visiting in Florida, Jacob's memories and the children's chatter in the living room kept him awake at night. In his grandparents' snug home, filled with Millers in every nook and cranny, Jacob's lone state set him apart.

"That's what *Daadi* said after supper tonight." Jacob knew where Ephraim's small talk was headed, straight to Betsy.

"Betsy Yoder is coming with her parents, too." Ephraim glanced his way. "She told Katie at our last Sunday meeting they'll be here just in time for Christmas."

"It will be nice to see her and her family." Jacob tugged on his suspenders. Not too much farther, and they'd be at the Bahia Vista stoplight. A hint of a chill drifted on the breeze, waving the fronds of a nearby palm tree.

"Nice? Is that all you can say, it'll be 'nice' to see Betsy?"

"She's a nice girl. Smart, pretty, and she bakes really *gut* pie. She'll make someone a *gut* wife someday. A little on the tall side, though." Jacob paused, and Ephraim did as well. "Happy now?"

"You need to talk to her, not just hang back in the corner like you're a mute."

"I'm not ready to talk to her. Not yet."

"Don't wait too long. She likes you, and she told Katie so. She's wondering why you keep staring at her and never saying anything."

"Like I said, I'm not ready. I don't know if I ever will be. I'm grateful to you and Katie for everything you've done for me, especially Katie helping with the children. I can do my own mending. Rebecca has become a good little housekeeper." Jacob felt his neck growing hotter with every footstep closer to the ice cream shop.

"I know that. And Katie and I are glad to help you. But it's time. Your children need a mother, and you a helpmate."

"Stop pushing me, Ephraim. I know what you're trying to say." Jacob continued the few steps to the street corner and the Bahia Vista stoplight. He didn't want the children to try to cross the busy street alone. They weren't used to watching out for traffic, not like this, anyway. They would make a few trips into town back in Ohio, but the town was far smaller than Sarasota and its infinite worldliness. The traffic, the constant reach of everything not-Plain into his Plain world. He didn't always understand how Plain people could live in the middle of it all. Life in Ohio felt much more in control.

Right. He almost laughed. Nothing had been in control since Hannah had left him. Left them all.

Ephraim kept silent, and Jacob knew he'd probably aggravated his brother.

God knew he'd accepted Hannah's death, and little Samuel's as well. The wounds inside him had scabbed over. Every so often, though, the pain would resurface and catch him when he wasn't paying attention, like the one time he'd cut his hand with a band saw when he was distracted at the cabinet shop. He couldn't help but pick at the scab as it healed.

He expelled a sigh before continuing. "Ephraim, I promise, after we leave Pinecraft, once we're home again, I'll go on. I don't know if it'll be with Betsy Yoder, but I'll think about it." Jacob figured he'd give his brother a shred of a promise. But he couldn't explain to Ephraim the restlessness he felt. His world was the same after losing Hannah and Samuel. His job at the cabinet factory, his home with the rooms Hannah had kept so spotless and filled with joy. Yet, his whole world had changed with the hole Hannah had left. If only an ice cream cone could help him forget his grief for a few minutes.

In sharp contrast to the tropical colors around them, their group stuck out like proverbial sore thumbs as they stood at the traffic lights and waited. Cars crisscrossed at the intersection. Big Olaf's ice cream parlor lay just across the street from them at the light.

Jacob sucked in a breath. He still hadn't grown accustomed to the traffic that zoomed through the heart of the Pinecraft neighborhood, and almost wished he had stayed back at the house with *Mammi* Rachel.

He wasn't scared of honking traffic, and ignored the pointing and stares as they crossed the street—tourists, *Mammi* assured him. The locals didn't mind the novelty of seeing the Amish and accepted the village as part of the city.

Jacob didn't want the children to see his reluctance to venture to the edge of the block. Everything in Florida was so . . . different from Ohio. Yes, different. That was the best word. But he could understand loving the scent of the ocean, the warmth during winter time when all far away to the north was quickly freezing over.

The children scurried into Big Olaf's and Jacob followed as they gathered at the ice cream shop counter, Zeke and Rebecca with their cousins, clutching their money as they decided what ice cream they wanted. True to form, Rebecca changed her mind at least three times before choosing her flavor. That would have earned her a gentle scolding from Hannah. The thought made Jacob smile.

"I thought you wanted a cone," Jacob said as Rebecca turned to face him with a dish of vanilla ice cream, covered with chocolate sauce and nuts.

"I did. But then I decided I wanted to take my time while I eat. You can't take your time eating ice cream cones, you know," she replied and grinned at him, the blue of her eyes matching the fading blue of the evening sky. Hannah's eyes.

Jacob tugged on one of her braids. "Truthful girl, you are."

They all turned to leave. Even Ephraim and Katie had ordered ice cream. But not for him. Jacob shared his son's disbelief at the idea of eating ice cream at Christmas. And walking in shirtsleeves to the corner ice cream shop.

They carefully crossed the road and began to meander back into the neighborhood and safety.

"I forgot a spoon!" Rebecca exclaimed and whirled back toward Big Olaf's. "I'll be right back."

"Mind the road," Jacob called out. "Wait, I'll walk with you." He strode back toward Rebecca and the corner.

"Oh, *Daed*, I'm not a baby. I can watch for the light and look for cars." Rebecca's long skirt swished a few inches above her ankles. Not too many years from now, she'd be putting her hair up under her prayer covering. Jacob wasn't ready for that.

Just six paces behind her, Jacob saw the light turn. Rebecca kept her focus on the ice cream in the dish and then glanced up at Big Olaf's across the street.

She stepped into the crosswalk. A dark sedan took the corner. Cars moved so, so quickly.

Jacob's throat clenched. He darted forward. "Rebecca!"

She froze and looked back at him, then at the car.

The thud wrenched a shout from Jacob.

Rebecca's scream stung his ears.

He reached the corner as Rebecca's dish of ice cream landed on the warm asphalt.

A compound femur fracture, a hematoma on the brain, a concussion. But no internal injuries. Jacob found one thing to be thankful for, besides the fact that Rebecca now breathed peacefully, sedated because of her injuries, in the intensive care unit.

How close they'd come to losing her two days ago.

The driver of the car, a young Mennonite woman returning home after visiting her grandparents, had dissolved into a heap on the pavement, sobbing upon leaving the driver's seat.

On Christmas break from college in Virginia, she'd borrowed her parents' vehicle and had been hurrying home to get ready for a date. She looked more *Englisch* than anything in her shorts, t-shirt, and flip-flops, but knew enough Dutch to speak to him and the family after the accident.

She hadn't seen Rebecca, who'd been walking with the light while the young woman turned. Children moved so quickly. The police weren't going to press charges. Jacob didn't think pressing charges would serve any purpose. This young woman deserved grace, and was suffering enough for one mistake.

Jacob sat up a little straighter in the cushioned chair in the intensive care unit. It had been his fault, really. He should have watched Rebecca more closely, should have kept her nearer to him, insisted she stop and wait for him to cross the street with her. He should have been firmer.

"She's always been the more willful one of your children," Ephraim observed.

"*Ach*, it's true. Hannah always knew . . ." Yes, Hannah had always known how to handle Rebecca. Gotte, *what am I going to do now?*

"You'll have to stay in Pinecraft, far longer than Christmas."

"A long time." But he had a job in Ohio, and had to support his family. Yet, he wouldn't leave his daughter. Not here. Not alone, her body broken and her brain swollen, although she'd be with family.

No, he would stay here in Sarasota, for as long as it took for Rebecca to get well again.

But Sarasota had turned out to be a far, far more dangerous place than he'd ever imagined. He had a nagging feeling Sarasota held more dangers for them still.

"Natalie, dear, I wish you'd change your mind and join us for Christmas dinner," said Grace Montgomery. "You shouldn't have eaten alone. Come for pie, or something."

Natalie Bennett held her cell phone close to her ear, but not too close. She stood in the lobby of Sarasota General Hospital.

"Too late, I'm already at the hospital. But thanks for inviting me." She tried not to smudge her clown makeup. She hadn't brought her emergency makeup kit to fix any damage to the face she'd taken great care to paint not quite an hour ago.

"At least come for dessert later, please?" Even over the phone, Grace's sound of longing and gentle insistence couldn't be missed.

"All right, I will." A few passersby glanced Natalie's way and smiled at her getup. "I forgot to give you and Todd your gift the other night at the office party."

"Sweetie, you didn't have to get us anything."

"I know. But I wanted to." She glanced around. "Hey, I'll call you later. People are probably wondering who Bubbles the Clown is talking to on the phone."

"Just come on over once you're through."

"You've got it. Merry Christmas." Natalie ended the call and slipped the phone into her tote bag, full of tricks and novelties for the children she'd soon visit. She also toted a mesh bag stuffed with oranges from the tree in her apartment complex's yard. The kids would love them. Right. Who was she kidding? She should have brought chocolate bars. Being in the hospital at Christmas was as much fun as getting socks for a present. An orange probably wouldn't help soothe things like chocolate.

Part of her wished she'd told Grace, her boss, mentor, and friend, about her lack of Christmas plans, but then she didn't want the sympathy. Maybe Grace wouldn't have felt too sorry for her. Grace, like most people attached to the circus world, knew the traveling life quite well. Holidays and roots weren't the same for them. Natalie knew full well. She couldn't miss what she'd never had, could she?

A Christmas tree had sprouted in the main lobby of the hospital, and its twenty-foot artificial glory twinkled like a beacon against anyone who dared say that Christmas had forgotten the sick and injured children of Sarasota. A Chanukah menorah glowed on the fireplace mantel in the seating area.

Natalie headed for the elevator and braced herself for the atmosphere awaiting her in the ward. If they lived in a perfect world, no one would be in the hospital at Christmas. No one would be sick. They'd all have their Norman Rockwell scenes around dining room tables, and moms and dads would yawn over their ham or turkey after staying up late putting together toys. Kids would giggle around Christmas trees and then pass out like the little boy in *A Christmas Story,* clutching his zeppelin. But not these kids in the pediatrics wing.

Natalie was used to nontraditional Christmases, and some of the children she was about to visit were, too. Chronic illness and severe injuries didn't take holidays.

But Christmas, Natalie had learned over the years, could come anywhere. Natalie didn't put up a tree or send cards, although she was fond of the Christmas music classics. Dad always played them when they were on the road with the Circus Du Monde. He and Mom would dance to "Rockin' Around the Christmas Tree" on Christmas night, wherever they were, and then Dad would hit the makeshift dance floor with Natalie.

Then they'd turn out all the lights and light one candle as Dad read the Christmas story from a Gideon Bible he'd swiped from a hotel somewhere. She never understood how the baby Jesus story related to dancing around a Christmas tree. Even now, the side-by-side secular and religious traditions sometimes didn't mesh well to her. But she discovered she loved the Christmas Eve candlelight service at church. It was there for the first time, three Christmases ago, the realization that God really loved *her*—Natalie Anne Bennett—hit her with full force. She'd spent the last two years figuring out what that meant, and how she ought to respond with her life.

Which meant she didn't need the Christmas tree or dozens of presents. What she needed was right here, hallways of children and their families waiting for a little joy. It was her way to give back in one of the best ways she knew.

Her throat caught at her own Christmas memories, and she took a deep breath as she pushed the button for the elevator. Bittersweet emotions didn't fit with what she was about to do. Clowns weren't supposed to be bittersweet.

Natalie took the elevator to the main pediatrics floor and checked in at the reception desk with the charge nurse who today wore a Santa cap. Multicolored twinkle lights flashed along the aqua blue counter.

"Hey, Miss Fran. Merry Christmas." She made her best clown's face for the nurse and held up an orange from her bag.

"Merry Christmas to you, too, Natalie." With a big smile on her dark face, the woman rounded the counter and gave Natalie a hug that threatened to crack her ribs. Natalie was careful not to get makeup on the nurse's scrubs. "Why are you here today? You should be with friends, or family."

"Same reason as you," Natalie replied. "For the kids."

"Ha, you're not gettin' paid double time today." Fran chuckled as she took the orange, returning to the other side of the counter. She tucked the orange next to a stack of files beside a computer monitor. "'Course, I'm not missing out, either. My Tonya's going to have the ham done by the time I get off tonight. And sweet potato soufflé, just like I taught her to make it."

"Sounds yummy. So, who do we have that needs a little cheer? Anything special I should know?"

"We have a new patient, just moved to the floor from ICU. 304. I think she could use some extra cheering up today. You might want to start with her and her family." An alert chime sounded at a console behind the counter. "Gotta run, sweet pea. See you in a bit."

Natalie called out, "See you," as Fran hit overdrive toward the room with a light flashing above the door. Natalie made her way to room 304.

People in less-than-festive clothing, women in long dresses, plain primary colors, wearing white head coverings, and a few men with beards, dark trousers and some in matching dark vests, clustered inside the sitting room. Amish, waiting their turn to visit someone. She made a clown's smile at them all and waved as she passed them in her rainbow striped clown suit and flaming red wig with long braids.

Natalie entered the hospital room with brisk steps and skidded to a stop. The little girl, the new patient Fran mentioned, lay on the bed, whispering something to her bearded father, who touched her head gently. Her right leg was in traction and a monitor flashed the girl's vital signs. Poor kid. Natalie definitely should have brought a chocolate bar.

Her father looked in Natalie's direction and stiffened. He stood. His blue eyes looked troubled. And like the people in the waiting room, he wore the classic dark pants of the Amish with a white shirt and suspenders.

"Hello." Natalie tried to stay in character. "I'm Bubbles the Clown, and I wanted to visit and cheer you up today, and wish you a Merry Christmas." She almost let her words falter at seeing the expression on the father's face. Did the Amish even celebrate Christmas? She probably ought to focus more on entertaining the little girl and forget mentioning the holiday anymore.

The father was tall, with sandy brown hair and beard, blue eyes, and a dark expression. The beard lent some age to his face, but Natalie figured he might be about her age, or maybe about thirty or so. A young woman next to him wore a dark blue dress with a white apron. She whispered to the man who stood beside the girl's father. Brothers, Natalie guessed, by the shape of their noses and eyes.

One bearded man in the corner wore dark trousers and a tropical print shirt, along with suspenders. Now *that* was something you didn't see every day. She tried not to stare at him, like the rest of them stared at her.

"Jacob," said the older brother. "It won't hurt for the children to laugh for a few minutes. Come on in, Miss, uh, Bubbles."

A small boy sat in the chair in the corner, his skinny legs tucked under his chin. "Can you juggle?" He had a bit of a singsong tone to his voice, with almost a German accent. He reminded her of a mouse, with his guarded expression and a hint of mischief in his round brown eyes. His thick brown hair sprouted a bowl cut that ended at his ears.

"Yes, I can," Natalie replied. She set her tie-dyed tote bag on the floor and snatched out three small rubber balls. "It's not so hard. See? Start with one ball."

The boy sat up straighter, then shifted to the edge of the cushioned seat. His eyes followed the journey as Natalie circulated the balls from one hand, to the air, then to the other hand.

"I wish I could do that," came a quiet voice from the bed. The little girl, older than her brother, shifted on the mattress. Pain shadowed her blue eyes.

"What's your name?"

"Rebecca."

"Well, Rebecca, I bet you could learn, quick as anything, after you get better." Natalie stopped the balls, ending up with two in her left hand and one in her right. "It takes practice, but if you stick with it, you'll likely be better than I am someday."

"Thank you for coming to visit today," said the young woman in the blue dress. She didn't seem much older than Natalie.

"My name's Katie Miller, and this is my husband Ephraim, and my brother-in-law Jacob. It's nice of you to visit on a holiday." Katie offered her hand, which Natalie shook.

"I'm Zeke," came a little voice from the chair. The little tyke with the big eyes and long legs smiled at her.

"Hi, Zeke, and Katie, and all the Miller family. It's nice to meet you, although I'm sorry it's here in the hospital, especially on Christmas day," Natalie replied. Katie. That had been her mother's name. But by the time Natalie had come around, she'd gone by Kat for several years.

"*Gotte* has a purpose in our being here," Jacob Miller said, and stroked his daughter's head. "I'm thankful He spared her life."

Natalie nodded. This wasn't her usual cheer-me-up visit. The kids had smiled at the juggling. "I brought you a present." She went to fetch her bag of oranges.

"How did you know to bring me a present, if you didn't know I was going to be here?" asked Rebecca.

"I knew some special kids would be here, and they should get oranges from the tree in my yard." Natalie drew two oranges out of the bag, and set the bag on the bed near Rebecca's feet. She gave the fruit a quick juggle, then presented one to Zeke and one to Rebecca.

"My *mammi* and *daadi* have grapefruit trees in their yard," said Rebecca. Her small hands massaged the pebbly surface of the orange. "But I like oranges better."

"Say thank you," reminded their father.

"Thank you." Rebecca smiled at Jacob, then Natalie.

What a tightly knit family. Natalie found she couldn't keep in character today. What was it about this family? She knew part of the answer lay at home, in a box her father had shipped to her just in time for Christmas. Too bad FedEx was so efficient. The box could have arrived after Christmas, and it would have been fine with her.

The orange slipped from Rebecca's grasp, tumbling onto the blanket. Rebecca's hands shook in a frenzy. Her head snapped back, her limbs stiffened. The vital signs monitor went crazy with beeps and alarms.

"Fran!" Natalie darted from the room and onto the floor. "She's seizing!"

The nurse was already flying around the desk, her bulky form moving with uncanny speed. Natalie had seen this before. She darted to the side to let Fran in. Another nurse dialed a pager.

The Millers joined Natalie in the hallway, and little Zeke was already sobbing. "My 'Becca."

Natalie squatted and touched his shoulder. "She's exactly where she needs to be right now, sweetie. She's being taken care of." Although she could make no promises for what lay ahead for the little girl.

"You're right," said Jacob Miller. He pulled Zeke closer to him. "We must find the others and let them know. We were taking turns, visiting her today."

The family filed toward the waiting room and left Rebecca to the doctor's care. Jacob, however, cast a worried glance at his daughter, then at Natalie. His look of sorrow pierced her heart.

Katie Miller glanced at Natalie. "We are going to go pray for Rebecca. Will you join us?"

Natalie nodded. "Of course." She ought to go to another room, and let this family do what they felt they must. But she followed them anyway.

When she entered the waiting room, the television set was off and the dark-clothed people were standing. A few of the women, about her age, wore pastel-colored dresses.

She bowed her head as they did, and one of the older men began to speak in another language. German, or Dutch, she figured. She didn't know the words, but felt the power and sincerity behind them.

Dear God, please guide the doctors. Take care of little Rebecca. I don't know what's wrong with her, but You do. Work through these gifted people who are caring for her now, Natalie prayed silently.

A warm, small hand slipped into hers and squeezed. Zeke Miller looked up at her with his mouse-eyes. Natalie squeezed back.

2

Natalie slapped her phone shut. She should have skipped checking her voice mail before going to Grace and Todd's house for dessert. After the incident at the hospital with little Rebecca Miller, her whole afternoon slid south. Way south. She'd left the waiting room not long after the final "Amen" had been said on Rebecca's behalf. She promised to come visit them again, at which Zeke beamed.

It wasn't that she hadn't witnessed a medical crisis or two while visiting children at the hospital before. She'd witnessed parents in tears, parents in denial, and angry parents who would rather curse God than pray for or believe in any type of divine intervention.

But this calm acceptance of what had happened to Rebecca rattled Natalie to her core. She'd glimpsed a flicker of fear and sorrow in Jacob Miller's eyes before he glanced away from her. So there was emotion, deep emotion inside that outward bravado. Was it bravado she glimpsed with him, or was he practicing something he knew he ought to feel, but didn't?

She ended up checking her voice mail after leaving the hospital. Dad had called from Los Angeles, where he lived with wife number two and their perfect children. One was stepmother Judy's daughter from her first marriage, and one was Natalie's little brother, Dad's longed-for son. She'd only seen him once and he was still young enough to carry a sippy cup. Natalie tried not to remember Judy was only five years her elder.

"Nat! It's Dad. Wanted to tell you hi and Merry Christmas. Hope you enjoy the gift card. I figured you could use it for, whatever comes in handy. And the stuff from your mom? I . . . well, I figured now was as good a time as any for you to have it. Hang on—" Squeals in the background punctuated his call, then laughter. "I still miss her, Kid, even though we couldn't stand being in the same room the last few years before, well, you know. We're going to toast Kat Bennett here today, and hope you will, too. Talk to you soon. Call me."

From that long verbal run, it sounded like Dad had already been toasting Mom, the day, and his favorite football team, probably with the help of a pitcher of mimosas that Judy had made that morning as the kids tore into their mountain of gifts. Dad had never been one for traditions, not while he and Mom and Natalie were on the road traveling.

It looked like the North Pole had transplanted itself onto the Montgomerys' front yard. She hurried past a leering inflated snowman in the yard, and up to the house covered with flashing lights. She stopped before knocking on the front door. She'd forgotten Grace and Todd's gift. Again. And if she went home, she knew she wouldn't venture out again.

Natalie rang the doorbell, and found herself swept inside by Grace, with a pair of Chihuahuas yapping around their ankles.

"You made it!" Bracelets clinked on Grace's wrist as she wrapped Natalie in a hug. "Burrito! Queso! Quit that. Honestly, these dogs. I'm going to call Animal Control before New Year's and have the beasts picked up and deposited on some other sorry family's doorstep."

"Ha." Natalie moved to pet one of the dogs. "You'd sooner ask for your arm to be removed than rid yourselves of these little guys." The dog, Queso or Burrito, she couldn't tell, gave her a friendly lick for once and then tore off along the hardwood floor with his brother, yapping about Natalie's arrival.

"True, true." Grace turned and gestured away from the entry. "I just made a pot of decaf. Don't tell Todd. He thinks it's regular."

Natalie laughed as Grace slipped an arm around her shoulders. "It's been quite the afternoon at the hospital. Normally it doesn't wear me out like this. I almost didn't come over, but I didn't want to sit home tonight."

"What happened? Is it because it's Christmas?"

They entered the great room, a sprawling combination of kitchen, living, and dining room looking out on an inlet of coast. Natalie wished she could afford a place like this. Good for Grace and Todd, investing in their Bird Key home while they strutted the high wire before retiring to open Pathway to the Stars Circus School. Authoring a best-selling tell-all of the circus life had netted Grace a superb nest egg.

And Natalie's own solo career was over before it really even began.

"No, it's not because it's Christmas. I met a family today. The little girl had just gotten out of ICU, and then she started having a seizure." Natalie shook her head. "Poor thing. Her family's Amish."

"Is that a bad thing, being Amish?" Grace took out a pair of mugs covered with holly and poured them both a cup.

"No, no." Natalie accepted the cup from Grace. "I meant, poor thing about the seizure. She's probably scared. Her little brother was, for sure. Even the father, but I think he masked that pretty well."

"What about her mother?" Grace slid the creamer across the granite island in Natalie's direction.

"Um, I didn't see if a mother was there. Or not." Her thoughts drifted back to Jacob Miller, hovering over his daughter, his firm resolve to stay strong reflected in his blue eyes. No mother there at the bedside. Natalie wasn't so sure about her own mothering instincts, but she knew for sure if it were her child, she'd be glued to her bedside day and night until she was released from the hospital.

"Hmm . . ." Grace's expression narrowed. "Okay. So this family got to you. It's all right. It shows how much you care. And you are definitely good with kids, for sure."

Natalie nodded. "Thanks. I do care. I admit I really miss my classes during winter break."

"Yes, I almost wish we'd kept the academy open this week, but it's useless to have classes with families on vacation." Grace poured cream into her coffee.

Natalie took a long sip of the coffee. "The time off will be good. By the way, I forgot your gift again. At this rate it'll make a good New Year's gift."

"Or save it for Valentine's Day." Grace laughed. "Hold on just a second." She left the kitchen island, and crossed the great room to the nearest floor-to-ceiling window where a glittering tree stood, covered in white lights. She picked up a gift-wrapped flat rectangle topped with a flaming red bow.

"Wow, now I feel bad." Yes, she'd make certain, next trip out, she'd give Grace and Todd their gift.

"Piffle. No worries." Grace brought the long wrapped gift back to Natalie and set it on the granite. "I hope you like it. I searched high and low for the right size."

Natalie plucked the bow from the package and tore off the first corner of the wrapping paper. A picture frame. Good. She'd been horrible about accumulating pictures over the years, probably because her parents didn't have many photos, or the photos they did have were in storage, or long gone.

Yes, the picture frame was a long rectangle of eight by ten prints, six of them. The first was of Natalie and her parents under the big top of Circus du Monde. Natalie touched the glass.

"I remember this one . . . I always loved that outfit." A pink leotard, with a matching ruffled skirt. But the cape. Oh, she'd loved the cape edged with sequins. She'd been five years old in that photo.

"I . . . it took some searching through the circus archives," came Grace's soothing voice, as if from a distance. "I hope you don't mind. The three of you looked so happy."

"No, I don't mind." Natalie swallowed hard. "I was just thinking of how few pictures I do have of my family. Now *this* other photo, I remember this one, too. It was the night I had my first solo act. I thought I was something else." Thirteen and so full of herself, with one hand on her hip and a saucy tilt to her head, her unruly brown hair pulled back and wrangled into a solitary braid hung over one shoulder. She had the first subtle curves of early womanhood.

Next, a photo of her parents, doing their trapeze act. No one could mistake the joy on Mom's face. The photo captured her in midair as she reached out for Dad, his hands ready to catch her. Natalie's heart twinged in her chest. She knew this first Christmas without Mom good-naturedly hollering at her on the phone several times a day would be hard. Somehow this made it a little easier than ignoring the reality altogether. Then there was the matter of the FedEx box from Dad, its contents still waiting for her to face them, and deal with them.

"You have a legacy here, Natalie. You're still a gifted artist, even though you're not a performer anymore." Grace sighed. "If I could do half the moves you younger ones do . . ."

"Ha." Natalie studied the details of the last photo, taken right before what she called The Fall. The photographer had captured a shot of her, performing an upside-down splits. She'd had hundreds of pictures taken during her all-too-short aerial silks career, but this one captured the same joy her mother's face held. The silks held Natalie more than thirty feet above the floor. No net. No fear, until . . . "I bet you still could."

"I know this Christmas is probably hard for you, but I didn't want you to feel like you're alone." Grace touched her arm.

"I don't, not really. Thank you . . . I love the pictures." Natalie nodded and blinked hard. *No tears*. "But you're right. It's been a hard Christmas this year. Seeing that Amish family today . . ."

"What is it?"

"My dad sent me a box, and it just got here yesterday. He told me he was sending some things that belonged to my mom. Things she had stuffed away somewhere." Funny how she thought she knew someone, and then everything could change with one box sent overnight from California.

"What do you mean? What about your mother? I don't understand. What did your father send you?"

"I figured my family had no skeletons in the closet, no secrets." Natalie took a deep breath and sighed. "That's not true. Because, going by what Dad sent me in the box, my mother, Kat Bennett, used to be Katie Yoder. Grace, she was Amish."

"Your daughter has had a traumatic brain injury, besides her compound femur fracture and internal bleeding," said Dr. Chen, the neurologist. "The MRI of her brain doesn't show any bleeding or a hematoma, but we do know she won't be safe to travel for quite some time, at the very least because of her fracture. It may be all she needs is time for the inflammation in her brain to subside, or she may need antiseizure medication permanently. We have no way of knowing right now, but we'll be monitoring her medication very carefully."

Jacob nodded. "I understand." The hospital noises swirled around them, asking for his attention. But Rebecca, not able to travel. He'd have to make arrangements. Ephraim and Katie were heading back to Ohio soon, as was their original plan. As had been his and the children's. The cabinet shop would open after New Year's, without him. He couldn't and wouldn't leave Rebecca. He couldn't expect his grandparents to care for a wounded child. After losing Hannah, he'd kept them as close to him as possible.

"We want to keep her for at least a week to make sure her scans stay clear, and then we'll release her after Orthopedics clears her. But she'll need close follow-up with specialists, including me." Dr. Chen's pager started beeping. He removed it from his belt loop and glanced at the display. "I think she'll do fine on the main pediatrics floor until her release."

"We'll stay here in Sarasota until you clear her to travel." He shook hands with Dr. Chen. "Thank you, thank you so much for what you've done for Rebecca. It's a miracle that she's alive."

"I must agree with you on that, Mr. Miller." Dr. Chen gave him a nod. "I'll sign off on her orders for now, but I'll be back if her condition changes."

Then he was gone, leaving Jacob alone in the conference area, a little nook with small café tables and chairs, used by physicians needing a quiet place to confer with their patients' families. He was glad for a few seconds alone. He could think better this way. Thankfully, the neurologist hadn't talked to him as if he were a dimwit. Maybe he only had the equivalent of an eighth-grade education, but he wasn't stupid. His gut told him it would be months before he and the children would board the Pioneer Trails bus for Ohio.

Mammi and *Daadi* would be delighted, of course, to have them stay, even though the reason was a tragedy. He and the children would fill up his grandparents' tiny home. He would make sure the children attended school in Pinecraft, or worked out home lessons for Rebecca once the doctor cleared her. And Zeke. Zeke would have a hard time going anywhere without his older sister.

Jacob leaned his head on his chin. Then, the matter of the hospital bill. He'd already contacted his bishop in Ohio. Together, they would all help pay for Rebecca's hospital bills. Local members from their district were already pitching in to help in large ways and small.

This also meant Jacob would need a job while he was here in Sarasota. He knew he couldn't spend all his time at the hospital. His grandparents had limited resources. He himself had some savings, but wasn't about to start tapping into them. Gotte, *so many things to think of and consider, but I know You are helping pave the way. I know You are working in this situation, but I still can't help but think I should have never left Ohio.*

None of this would have happened if he hadn't come to Sarasota. What's done was done, and there was no taking back his decision. However, his daughter's pain was too high a price to pay for a week or so of self-indulgence.

He needed to return to Rebecca's room. She'd been through much, and Hannah would have been pleased at how strong Rebecca had been through the whole ordeal.

As soon as Jacob left the consultation room's carpeted area and stepped onto the tiled hallway, he nearly collided with a young woman in a sky blue dress and white apron. She held a small bouquet of flowers.

"Betsy."

Betsy Yoder's brown eyes grew round in her face. A pink glow shot to her cheeks. "J-J-Jacob." Her free hand smoothed the top of her prayer covering and patted down a few stray hairs. "I'm here to see Rebecca. I heard she's out of ICU."

"Yes, yes she is." He sidestepped and increased the space between them, like a crab they'd seen scuttle from the water. "We had quite a scare yesterday. She had a seizure."

"Oh, no!" Betsy's long strides matched his, her flip-flops slapping the floor. Taller than a lot of the women in his Order, she had an air of both responsibility and warmth. Jacob glanced at the flowers she held. Too bad she hadn't brought one of her legendary pies, but food like pie was probably off limits at the hospital. His stomach growled.

"She's doing better today. I just had a meeting with the neurologist. It looks like we'll be staying here in Florida for a while." He nodded at a man passing by, who stared at the pair of them curiously.

"But what about your job?" Betsy stopped when Jacob paused outside Rebecca's doorway. "How long do you think you'll have to stay here? Not that it's bad at all. Sometimes I think I'd like very much to stay in Florida."

He felt a warm hand on his arm and looked down. Betsy pulled her hand back and clamped it firmly on the bouquet. "I'm not sure how long we'll be here. Months, probably. I'm going to see about making a phone call to the cabinet shop. I hope they'll hold my job for me. They probably will."

"Of course they will." Betsy nodded. "They have to." She clamped her lips together.

Jacob entered Rebecca's hospital room. Over the past few days, it started to fill with cards and encouraging notes, just as *Mammi's* refrigerator brimmed with food from the neighborhood.

"*Daed.*" Rebecca's smile lit the room and rivaled the Florida sunlight streaming through the window. "And Betsy, too."

"Flowers for you, to brighten your room." Betsy held out the bouquet, and Rebecca clutched it and held the flowers to her nose.

"Thank you. They're very pretty." Rebecca set them on the tray table close beside her bed, next to the orange the clown had brought her three days ago. Rebecca didn't want to eat it, but just look at her "gift" from the lady clown.

Was Christmas only three days ago? Jacob's days had started to run together, ever since the accident. With his everyday routine gone, he fought to hold onto some sense of order. Morning prayers helped, and a walk around the neighborhood before going to the hospital.

The people of Pinecraft meant well, asking about Rebecca. But it was hard for him to have a moment of quiet thoughts before the day's onslaught of hospital news overtook him. If only his parents were here to help. They'd had to leave for Ohio the day after Christmas, but he promised to keep them informed of Rebecca's condition and progress.

"Do you need anything, Rebecca?" Betsy asked.

"I miss my doll."

Jacob touched the top of Rebecca's head. "I'll bring it later. I promise."

Betsy busied herself with adjusting Rebecca's pillows. For some reason, the gesture made Jacob's throat tighten. He hadn't asked for her help and the motherly action made him shift on his feet.

Had Betsy been talking to his sister-in-law? He knew he'd told Ephraim the other day he would prepare himself to "move on" once they returned to Ohio. But he wasn't about to have someone push him into it. No matter how pretty her hair and efficient her mannerisms, no matter how much the idea of her pies made his mouth water, Betsy Yoder couldn't make him give her a second glance.

"*Daed*, are you all right?" Rebecca's voice sounded concerned.

"I am just fine, just fine." He glanced at Betsy. She'd quit fluffing the pillows and fussing over the blankets, and now stood back a step from the bedside. "Don't worry about me."

"I wonder if the clown lady will come back."

"Clown lady?" Betsy asked.

Jacob opened his mouth, but Rebecca continued. "A clown lady came on Christmas day and brought me the orange. I . . . I had a seizure while she was here. I hope it didn't scare her."

"She didn't seem afraid. I think she's seen it happen before." Jacob tried to reassure her. "She visits a lot of sick kids."

A soft knock sounded in the doorway. "Excuse me? May I please come in?"

Jacob shot a look to the source of the voice. A young woman, with long dark hair streaming past her shoulders, stood in the doorway. She wore a pair of pink cropped pants and a simple white blouse. She carried a familiar-looking tote bag in a kaleidoscope of colors that reminded Jacob of wildflowers.

3

Of course, Mr. Miller and his daughter looked at Natalie as if she'd entered the wrong room. They'd never seen her before like this, in her street clothes and without a load of clown makeup clogging her pores.

Natalie cleared her throat. "I met you on Christmas Day, Mr. Miller. I, um, was the clown who visited you."

Natalie's visit today had two purposes. First, she wanted to see how Rebecca was doing. Also, Natalie hoped the elderly couple would be present, or at least Rebecca's Aunt Katie. She might get a few answers to the questions raised by the box Dad had shipped to her.

Mr. Miller blinked and tugged on his suspenders, then glanced at his daughter. They weren't the room's only occupants. A young woman stood, her eyes round in her smooth complected face as she assessed Natalie.

"You came back," said Rebecca Miller. "I'm sorry I got sick in front of you."

"Don't worry about it. You couldn't help it." Natalie approached her bedside. "I wanted to see how you were doing today. I've been praying for you. And your family."

"She's doing much better, thank you." Mr. Miller wore the same guarded expression she'd seen on Christmas day. Natalie almost wanted to make him smile to see if his eyes would light up. She shrugged off the thought. What this family had been through.

"I don't know your name, Miss, um, Bubbles . . ." Rebecca snapped Natalie's attention from Jacob Miller.

"I'm Natalie Bennett. You know, Bubbles isn't my real name." She reached for Rebecca's hand, and shook it.

Rebecca gave a soft laugh. "I knew that. Right, *Daed*?"

Jacob nodded, but didn't look at Natalie. Instead, he appeared to study the other young woman.

Natalie took a few mental steps backwards. She'd interrupted something with Jacob Miller and this woman, who stared at Natalie's pink capris. Worse, she hadn't thought things through. A hospital room wasn't the place to start any search for her roots. Not now, with a little girl recovering here.

She wished the small crowd present on Christmas day had shown up today. "Well, I might just have to come back again and help you juggle sometime."

"You . . . you work as a clown?" The other woman in the blue dress finally spoke.

Natalie nodded. "I volunteer here once a week in the pediatrics ward. Normally, I'm a circus school teacher here in Sarasota. Pathway to the Stars."

"Really?" The woman's eyebrows shot up to the top of her forehead. "How did you come upon that job?"

"I grew up in the business. I used to work in the circus, too." Natalie glanced from Jacob, to Rebecca, to the woman again. "My parents were both circus performers, and I used to do aerial silk routines."

"Really?" The woman repeated herself. "I've never met a circus performer before. Have you, Jacob?"

"No, I haven't." Jacob looked as though he wanted to be anywhere but there at the present moment. Of course, he must. Who'd want to be visiting their child in the hospital?

And this woman hovered near Rebecca as if she wanted to ward off any bad influences Natalie might bring to the child. Ridiculous. But the woman took a step closer to Rebecca and stood near the head of the reclining hospital bed, currently elevated so Rebecca could sit up.

"They have a high wire act, too," the woman said.

"Oh, I hope I can get home to see that." Rebecca looked down at her blankets and scrunched the fabric with her fingers. "I'm sorry for causing so much trouble."

"Nonsense." Jacob shook his head. "Christmas came and we enjoyed our time together. And I promise you, when we get you back to *Mammi* and *Daadi's* house, we will go to the beach, and get ice cream again, and watch the older kids playing volleyball at the beach. And go to the singings and play at the park."

"I can't wait to go home." Rebecca glanced at Natalie. "I hope you'll come and help me juggle when I get home."

Natalie cleared her throat and dared not look at Jacob or the woman across from him. "Maybe I will. I'd like that. It sounds like your father has a lot of fun things planned to help you get better." She picked up her bag and took out a set of juggling balls. "I tell you what. If your dad doesn't mind, I'll leave two of these balls with you. I want you to practice tossing from one hand to the other. Your hands will learn how to do it. Of course, if your doctor tells you to rest, I'm sure you'll listen to him."

"Of course, she will," came Jacob's terse response. "My daughter knows how to listen to authority."

Natalie nodded. "I'm sure she does. You have very polite and respectful children, Mr. Miller." It was her cue to leave. "I hope to see you again, Rebecca. Or maybe Bubbles will come back before then and see how you're doing on your juggling."

She couldn't resist shooting a grin to Jacob and the young woman, who she guessed to be about eighteen, maybe a little older. Clearly, if there wasn't a Mrs. Miller in the picture, this lady in blue would step up for the position. Maybe that was why Jacob looked like he wanted to tuck his daughter in his arms and run from the hospital.

He also looked like the kind of man who'd make up his own mind and let said lady in blue down gently, if need be.

"Thank you for coming by, Miss Bennett." Jacob finally met her eyes. Eyes that blue weren't legal. And she didn't need to think about them, actually. If anything, she needed to wish him and the would-be Mrs. Miller in the room all the best.

Next time she came to the hospital, she'd talk to his sister-in-law about finding out some information about the items her father had sent to her.

Mom, Amish? Kat Bennett was once Katie Yoder? It was like learning her dad had bought a house and a minivan. Okay, so he was a stuntman in L.A., but the very idea of her father putting down roots somewhere was nearly as ludicrous.

Natalie merely waved at Fran on her way out and didn't stop at the desk. *God, I don't know who I am anymore, or who my family is anymore.*

What little she did know about the Amish, she knew the families stuck together. She didn't know if she considered it stifling or comforting. But look how the Millers and those connected with them gathered when Rebecca had been injured.

Jacob Miller, I almost envy you . . . Natalie bit her lip and headed for the elevator.

Things like pink cropped pants were just one of the reasons Bishop had given Jacob an unspoken warning against visiting Sarasota. Now, Jacob realized he was doomed to be here for who knows how much longer.

How could he not help but notice Natalie Bennett?

He managed to escape from Betsy and her smiling face before anyone saw them get off the bus together. This never would have happened, had he taken Henry Hostetler's offer of a hiring a driver to take him to see Rebecca. But it was cheaper to ride the city bus.

And so, he and Betsy had ridden the thirty minutes or so, side by side on a bus seat back to Pinecraft. A few other Plain people rode too, interspersed among the *Englisch*. And what they would all say about seeing him with Betsy . . .

He hurried along the sidewalk and headed toward the Bahia Vista traffic light

"Hello, Jacob Miller!" Henry Hostetler waved as he approached, bicycling across the street. "How's Rebecca doing today?"

"Much better than yesterday." Jacob glimpsed Betsy hurrying to meet some of her friends near Big Olaf's ice cream shop. They circled around Betsy like a flock of birds with their varying colors of dresses and white head coverings. A few of them glanced his way. Just what he didn't need right now. Giggles drifted in his direction on the balmy air.

"That's good news, Jacob." Henry stopped his tricycle and adjusted his dark round hat. "We've been praying for her. I suppose you'll be heading back to the hospital later?"

"Yes, I am." This time he wouldn't go alone. If Betsy were to happen back to the hospital, he wouldn't face her by himself. Also, if Natalie Bennett came back, too, in her pink pants with hems skimming her shins, and her long hair swishing as she talked.

Like the women of his Order, Natalie Bennett wore her hair long, but unlike the women in his Order, she wore it down, the walnut-colored strands of silk flowing past her shoulders. Rebecca's face glowed when Natalie had entered the room. Miss Bennett. He reminded himself of her proper name. Even Bubbles the Clown would do.

In his imagination, Natalie's dark hair transformed into Hannah's locks of burnished gold. Every night, the only time Hannah wore her hair down, she would brush her hair by the glow of the lamp. Jacob would sit reading his Bible in bed, but the rhythmic movements of Hannah's hand and the hairbrush kept drawing his attention from the pages.

So beautiful. The gold blended back into brown.

This was why he should have never come to Florida. The past and present jumbled together in his brain like the eggs *Maami* scrambled for breakfast and served with freshly fried thick slices of bacon, fried potatoes, and buttered wheat toast.

"You okay, Jacob?" Henry's voice jerked Jacob from his thoughts.

Jacob nodded. "Things aren't working out as I planned. We were only supposed to be here for two weeks. I have a job I must get back to."

"Ah, that's very true." Henry shifted on the tricycle seat and squinted across the street at a neat row of cottages. "Life seldom unfolds as we think it will. Even living so simply, troubles bore their way into the sturdy planks of our plans. But God in His wisdom has our interests in mind, far better than we could contrive on our own."

Jacob shivered at the sudden turn of the breeze. "I wish I knew why. I wish I could accept *and* understand at the same time." Losing Hannah and Samuel. And now the sweetest child with her mother's spirit lay miles and miles away from them, in a room among strangers. The only reason he'd left her was to return to the village to speak to someone about a job.

"Sometimes, we don't." Henry shook his head. "No, many times we don't." Of course, Henry spoke truth from his own life, widowed nearly twenty years, his children grown and living in Indiana.

"I . . . I realized I don't want to be alone, Henry."

"Like me, you mean?" Henry chuckled. "Oh, in all these years after losing Mabel, I may have felt alone during some dark times. But truthfully, I've never been alone. I've found joy and purpose, and community here."

Jacob nodded. "*Daadi* said you have a *gut* life here." But that's not what he wanted. Not in the least. He couldn't accept the being alone part. Giggles from the girls outside the ice cream shop rang off the walls of the shop.

"Listen to me, now." Henry's hand on his shoulder felt warm. "You're still young. Your children are still young and not a couple years from leaving the house, as mine were when Mabel's days were finished. I know there's a fine future ahead of you, Jacob Miller. Keep your eyes open and be ready. It might just surprise you."

"I'll try to do that, Henry."

"And now, I must be off. Time for shuffleboard. Josiah Fry says he can best me. Ha, ha, I don't think so." Henry rang the bell on his tricycle as he pushed off along the street and resumed his journey, headed in the direction of Pinecraft Park.

Jacob trudged along to his grandparents' house. He should have asked Henry about a job. The man wasn't quite as old as his grandparents and still worked around Sarasota, doing maintenance and home repairs, along with light construction. Jacob stopped at the neat little house that his grandparents owned, a simple white clapboard cottage with four rooms, each divided evenly with the back two rooms donating some of their space to the bathroom.

Forget his troubles in Florida, Ephraim had told him. Enjoy a few moments with his children away from everyday life. A flash of pink caught his eye, flamingo pink. The same pink as Natalie's pants. Of course it wouldn't be her. It was a local Mennonite girl's pink dress. He would never get used to the colors used with abandon here in Sarasota.

Pinecraft was supposed to be the Plain people's refuge from the world. Jacob sighed as he headed up the walk to the house. Even this refuge had distractions. He wanted to be on the farm in Ohio. He didn't care if there was a foot of snow on the ground. Just to be back, among all that he knew. Maybe now he could fight the pain of memories.

Gotte, *please help me. I can't do this. Where can I go for some peace? This storm has raged far too long.*

He didn't feel or sense any response. No answers from above, and nothing but questions rolling through his mind like the endless waves along the shore he wished he'd never seen.

4

"I'm thinking about staying in Pinecraft when my parents leave," Betsy Yoder announced. Maybe it wasn't wise to voice her thoughts just now, but surrounded by her friends in the happy atmosphere of Pinecraft Park's sandy volleyball court, the words came right out.

She waited for her friends' reactions. Miriam dropped the volleyball in mid-serve.

"No, you can't be serious. Staying here, with all the old people?" Miriam raised her hands, as if in surrender. "What can you be thinking?"

The others flocked around her, murmuring similar sentiments. Florida in the winter was an exciting diversion from what waited back in Ohio. The young women had the chance to soak up sunshine in wintertime and let the scent of Hawaiian Tropic fill the air. They wore flip-flops, suntan lotion, and enjoyed many modern conveniences not exactly allowed back home.

"I need a change." She picked up the ball that Miriam had dropped. How could she tell them something she couldn't explain herself, completely?

"But you're twenty, not eighty."

"I know."

"I'd stay, if it wasn't for someone at home," interjected Betsy's youngest sister, Emma.

"Who? Who? Do tell us." Miriam practically pounced on Emma's statement.

"Eli Troyer. He would have come, but he decided to stay and do extra work, and save the money." Emma tossed them a knowing look. A few of the girls squealed. And Betsy tried not to sigh.

Emma, pulling the conversation to herself, as usual. The others would quit bothering her about staying in Pinecraft. This was a *gut* thing.

"Still, though, this place shuts down in the summer. Nobody's around. Nobody except *old* people," said Miriam, waving her arms. A few of the older folks over at the shuffleboard court glanced in their direction. Some laughed and shook their heads.

"And newlyweds," Emma added with a grin. No doubt she'd already considered that possibility for herself. And Eli. Why else would he stay in Ohio, but to work and save money to buy them a house?

"There *are* younger families who live here, not just older people. Plenty of people live here year-round. Sarasota is a good-sized city," Betsy said. She knew she'd encounter disbelief from her friends at her idea, but not the outright opposition.

"But what would you *do*?" Miriam asked.

"Clean houses. My *Aenti* Chelle says I can make several hundred dollars a week, easily. The *Englisch* pay Amish housekeepers very well."

"What did your parents say?"

"I haven't told them yet. Or, asked them, rather."

"Then nothing's settled," Miriam said. "Besides, hasn't Gideon Stoltzfus been walking you home from the singings? You wouldn't return to Ohio, even for him?"

"Yes, he walked me home. Once." Betsy nibbled her lower lip. "But it won't happen again. I can't go back to Ohio for him." She didn't want to admit to any of them why she'd concocted the idea to stay in Pinecraft. Yes, the Millers were staying in Florida after the horrible accident. They had to. No one knew when Rebecca would be well enough to make the hundreds of miles trip in a hired vehicle, let alone the confines of a Pioneer Trails charter bus.

The idea of returning to Ohio and not seeing Jacob and the children, well, she couldn't bear that. She hadn't confessed it to anyone, not even Miriam, her dearest friend. Miriam might understand; she and Isaac Troyer, Eli's brother, were inseparable and likely would be wed next winter.

Yet Jacob Miller was different. Older than her, settled, and experienced. He was a man in the eyes of the elders. Maybe if she stayed here, in Pinecraft, Jacob would notice her for more than her delicious pies.

"So, when will it be *your* turn to be a newlywed, Emma Yoder?" someone in their circle asked.

This time, Betsy did sigh. Enough. Her mind was made up. If others thought her youngest sister was marrying before her, well, that only added to the urgency of what should come next.

Natalie's pores didn't care much for the clown makeup, not when the mercury rose to 86 degrees on January third. Yet another reason she loved Florida in the winter, so she wasn't about to complain. This trip to the hospital, though, she waited until she arrived to apply her makeup in the ladies' room instead of making the trip in full Bubbles makeup.

She was ready to visit the children's wing, especially to see Rebecca Miller and little Zeke with his mouse-eyes. What brave children. Kids were resilient and often braver than their parents, Natalie had discovered. She found it easier to focus on the children instead of the parents when facing illness head-on.

Natalie skittered to a stop when she entered Rebecca's room. The blankets on the bed were thrown back, the room vacant. Natalie went to the desk.

Fran was off duty and her seat was filled by the day nurse, Brenda. "Where's Rebecca Miller?"

"Outside, in the courtyard with her family, getting some sun," replied Brenda with a toss of her head. "I don't blame them one bit. It's better than the two days of rain we just had."

Natalie nodded. "Thanks." She headed for the children's courtyard before she lost her nerve. A shyness crept over her in spite of her clown makeup when faced with encountering the Amish family. Children were children, but the adults . . .

She'd read up on the Amish and knew they didn't use modern conveniences like electricity and gas-powered vehicles and technology, although she'd heard of exceptions here in Sarasota. They dressed Plain, especially the women. She'd seen the other young woman stare at her pink capris the other day.

Natalie found her way to the courtyard, where laughter echoed off the walls. She forced her legs to move in the Plain family's direction. Little Zeke was hunched over, palms on his knees, as he studied the koi in the pond.

"No, those wouldn't make a very *gut* supper," she heard a warm tenor voice say. Jacob Miller.

"I want to eat some alligator, *Daed*," said Zeke.

Jacob swung to face Natalie. "So the clown has found us outside." This time the older couple was with him, and the other man she figured to be his brother along with his friendly sister-in-law.

She gave them her exaggerated nod, wide smile with her lips sealed, and waved. “I wonder how Miss Rebecca is doing today. Better, I hope?”

“Much better,” said the little girl. “I’ve been practicing my juggling too, with the balls you gave me.”

“Have you, now?” Natalie pulled out a trio of oranges from her bag, then started moving the three pieces of fruit in a circle above her head. “I suppose this doesn’t impress you, then?”

“I keep dropping one,” said Rebecca. “I did try juggling my fork and spoon.”

“Once,” echoed Jacob, giving her a hint of a smile.

“How ‘bout a knock-knock joke?” Natalie ventured. Did Amish know about knock-knock jokes? She was about to find out. “Knock knock.”

Rebecca gave her father a questioning glance. “Say ‘Who’s there?’” he whispered.

“Who’s there?”

“Banana.”

“Banana who?” whispered Jacob in Rebecca’s ear.

“Banana who?” Rebecca parroted as Natalie kept up the juggle.

“Knock-knock.” Even Natalie chuckled, though she’d told the joke hundreds of times.

“Who is it?”

“Banana.”

“Banana who?”

They repeated it again, and Natalie grinned. The goofier the joke, the more a younger one loved it.

“Knock-knock.”

“Who’s there?”

“Orange.”

"Orange *who*?"

"Orange you glad I didn't say banana?" Natalie ended her juggle and gave Rebecca one of the oranges with a bow.

Rebecca clutched the orange, her confused expression replaced with a laugh and a smile. "Orange you . . . aren't you. That's funny."

"Do you like balloons? I can make a balloon animal for you. What's your favorite?"

"A kitten." Rebecca frowned at her orange. "We have barn cats at home, but *Daed* says no cats in the house."

"Well, the cats probably help by keeping the mice outside." Natalie glanced at Jacob as she opened her tote bag. She could make a simple black-and-white cat, or an orange tabby.

"Miss Bennett is right," Jacob said. "The cats are workers, not pets."

He remembers my name.

She felt as if she stood before the family, no clown makeup, and her Bubbles persona had somehow slipped. "Do . . . do you want an orange cat or a black-and-white?"

"Orange."

"You got it." Natalie blew up the slim long orange balloons, then started twisting them. Zeke moved closer. Of course, she wouldn't forget him.

"And you, Mr. Zeke, be thinking about what you want me to make for you."

Zeke nodded, his eyes focused on her hands, wrangling the pliable balloon into the shape of a cat's body. Then some legs and a perky tail came next.

"Can you make a blue fish?" The question came out softly.

"I can certainly make you a blue fish." The expression on his face plucked at the strings of her heart. Another family passed them, hovering around a young girl in a wheelchair, her head bald.

The Millers weren't the only family she should spend time with. The adults talked quietly among themselves, Natalie picking up an occasional word in German, or whatever dialect they used.

The oldest Miller woman had warm blue eyes in a wrinkled face, her gray hair caught back neatly and covered with a white bonnet. Her cape dress of navy blue almost had a formal air about it, as did her white apron that covered her dark dress.

Ask her. But Natalie's fingers trembled as she fashioned the kitten's whiskers. Surely, they would help her learn more about Katie Yoder who became Kat Bennett. As in, find her family. Yoder, she knew, was a common enough name, almost like Smith or Jones. And how many Katies could there be?

But then, she had no right to ask them anything. This was only the third time they'd encountered each other, the longest period of time she'd spent with them. Don't get too attached to the families you visit, she reminded herself. They passed through the hospital doors, all with their own stories, some with happy endings and others not-so-happy.

"Here you are, one orange kitten." Natalie handed the balloon figure to Rebecca. "Now for the blue fish." She felt the other family's eyes on her and heard excited whispers about "animals."

"I'm going home soon," Rebecca announced.

"Now, the doctor hasn't said for certain yet," Jacob said. He glanced at Natalie. "We're also getting a hospital bed for the house."

"I know you'll be excited to be home again."

"Well, my *mammi's* home. My real home is in Ohio."

"Ah, I see." She paused and blew up a pair of aqua-colored skinny balloons.

"We were only here for Christmas vacation, and then I ruined Christmas for everyone." Rebecca's eyes pooled with tears.

"Hush, no, you did not," spoke the older woman. "We were together and God watched over you for us. For that, we had a thankful Christmas."

Such grace in the face of tragedy. "Well, I am thankful to have met you all," Natalie ventured as she formed half a balloon into a fin. She forced herself to swallow around the lump that had swelled in her throat. Not clownlike behavior, not at all.

⁂

"A sweet, kind young woman," said *Mammi* Rachel after Natalie Bennett had moved on to visit with the other family in the courtyard. "Brave, to visit us here in the hospital, too. Some people don't like hospitals. I don't."

Jacob nodded. The children were dueling back and forth with their cat and fish balloon animals, making appropriate noises for both. He didn't know how someone could visit sick children, day after day, and not have it affect them deeply. Yes, Natalie Bennett was sweet, and kind. Her presence had hit him with a splash of joy.

Despite his *mammi's* words about *Gotte's* hand being upon Rebecca and preserving her life, and how Christmas was *not* ruined, it was hard enough to see his daughter suffering. Moments of laughter, like now, helped mask the pain, along with medication. But tonight would be hard, when Rebecca cried out for her *mamm*, and Jacob could do nothing except whisper words of comfort and prayer. That's when the deepest wounds of his heart yet again lay bare and sensitive to the waves of memory. Whenever the children fell ill or upset, Hannah always knew what to do.

"She's lonely," *Mammi* said. "I will remember to pray for her, for *Gotte* to settle her with a family."

"I imagine she already has a family." Why the conversation had turned to the clown visitor, he didn't know. She kept glancing toward them as she entertained the other family in the courtyard.

"Probably. There are few of us who don't," quipped his *daadi*.

"Can I come home yet, *Daed*? I promise I won't cry when I take my medicine." Jacob couldn't miss the longing in his daughter's voice.

"As soon as the doctor says you can come home, you can be sure we'll have Henry Hostetler come with his big blue van right up to the front door of the hospital." He tried to make it sound like an adventure, but at the last conference he'd had with the doctor managing her case, they had a long road to travel before they could dream about returning to Ohio.

Forgive me, Gotte, *for the folly of making this trip. But don't let my daughter suffer for my decision.*

The family started chatting about all the fun things Rebecca could look forward to once she returned to Pinecraft.

Ephraim tugged at his shirtsleeve. "You're a hundred miles away. What's going on?"

He studied his family and shrugged. "Nothing, not really."

"Walk with me, little brother." Ephraim gestured along the paved walkway that made a gentle curve from one side of the courtyard to the other. Carefully cut greenery lined each side of the path. Nothing like their property in Ohio, where the focus was on the immense vegetable garden. His garden had remained scant and small. Hannah had been the one to tend to it.

Another unbidden memory.

"I've told *Gotte* I am sorry, sorry for ever coming here." He might as well be the first to speak.

"What? You think Rebecca's accident was punishment?"

"Yes. No. I don't know. Before we left Ohio, at the last Sunday meeting, Bishop Troyer pulled me aside." Jacob sucked in a deep breath. "He warned me about coming to Florida. He said it was worldly and dangerous. He told me to beware, or suffer the consequences for any compromise."

Ephraim shook his head. "Of course, we must be careful. Bishop only has your best interests at heart."

"It's because I almost left, isn't it?"

"That was a long time ago and you hadn't been baptized yet."

"That's not the time I'm talking about." He'd ventured, a bit, into the world, almost saving up enough money to buy a car. But he'd stopped himself.

However, after losing Hannah, grief had bitten into him so hard that he wanted to bundle the children into a hired vehicle and go—anywhere. There were plenty of groups throughout the country where ex-Amish could find refuge and help. He would have started with nothing, but still had the children and hope that life would get better. And, the memories wouldn't assault him at every turn.

"But you didn't leave," Ephraim reminded him. "This is not a punishment, Jacob. Sometimes things happen, but not apart from *Gotte's wille*."

Jacob wanted to scoff at the words. *Gotte's wille*. Sometimes trying to live with grace, no matter what the circumstances, was too hard for a man. No one could tell him how to bear this burden without questioning.

5

Daddy, Happy New Year." Natalie used her perkiest tone and the words came out just fine, even after she debated with herself for fifteen minutes before dialing the phone. "I know it's January fifth, but, better late than never, right?"

"Honey, it's good to hear from you." His voice cracked a little. It was just after eight in the morning on the west coast. "Are you doing okay? You're calling awful early."

"Sorry, did I wake you? I thought you'd be up, chasing after TJ."

"We're up, we're up. He loves the train set you sent him. Tried to bring the tracks and engine with him to bed the first night."

"Good, I'm glad." She swallowed hard and shifted on her bed, tucking one leg underneath her. "Um, I wanted to talk to you about the box of Mom's things you sent me." The box sat beside her now, its contents still shaking the foundation of what she'd always believed her quirky family to be.

A white prayer *kapp*, flat and folded. A cape dress in a lovely shade of Wedgwood blue, a white apron. An unfinished quilt top, made of scraps of fabric in a rose garden pattern. A genealogy page from a family Bible that contained her mother's birth date. When she held these items up to the mental image of what she knew about her mother, they didn't mesh. Not a bit.

"Dad? You still there?"

"I'm here. I, uh, I'm not sure how much I can tell you about your mother's family. She didn't tell me much. I knew better than to try to drag any info out of Kat Bennett."

"She *was* stubborn. Or, as she'd say—"

"Resolute," her father said with her simultaneously.

They both laughed and Dad didn't seem quite so far away and she felt a glimmer of the family she once knew, something had crumbled when Kat and Clive Bennett decided to head for Splitsville. Sure, Natalie had been old enough to be on her own at the time, but she'd assumed the union of the Flying Bennetts would last beyond the big top.

She'd assumed wrong.

"Dad, did Mom ever talk about being Amish, or mention where her family lived? I mean, she always told me she was an only child and her parents were dead."

"I know." Her father's laugh had disappeared and a sigh came across the line. "I let her. It was her business, after all. But I think they were from somewhere in Ohio.

We were young. She was only seventeen when we met, out with her friends and looking for a job and adventure in the circus. Her blue eyes, her innocence in spite of her tough-girl image . . ."

The story tumbled out of her dad, but Natalie had only heard her mother's version over the years.

"My parents were super-strict and so was their church, so I left as soon as I was old enough. Then I met your dad and the rest is history," Mom used to say.

It was pointless to vent to him, to ask why Mom had never said more about her family—a whole *family* that she'd left behind. Dad would say what he was saying now, it was her mother's business, and Kat Bennett had a right to her own secrets. But the idea that there was a family out there—Amish—well, they were Natalie's family, too.

"I was thinking about looking for them, Dad. I met an Amish family while volunteering at the hospital and they're really nice. Maybe they'd help me look for Mom's family, or know someone who might know them."

"Ah, Honey, it's probably best if you leave it alone. That's a whole world, closed off to outsiders. They keep themselves to themselves. And some of them have some pretty weird ideas. Katie Bennett might have died last year, but Katie Yoder died decades ago to her family. If there was one thing she didn't want to talk about, it was probably the whole shunning thing."

"Shunning."

"If you turn your back on your Amish family, you're dead to them. Or something like that. I always thought she was being figurative when she said her family had basically shunned her."

"Yes, I've heard of that."

"Not to change the subject, but I was going to tell you some more good news—wanted to wait, but Judy said I could."

"What's that?"

"You're going to have another little Bennett sibling by the summertime."

"Wow, um, congratulations. I should see about getting out there to visit you all."

"You should. It'll be harder for us to travel with a passel of kids, and Judy gets sick on planes."

They ended the call after some more chitchat—on her part. Her hand trembled as she pushed the End button her phone and stared at the box beside her.

Natalie reached for the Plain dress and sniffed. The faint scent of lavender. "Lord, I feel so adrift right now. I thought it would be easier, being a Christian. But the more I learn, the more alone I feel." Sure, she had a church she enjoyed and a small circle of casual friends. But they all had family affairs of their own to attend to this time of year.

"Thank You that Christmas is over for now." She placed the dress back in the box with the other items. Next trip to the hospital, she'd talk to the Millers. Surely, one of them would help her. If they said no—well, she wouldn't think about that.

Rebecca Miller stared at the bed taking up part of her *mammi's* living room. She'd never seen such a fancy bed, ever. It even had a motor on it, like the one in the hospital.

She wouldn't have to share a bed with her cousins Abby and Maybelle while they were here visiting in Florida. *Daed* had said she would find something to be thankful for about having a broken leg. The thick cast made her leg feel like she had an anvil tied to it. Getting her own bed to herself, well, that was a *gut* thing. Abby hogged the blankets and Maybelle talked in her sleep.

"That's a big bed, *Daed*," she said as she looked up at her father. He smiled at her, but his eyes still looked sad, just like they'd always looked since her *mamm* died.

"Up you go, try it out. We need to make sure you get your rest." He touched the side of her head.

"Don't worry. My head doesn't hurt today." She would do her best not to scare any of them. She didn't want to go back to the hospital. Ever. Except maybe to see the pretty clown who juggled. She made sure nobody touched the kitten that Miss Bubbles had made for her. She would keep it forever. Even if she never saw Miss Bubbles again.

Even Zeke looked sad as they left the hospital. "We didn't get to say goodbye."

"I know." But she was tired of sleeping in a noisy place like the hospital. They were always waking her up, too. "But we got to say goodbye to Miss Fran. She's the nicest nurse in the world."

Mammi made all her favorite foods for supper that night and *Aenti* Katie made her delicious apple crumble for dessert. She wanted to go to the park, but knew there wasn't a way to get her there, not with the wheelchair she had.

When nighttime came around, instead of being tucked into the room with her cousins who were set to leave Pinecraft early the next morning, Rebecca found herself snug in her hospital bed in the front room, her leg propped up like it had been in the hospital.

Her leg ached, but she wasn't going to cry and be a big baby. She had put the family through so much trouble, and poor *Daed*, he had enough worries. Rebecca strained to hear whispers around the family table in the kitchen.

". . . start working for Henry Hostetler first thing," said her *daed.* "I was able to make a phone call to the cabinet shop. They understand I won't be coming back for a while."

Rebecca frowned. Her fault. She reached for Molly, her doll. No Molly. Did they pack everything from the hospital? But Rebecca hadn't needed much. Molly wasn't even the best-stitched doll. A faint memory of her *mamm* came around again, giving her the doll on Christmas, long ago.

Molly was gone. Now she really *would* cry. She tried to be brave, but tonight her trying wasn't *gut* enough.

"The Mullets are having a singing tonight. We should go," said Ephraim.

"But Rebecca . . ."

"I will sit with the children tonight," said *Mammi*. "You three go, get your grandfather out of the house as well."

"I don't know." But the Mullets were known for their hospitality, along with the guarantee of hot *kaffi* and hot cocoa for their guests. The music would do them all some good. The Pinecraft residents would also be glad to know Rebecca was safe at home, at last. It would save Jacob the chore of repeating the story a few dozen times.

Jacob paused at the hospital bed in the living room. Rebecca slept, her breathing even, one hand gripping the sheets in a crumple.

"If she needs anything, I will be here." *Mammi's* words should have reassured him. "Go. She sleeps."

They want out into the January night and joined others in the neighborhood heading for the Mullets' home but a few blocks away. A hint of remaining warmth from the day lingered on the pavement. The first streetlights clicked on, their light filtered through the Spanish moss that hung from trees.

A beautiful night. A romantic night, Hannah would have told him. Ironic. She used to tell Jacob about winter vacations spent in Pinecraft as a young girl, visiting her friends and family. Cousin to Betsy Yoder, who he just now caught sight of, walking with some of her friends toward the singing.

They made their way past a score of bicycles lining the driveway and parked in the front yard. No horses and buggies allowed in Sarasota, but bicycles seemed to multiply like rabbits whenever something big was going on in Pinecraft.

Singings were a little different in Pinecraft than Ohio, he'd realized. Amish from all orders and various districts as well as

Mennonites from different parts of the country gathered in the courtyard that lay between the Mullet family's complex.

Someone was tuning a guitar, one of the Mennonites from Kentucky, he was told.

"It's the Ohio Millers!" a voice called out. Henry Hostetler, who tonight wore a yellow Hawaiian print shirt. "How's that little girl of yours doing?"

"She's home in bed, resting," Jacob replied, but was quick to add, "My *mammi* is helping watch over her tonight."

"That's great news, great news, to be sure." The older Mennonite man nodded. "We're thankful for answered prayers."

"Us, too," Jacob said, glancing at his brother and sister-in-law. "They're leaving on the next bus for Ohio."

Some from the neighborhood crowded round, murmuring their own plans and regrets to see part of the Miller family leaving.

"I get to keep my grandson and his children for a while longer," said *Daadi*.

Jacob nodded and studied the others in the courtyard. Some had brought their own chairs; others perched at the perimeter on their wide bicycle seats to join the singing. Betsy was staring at him. Of course, at some point during the night, he'd find himself speaking to her. She was one of Hannah's cousins, after all. He couldn't be rude. He needed to share his gratitude for her visiting Rebecca in the hospital.

"Hot coffee and hot chocolate at the corner table, if anyone wants some before we get started," called out Matthew Mullet, a friend of his father's. "Tonight we're going to start with Harold Stoltzfus and his family from Pennsylvania, who have brought their guitars and one banjo." After the Mennonites had their turn, another family would follow, the Frys, also from Pennsylvania, who would lead the group in some traditional hymns.

A few stepped forward to get warm beverages, but Jacob stayed where he was. The evening chill was coming upon them, reminding them while this was Florida, it was still January.

He wasn't accustomed to the musical instruments. Then the music started and he found himself tapping his foot. Bluegrass, he knew it was called. Or something like it. The song was called "Pickin' Cotton" and featured a banjo solo. Happy music.

Somehow, during the evening, Betsy had sidled her way closer in his direction, and once Matthew Mullet made announcements for an intermission, she was standing next to Katie.

"My parents are leaving on the next bus, too," she announced to their small circle. "I didn't know that," said his sister-in-law. "We wish we didn't have to leave Jacob and the children here, but Ephraim's shop is set to reopen after their winter break so we don't have much choice."

"I'm staying." Betsy's announcement made them all stare at her.

Surely Jacob's ears had deceived him. "You're staying? Why?"

Her cheeks shot full of red. "I have a job. Cleaning houses with my *Aenti* Chelle. I start Monday."

"A job." Katie shook her head. "But, your parents are leaving."

"I know. Since I'm staying with my aunt, my father said it was fine, but to make sure I attend services on the weekend."

"It almost sounds like *Rumspringa*," Katie said.

"Oh no, not at all. I've been baptized and I'm not leaving anything. I think I'll be more useful here. I like the sun and the beach. I like the idea I can earn some money." Betsy's blue eyes glanced toward Jacob. "How long are you planning to stay?"

"I'm not sure. It depends on how long it takes Rebecca to be well enough to travel by van or bus. The doctor also wants her to avoid traveling because of her brain injury. For now."

Betsy Yoder, staying on in Pinecraft. Cleaning houses. His poor tired brain was trying hard to process the idea.

Some would say this was a sign, others would say it was a young woman's shrewd attempt to remain behind and see what happened next.

What was her father thinking, allowing her to stay? The Yoders had family here year-round, as did quite a few of the visitors. Or friends, or friends of friends. But Betsy was a farm girl, unaccustomed to life in the city.

"*Kaffi?*" Betsy asked.

Jacob yanked his focus away from his thoughts. Ephraim and Katie stared at him. Betsy was asking *him* if he wanted coffee. Oh, this was a bad idea tonight. He should have stayed home.

Instead, he opened his mouth and said, "Yes, please."

She nodded and ambled toward the refreshment table, her flip-flops snapping on the pavement.

"You know why she's staying." Katie's voice was low.

"I haven't asked her to."

"Well, I think she's holding out hope . . ." His sister-in-law's voice fell silent as Betsy returned with two Styrofoam cups of coffee, steam trailing away from the brims.

"Here you are." She extended one cup to him. "Cream only."

She knew without asking how he drank his coffee. Jacob stifled a groan. "Thanks." A group of singers marched to the area serving as a stage, of sorts. Not that anyone was showing off, in particular.

The quintet of three men and two women hummed, getting their voices in tune. Jacob closed his eyes and listened to the harmonies, then sang with the rest of the group. The familiar hymn brought him back to Ohio, another unbidden memory. The same hymn they sang during the singing, after which he first took Hannah home by buggy.

Under a starlit night, they'd talked and laughed, the sounds mingling with the clopping of his horse's hooves. Jacob opened his eyes and scanned the crowd. Friends, distant relatives, a few strangers. The night breeze lifted the fronds of the nearest palm tree in a gentle hiss.

The unknown lay before him. Betsy sipped her coffee and studied him over the edge of her cup. Something familiar flickered in her eyes, then was gone.

6

It wasn't her day to volunteer at the hospital, but Natalie hoped to make this a quick errand. She had baked some loaves of her apple bread, wrapped carefully with plastic wrap and tied with a simple ribbon bow. Before she left her apartment, she tucked the still-warm trio of loaves into her tote bag.

She zipped along to the pediatrics wing and waved at Fran as she entered Rebecca's room. As before, she stopped in the doorway when she saw an empty room. But this time, she saw crisp fresh linens on the bed, the furniture neatly arranged and not helping a family keep vigil.

"They released her last night." Fran stood by Natalie's shoulder in the doorway.

"Oh." She stepped into the room anyway, then strode to the window. "I . . . I brought them some apple bread." As if that made any sense to Fran.

"I know, hon, you got attached." Fran's soft voice brimmed with understanding. "This family more than others."

"Yes, I did." She didn't care to explain the reasoning, or the hope she held inside her tote bag, hope that the Millers would help her find Katie Yoder's family. Her family.

The phone buzzed at the desk, and Fran left the doorway. Natalie sighed as she entered the room. She sank onto the chair nearest the bed. Well, she thought it was a good idea to ask the Millers about her family. A dark object on the floor, under the corner of the bed, caught her attention.

Natalie got down on her hands and knees, reaching for the dark whatever-it-was. Her fingers touched fabric. She pulled out a doll, wearing a smaller version of the cape dress and apron worn by its owner.

She stood, hugging the doll to her chest. She snatched up her tote bag, and left the room. Fran was hanging up the phone when Natalie stopped at the desk.

"You know I can't give you an address. HIPAA." Fran frowned at the computer monitor in front of her. "I almost wish I could. But I'm not getting fined, losing my job, or going to jail for nobody."

"I know. I wouldn't ask you to, either." Patients had rights to privacy, with good reason. Natalie understood patient privacy rights. She held up the doll. "I'm going to track them down, somehow. Sarasota's a big city, but I know I can find their neighborhood."

"Yes, ma'am. Yoder's restaurant on Bahia Vista would be a good place to start."

"Yoder's?"

"Uh-huh. They have a restaurant, fresh market, and a gift shop. I bet someone there might know something about the Millers. Or someone who knows where they live." Fran licked her lips. "We've been to Yoder's for supper. Had the fried chicken, with greens and mashed potatoes. Yum, yum, yum."

"Good idea. I'll start there." She smiled at the nurse. "Thanks."

"Bring your appetite when you go and save room for pie," Fran called out as Natalie left the floor.

Natalie waved, fighting off the sensation of wobbly knees trying to take over. Within minutes, she plugged Yoder's and Bahia Vista into her phone's GPS and was heading across the city.

Bahia Vista was a long east-west four-lane street bisecting part of Sarasota. After a series of stoplights, Natalie saw a sign for Big Olaf's ice cream parlor. In front of the neat white building sat a few women in clothing of the Plain people as well as bearded men wearing dark trousers with suspenders. She'd found Pinecraft.

On the other side of the stoplight stood signs for Yoder's Restaurant, so she pulled into the nearest vacant parking spot. "You have arrived," observed her phone. Yes, she'd arrived, all right.

Natalie opened her tote bag and looked at the doll inside. "Well, let's see if we can find your little momma."

She saw a window for placing orders to go, but her stomach growled. Maybe she should go ahead, sit down, and have lunch inside. If she was here long enough, maybe the Millers themselves would come walking in.

A stream of women in cape dresses with others in regular street clothes made a short line outside the restaurant. Natalie tried not to stare at the contrasts. She exited her car, clicked the lock, and watched as a Plain family crossed busy Bahia Vista Street on bicycles. The mother drove a three-wheeled tricycle, towing a small wagon large enough to hold the toddler that rode inside. They could have been on a movie set. But no, this was real.

A sweet Mennonite woman stood at the hostess desk as Natalie followed the line. "Just one?"

"Just one." Natalie shifted her bag on her shoulder. Silly. What had she expected, to find the Millers coincidentally inside and have a joyful reunion as she returned the doll to

Rebecca, then asked about her mother's family? But she had to start somewhere, and might as well begin her search on a full stomach.

The waitress, an older woman in a dark polo shirt and khaki trousers, brought her a glass of ice water. "Now, are you ready to order?"

"I'm having a hard time deciding. What's your favorite?"

"The meatloaf, with seasoned green beans and potato casserole. You'll like the cornbread muffins, too."

"Okay, I'll have that."

As her waitress scribbled on her order pad, Natalie plucked up her courage. "Do you—do you happen to know a family named Miller, visiting from Ohio?"

"I know several Millers. It's a popular name around here. My maiden name is Miller, in fact."

"Oh. Well, I'm looking for the family of Rebecca Miller. She's about seven years old and was just released from the hospital with a broken leg. Her father's name is Jacob, and her aunt's name is Katie."

The woman nodded. "Ah, I think I heard about that one. Little girl was struck by a car, at the traffic light right out here. Just before Christmas." She shook her head. "I don't know the family, though."

"Oh, I see."

"But, tell you what. I can ask back in the kitchen. Etta Yoder knows everyone in Pinecraft."

"Is she of Yoder's restaurant?"

"Oh, yes, she is. The whole family runs the business."

"Well, I'll ask her, then. Thank you, thank you very much."

Her waitress left and scurried toward the kitchen, and Natalie allowed herself to study the kaleidoscope of different wardrobes worn by her fellow diners. She noticed not all *kapps* were alike, and not all cape dresses were, either. The worlds of the *Englisch* and Amish blended here in the restaurant as locals and tourists alike filled the tables.

A white-haired woman wearing a slate blue cape dress and sheer white *kapp* stopped at her table. "Excuse me, are you the one asking about the Millers?"

"Yes, that's me. Are you Etta?"

The older woman nodded. "I am. You're looking for the Millers who live on Birky Street. I've known Rachel Miller for over forty years, and it about broke my heart to hear of her great-granddaughter getting injured."

"I'm Natalie Bennett. I met them while Rebecca was in the hospital. Rebecca left her doll, and I wanted to return it to her."

"Ah, I see. Well, I'm sure they'll be glad to see you."

"I hope so."

Etta nodded. "Enjoy your meal."

"Oh, I plan on it." In her hurry to get out the door this morning, she'd skipped breakfast. "Thanks for your help."

If it wasn't for her being so hungry, she'd have asked them to box her meal and she'd take it to go. She should've called Grace to join her for lunch. The older woman would have had a ball and probably would insist on going through every inch of the gift shop next door. But then, this quest was something she wanted to make on her own.

Natalie savored the restaurant's peaceful lunchtime bustle, then forced herself to take her time eating. Soon enough, she'd find the Millers, thanks to Etta. Her waitress was right; the meatloaf had perfect seasoning and practically melted in her mouth. The green beans convinced her beans weren't such a bad side dish after all, and she could eat the cheesy casserole all day long.

"Room for pie? Coconut cream is our special today," her waitress asked as she picked up her plate and flatware.

"No, I'm stuffed. Completely. But I'll be back for sure some other time."

"I'm glad you enjoyed it. Here's your check. They can help you out at the register."

Natalie headed for the register, lugging her tote bag. This place was a treasure; not quite touristy, it wouldn't fall for that.

She noted a brilliantly colored magazine next to a shelf of cookbooks and other books about the Amish for sale. *Cooking and Such*. She grabbed a copy. One of these days, she'd promised herself to brush up on her cooking skills. If it turned out half as delicious as the layer cake looked on the cover, she'd be doing well.

Birky Street. As she handed her check to the cashier, she asked, "Can you tell me where Birky Street is?"

"Sure, just cross at the light out here at Bahia Vista and Kaufman, go straight across and it's the first street on your right," the *Englisch* girl running the register replied.

"Thanks." Natalie held up the magazine. "I'll take this, too."

Etta entered the area behind the registers. "There you are. The Millers' home is the white house with blue trim. They usually have a small table out front by the driveway with grapefruit for sale."

Within five minutes, Natalie was back in her car, maneuvering her way to Birky Street. "White house with blue trim, table with grapefruit."

No sidewalks here, so she made sure she gave pedestrians and bicyclists enough room as her car crept along the street. She could see why bicycling or walking would be an easier way to get around the neighborhood. Birky Street.

She took a right and kept driving. There it was, white house with blue trim. A trio of palm trees separated it from the house beside it. The house had a driveway, but no cars, just an assortment of bicycles tucked underneath a carport.

As she left her car, she felt as if a flock of seagulls had started batting their wings inside her stomach. What was wrong with her? Put her on a circus platform in a coliseum or beneath a big top full of thousands, and the thought exhilarated her. Here she was just returning a doll to a little girl and asking a favor of near strangers, and she wanted to dash back to her car and the security of home.

The older woman, the grandmother Mrs. Miller, answered the door. "*Ach*, you're the young lady from the hospital."

"Yes, I found something that belongs to Rebecca." Natalie slid the doll from the tote bag.

Mrs. Miller pulled the door open further. "Well, come in, come in. Rebecca has been missing her doll."

Natalie entered the home. The aroma of pie crust and fruit filled the room. A hospital bed also took up part of the room as well.

"Miss Natalie, it's really you. I thought I would never see you again. Ever." Rebecca clapped her hands. "How did you find me?"

"I had lunch at Yoder's, and Mrs. Etta Yoder told me where you lived. Here." Natalie waved the doll in the air. "I found someone in your old room. I think she missed you."

"Molly!" Rebecca reached for the doll. "I thought she was gone forever."

"Thank you for doing this for Natalie," said Mrs. Miller. "Would you like some lemonade? Fresh squeezed."

"Yes, it sounds delicious. Thanks." She watched the Amish matron retreat from the living room. The house seemed curiously empty. Rebecca's hospital room always seemed to have a throng of family and visitors.

"I can't wait till I can go to the park again." Rebecca sighed. "Maybe tomorrow. That's where Zeke is with *Daadi*. Playing bocce. Zeke's too young to play with the old men."

"Ah, I see. Do you have a wheelchair you can ride in?"

"It's supposed to get here today. My *daed* helps carry me in the house."

Natalie wanted to ask about Jacob, but didn't.

Mrs. Miller reentered the living room. She held a glass of lemonade. "Here, please, sit down for a few minutes."

"Thank you." Natalie accepted the glass and sat down on the nearest cushioned chair. A fan circulated air in the room. "You have electricity here."

"Yes, we do. We can have things like electricity here in Pinecraft, if my husband and I were living in Ohio, we wouldn't have. Well, in Ohio we power our lamps and stove with gas."

Natalie nodded, setting her glass on a nearby coaster. She reached for her tote bag and for the apple breads. "Here. I made these for you, Mrs. Miller. I hope you enjoy them." She pulled the loaves from the bag.

"Why, thank you. Please, call me Rachel. If anything, we should have done something for you, to thank you for helping Rebecca smile while she was in the hospital. But my grandson has started a new job here, so he probably didn't think of it."

"Well, I brought the bread mostly because I have a favor to ask."

"Oh?" The older woman's eyebrows raised. "What is that?"

Natalie inhaled a deep breath before continuing. "I recently learned that my mother used to be Amish. She never told me. All the time, growing up, I thought my grandparents on my mother's side were dead and she had no other family. I'd ask my mother for more help, but she passed away last summer of cancer." The words caught in her throat.

"I am sorry she lied to you."

Lied was a strong word, but yes, hiding your family from your only child, that was a lie. Anger threatened to bubble up inside, but Natalie quelled the heat. "Thanks. I don't know why she felt she had to. Anyway, my father sent me some of her things, some of her Amish things, including a family genealogy of sorts taken from a Bible, I believe. I was hoping you might be able to help me look for her family."

Rachel nodded slowly. "I see. What was her name?"

"Katie Yoder. I think her family was from Ohio, but that's all I know."

Rachel frowned. "*Ach*, that's not much to go on. Katie Yoder is about as common as the *Englisch* Jane Smith. Do you have the genealogy page with you?"

Natalie picked up her bag, rummaged through the contents. She'd left it on the counter at home, probably. "I'm afraid I don't." But then, she'd been afraid of being turned down.

"What else did your mother leave for you? You said she had more things."

"A dress, and her *kapp*. And an unfinished quilt top."

Rachel's eyes lit up. "Now, I would like to see the quilt top. Do you know its pattern?"

"I don't. I'm not much of a seamstress." An understatement, except she had enough skill to mend small tears and sew on buttons. "I'm honestly not sure what I should do with it."

"Do? You could finish it."

"Finish it." She hadn't thought about that. She wouldn't know where to start.

"Of course. It's likely the quilt was supposed to be a gift for someone. Or, for her own bed after her wedding."

Natalie nodded.

"My *daed* started a new job today," said Rebecca. "It's not making cabinets but fixing things. He says it's good honest work."

"*Yah*, it is," Rachel replied. "*Ach*, the house will be so quiet when you leave for Ohio."

That answered her question about where Jacob was. "How long do you think Jacob and the children will be here?" Natalie allowed herself to ask.

"That I don't know." Rachel rose from her chair and moved to Rebecca's bedside. "Her *onkel, aenti*, and cousins left on the Thursday bus."

A knock sounded at the front door.

"Oh." Rachel glanced at the door. "I'm not expecting company. But you never know around here. Someone may be coming by to welcome Rebecca home."

Instead, it was an efficient-looking woman in a polo shirt and khakis. "I'm from Palm Grove Medical Supply. A wheelchair for Miller?"

"We are the Millers," said Rachel. "Do we pay you?"

"No, no. We bill," said the woman. Rachel signed a paper on the clipboard.

Natalie rose. She should go. She'd enjoyed the lemonade and the conversation, but clearly it wasn't a good time.

"Wait here, Miss Natalie. We're not through talking yet." Rachel's tone made Natalie want to behave, to visit and chat.

But she waited while the medical assistant showed them the features of the wheelchair, how to lock the wheels, and only after Rachel showed she could negotiate the chair through the living room did the assistant agree to sign off and leave.

"Now, to bed with you for now, unless you'd like to sit on the couch," Rachel said as she helped Rebecca out of the chair.

"Couch, like the grownups." Rebecca hobbled toward the couch. "I wish I could use crutches. I don't want people to have to push me to go places."

"Not until your father gets home." With Natalie's help, Rachel made sure Rebecca was seated with her broken leg, now in a long cast, propped up on an ottoman with a pillow. Once Rebecca was settled, Rachel turned to face Natalie.

"About your *mamm*, and the quilt top. I think I can help you with both. Why don't you stay for supper? I know the *kinner* would like that. We can take our time and talk."

The front door clicked open and Zeke bounded inside. "Becca, I saw an alligator. A little one, but it was *real*." He was followed by the elder Mr. Miller, who stopped stock-still in the doorway for a few seconds when his eyes met Natalie's.

He glanced at Rachel and said something in Pennsylvania Dutch. She stood and followed her husband into the kitchen, where whispered voices rose and fell. Natalie knew the word *Englisch*, and understood *Katie* and *Yoder* easily enough.

"I'm glad you're here," Rebecca said. "I'm glad you brought Molly, too."

"When I saw your doll on the floor, I knew you probably missed her, so I had to look for you. It was easy as going to Yoder's Restaurant."

"Are you trying to find your family, too?"

Natalie nodded. "Something like that. My mother never told me she used to be Amish. I want to find my grandparents, if they're still alive."

"How long was your *mamm* sick?"

"A long time. Several years." Natalie shifted on the cushion. Surely, this wasn't the best conversation to have with a young child.

"My *mamm* died, too," whispered Zeke. "She was having my little brother. Too soon, *Daed* said."

Her heart seized up. These children, to have tasted grief so young. Here she was, twenty-eight, and even now, it sometimes ripped through her. To lose a little sibling at the same time. What Jacob must have gone through as well.

"I am sorry, both of you," was all Natalie could manage. "I was blessed to have had my mother as long as I did."

"*Daed* said she is probably in Heaven, she was such a good wife and *mamm*," Rebecca said. "But I miss her. My *Aenti* Katie says it is time for my *daed* to move on, me and Zeke need a new *mamm*, but I don't want one."

"Oh?"

Rebecca shook her head. "I am in my second year of school. If I work hard, I can finish early and help my *daed* in the house, so he doesn't have to do it on his own. I can already do all the laundry."

Natalie couldn't resist a smile at the little girl's grownup-sounding plan. "That is sweet of you, wanting to help your dad."

"Do you have brothers or sisters?" Zeke asked.

"Actually, I do." Natalie paused. How to explain divorce to children, especially Amish children? That her father had tired of bickering with her mother, then found a newer, younger version to start another family with?

"I have a younger brother, half-brother. My parents, ah, divorced about five years ago, and my dad married again. So, now I have a younger brother. I've seen him. Once, after he was born. He's three now."

"Three? But you're old enough to be a *mamm*, and have a little boy who's three."

Natalie tried not to sigh as she nodded. Yes, the more than two decades' age difference wasn't lost on her either.

"Do they live here?"

"No, California."

"*Ach*, I've never been to California, only here. And in Ohio."

The older couple reentered the living room and Natalie rose as Mr. Miller approached her. "I found Rebecca's doll in the hospital room and returned it to her.'"

The elderly man eyed her worldly clothes, or worldly to him, anyway. "It was just a doll. But thank you. Rachel says you're staying for supper."

"Um, yes sir."

He nodded. "That's some fine apple bread you brought us. Should go nice with a cup of *kaffi*." With that, he strode back toward the kitchen.

Rachel chuckled. "That's my Isaiah. He always does like a *gut* bread."

Yet his unspoken disapproval lingered in the air.

Jacob's muscles reminded him that he'd been on vacation, sort of. Not counting the trips back and forth to the hospital. But the sitting and indulging in his great-grandmother's cooking were making him soft. Today while he perched atop the roof of a Sarasota *Englisch* family, he had confirmation of his inactivity.

He shifted on the front seat of Henry Hostetler's minivan. "Same time tomorrow?"

"Same time," Henry said as he turned onto Birky Street. "And don't worry about packing a lunch. Chelle is sending lunch for all of us tomorrow."

"I'll remember that." Jacob flexed his arms. "It feels *gut* to be working again. Thank you for the chance."

"I've been looking at expanding the business, so it's all hands on deck." Henry pulled up into the driveway. "Looks like you have some company."

Rebecca was sitting in a wheelchair on the front sidewalk, grinning as Zeke was bent over backwards in the front yard, his belly up to the sky as he tried to mimic the actions of a young woman whose long dark hair touched the ground.

She pushed her weight onto her hands and let the momentum carry her feet backwards over her head.

Natalie Bennett, doing some kind of a back flip in his front yard. Or rather, his grandparents' front yard.

She popped up onto her feet and stared at him as he opened the door to the minivan.

"Looks like you've got company," Henry observed again. "Pretty company."

"Looks like it." He picked up the small cooler he'd use to hold his lunch. "I'll see you in the morning."

"See you." Henry waved at the children. "Tell your family hello."

Jacob nodded as he shut the door. "Will do."

The van careened along down the street, halting at the stop sign long enough to be called a legal stop, then hanging a quick left toward Bahia Vista.

"*Daed!*" The sound was the best thing he'd heard all day. Zeke ran to him and jumped into his arms.

"How's my Ezekiel doing today?"

"Very *gut*. *Daadi* took me to the park and we saw an alligator in the water."

He set his son down. "Did you now?" He'd never seen an alligator before, only in pictures.

Natalie stood to the side, her face flushed.

"Miss Natalie found my doll at the hospital, and then she found us," announced Rebecca from her wheelchair. "*Mammi* has invited her to stay for supper. Miss Natalie's *mamm* used to be Amish when she was young, but she never told anybody."

"I see." Natalie Bennett's mother, formerly Amish? He tried to process his daughter's chatter.

"Hello, Mr. Miller." Natalie crossed her arms. "It's nice to see you. Congratulations on the new job."

"Ah, yes, thank you." He nodded. "It will help pass the time while Rebecca recovers."

"But I have a wheelchair now, *Daed*. It can help me get around."

"That's true, but you have more than a broken leg to recover from." He passed by Miss Bennett, unsure of what else to say to the young woman. He stopped and turned to face her. "Thank you for bringing the doll. My Becca was missing her very much."

"You're welcome." A smile quirked the edges of her mouth and the breeze lifted the wispy ends of her nut-brown hair.

If Natalie Bennett were a proper Amish woman, she would wear her hair up in a bun or a twist, topped with a prayer covering. The glory of her hair would be evident only to her husband, not streaming past her shoulders for the world—for him—to see.

But then, Natalie Bennett wasn't a proper Amish woman. He almost found himself almost wishing she was.

7

The children's chatter and laughter buoyed Jacob's spirits during supper, although his mind and awareness couldn't ignore the young woman across the table from him. She and *Mammi* talked about a quilt, and Miss Bennett kept reinforcing the fact she wasn't much of a seamstress.

"I still say you should put in your mother's quilt."

"Put in?"

"Finish it." *Mammi* stressed the two words. "She began it. You can put it in."

"I—I suppose I could. I wouldn't know where to start. Or how."

"Do you work during the day, like most *Englisch* women, at a career?" *Mammi* asked.

"I teach at the circus school a few mornings a week and every afternoon. My hours can be a bit different than most career women."

"I tell you what," *Mammi* said. "Bring your quilt top to me and I will start helping you on mornings when you are free. I have a quilting frame we can open up while we work on the quilt. The work will be yours, though."

Miss Bennett nodded. "Fair enough. But I would hate to mess it up."

"And now, the matter of your family. Next time, bring the papers you have and we'll see what we can do. Right, Isaiah?" *Mammi* glanced at *Daadi*.

"Yes, we can."

"Her *mamm* used to be Amish a long time ago," Rebecca said. "But she died."

Natalie nodded, her gaze focused on her plate. "Last summer."

"I'm sorry to hear that." Jacob took a bite of grandmother's potpie, fresh from the oven less than an hour before. The comforting food did a little to take the pang off a ripple of grief running through him.

Their eyes met and he saw his own grief reflected in Natalie's brown eyes. Maybe grief was the connection he felt with this young woman. Grief had cut into their worlds, slicing the natural order of things into shreds he wasn't sure could be stitched together again.

A very unAmish sentiment. He reminded himself *Gotte's wille* had taken Hannah earlier than any of them had planned. Surely, Natalie Bennett had anticipated having her mother around for a long, long time. Sometimes *Gotte* had other things in mind than what they wanted.

"Mrs. Miller, this was the best potpie I've ever had," Natalie said. She paused long enough to wipe her mouth with a paper napkin. "Although I have to say the only potpie my mother served was the little round frozen mini-pies. You know, one pie per person."

Jacob shook his head as he took another bite. He couldn't imagine living in a world of instant food everywhere, microwaved this, frozen that. Of course, once in a blue moon they'd indulge the children in fast food, but it wasn't a typical part of their regular diet. The dollars wasted could be put to better use than a meal devoured within minutes.

"Frozen potpie?" *Mammi* mimicked Jacob's head shake. "I can see that freezing leftovers would be a wise idea. But prepackaged potpie?"

"I guess my mother didn't like to cook." Natalie smiled. "You think she'd have held onto some part of her roots . . . If you don't mind, may I take you and the children for ice cream, to that place by the traffic light—Big Olaf's? Just to say thank-you for supper." Natalie's eyes shifted from Jacob to his grandparents. He tried not to stiffen, but let his fork settle onto his nearly empty plate with a clink.

Daadi sat up straighter on his chair at the head of the table and cleared his throat. *Mammi* stood and began clearing empty plates from the table.

"Oh, ice cream," Zeke said. "May we, *Daed*?"

"I'm feeling all right now. Please?" Rebecca pleaded with him.

Evidently, Natalie didn't know about the parental rule about not suggesting anything in front of children, any hint of fun that must be approved by adults, especially if she didn't want the children's pleading to follow. But then his children never pleaded. This was the closest they usually came to pleading. And of course, Natalie had no way of knowing about their outing for ice cream, the night Rebecca was struck by the car.

"If it's not a good evening, I understand," Natalie said.

"It's not that," Jacob said. "We were . . . we were coming back from getting ice cream at Big Olaf's when the accident happened."

"Oh, I'm sorry I suggested it."

"You didn't know." He tried not to glance at his children. Zeke stopped squirming and finished the last of his milk. Rebecca looked pale, but resolute.

"It was a Mennonite girl, home from college. She didn't mean it," Rebecca said. "I wasn't watching the cars."

"Well, we can all go," said *Mammi*. "I have a taste for that cookies and cream flavor."

Never mind Jacob knew she'd baked a coconut cream pie this morning. She'd already started on her cooking when he met Henry Hostetler at the front curb.

"I guess we're getting ice cream," Jacob said.

"Hooray!" Zeke clapped, bouncing on his chair.

Within fifteen minutes after some low grumbling from his *daadi*, they had Rebecca settled in her wheelchair and were heading in a pack toward the Bahia Vista light. There were the Yoders—Betsy's parents—out for a walk after supper. They waved the family down before all of them reached the corner of Birky Street.

"We heard the news," said Mr. Yoder. "Welcome home, Rebecca."

"Thank you," she said. "I get to ride in a wheelchair until I'm allowed to use crutches."

Ach, a child's exuberance in the face of obstacles. Tonight, Jacob would let her enjoy the moment. He shook hands with Mr. Yoder.

"We appreciate what everyone's done for us. Thank you, and thank the rest of the elders." Without the help of the others, he didn't want to think of the growing dollar amount of Rebecca's hospital bills, and what lay ahead of them.

Mr. Yoder nodded. "We are thankful that we were able to help."

"We're leaving on the next bus," Mrs. Yoder said. "Please keep in touch about your progress."

"Of course we will," said *Mammi*.

"I do have a favor to ask of you," Mrs. Yoder stepped forward, a frown crossing her face. "It's about Betsy."

"Is everything all right?" *Mammi* asked.

"She is staying behind in Pinecraft when we leave."

Jacob didn't miss Natalie's expression of curiosity. Her eyebrows were up as she looked at him.

"No harm in that. The winter will bring plenty of visitors." *Mammi* nodded. "It's an exciting time for the young people, for us older ones, too."

Mrs. Yoder gave Jacob a pointed glance. "She is cleaning houses and staying with my mother's youngest cousin on Schlock Street. Until she goes home, it will be nice for us to know she is watched over, besides her staying with Rochelle."

"You can be sure we'll watch out for her," said *Mammi*. "I'm sure she'll be ready to go home by early spring. The crowds disappear and it's just not the same without them."

The conversation drifted to small talk. Jacob studied Natalie, who was the subject of some curious glances from the Yoders.

Yoder. At supper, she'd mentioned her mother was a Yoder.

"Mr. and Mrs. Yoder, do you know of a Katie Yoder who left her Order some years ago?" he asked. Natalie's posture snapped to attention and she drew closer, away from the children.

The couple exchanged glances. "No, I don't believe we do," said Mr. Yoder. "We would definitely remember the name, and remember to pray for her to return home to her family."

After saying their goodbyes until the Millers returned to Ohio, they continued on their way. Zeke led their small band, bouncing on his feet.

"Ice cream, ice cream, I'm getting ice cream." His brown hair shook as he bounced. Then came a stream of Pennsylvania Dutch.

"Thank you for asking about my mother," Natalie spoke beside Jacob. "Next time, I'll be sure I bring more information. Such as her parents' and siblings' names."

Jacob nodded. He recalled his great-grandmother's words to him about Natalie being lonely, and praying *Gotte* would settle her in a family. He would definitely pray the same thing. If he didn't have his family, going through what he'd gone through in losing Hannah . . . thank *Gotte* for His providence.

They came to the traffic light. Cars crisscrossed in front of them on Bahia Vista, just as they had that night—was it only weeks ago? He took a deep breath. It would be different this time. Of course it would be.

Everything was different after crossing this street on foot for ice cream once before. The evidence surrounded him even now. Rebecca, injured and facing months of recovery, and a volunteer hospital clown searching for her Amish roots who stood close by.

"*Daed,* are you ready for ice cream?" Zeke said, tucking his hand inside one of Jacob's.

"*Yah.*" That, and whatever else lay ahead. Even Betsy Yoder staying behind in Pinecraft.

Betsy put her feet up on *Aenti* Chelle's chaise lounge in the breezy lanai. Aunt Chelle was her grandmother's youngest cousin, but had left the Order with her parents when they became Mennonite before she turned nineteen.

Once upon a time, *Aenti* had been set to marry, but something had happened, something still not spoken of in Yoder family history to this very day. It was bad enough for Aunt Chelle to leave the northland and spend her time here in Pinecraft year-round.

In spite of that slice of the Yoder family not being part of their Order, they still remained Plain, part of the conservative branch of the Mennonite church. *Aenti* Chelle wore lovely cape dresses in tropical colors and a bright-white head covering, but no apron. Betsy had only seen her *aenti's* hair down on rare occasions in the evening. She drove a van that usually brimmed with supplies and tools for her housecleaning business.

Betsy and her *aenti* had both logged a full day's work as *Aenti* let Betsy shadow her while visiting clients.

"My feet are sore," Betsy said as her *aenti* stepped out to the lanai. She took a sip of Aunt Chelle's fresh-made lemonade and watched the palm trees wave in the twilight outside.

"It's a lot of time on your feet, I know." Aunt Chelle held her own glass of lemonade. "You're sure you want to stay?"

"I do. I have to. I need to."

Her *aenti* nodded as she took the chaise lounge opposite Betsy's. "Ah, this is my favorite room in the house, you know. Up first thing in the morning, drinking my coffee and reading my Bible, having breakfast, feeling the breeze."

Aenti Chelle fell silent. Despite her typical cheer while at work, *Aenti* bore a quiet sadness that only showed up occasionally when she and Betsy were alone. Like now.

More than once since Betsy had lugged her suitcase from her parents' vacation rental home to her aunt's home, she'd intended to ask why her aunt had never married.

"I like this space. A lot. We couldn't use this year-round in Ohio." Betsy paused. "Thank you, for letting me stay. It's important to me, that I'm here right now. Have you . . . have you ever been in love?"

Aenti Chelle gave a quiet sigh before answering. "Ah, the things people do for love. Or, not."

"I have to stay, if not for love. It's important to me," Betsy repeated. "Otherwise, I'll never know. Haven't you ever felt that way? If you *didn't* do something, you'd live with the regret of not knowing what might have happened?"

"I've done that already, my sweet niece. I've lived with the choice of *not* doing something." Her *aenti* shrugged. "But God has honored my choice, and here I am."

Betsy wanted to ask more about *Aenti* Chelle's choice, or lack of choice, but thought better of it. "When your family left the Order, what happened? Did the rest of them turn away from you?"

"Some did, although here, my membership in the Beachy Amish Mennonite church has prevented my shunning, and my parents, as this church is very conservative. My bishop at the time said I wasn't leaving our Plain life, although I left the Order." Her aunt studied her face. "You're not thinking of leaving, are you?"

"Oh *no*. Not at all. I've been baptized and I'm not running anywhere. I didn't even want to go on *Rumspringa.*" Betsy sighed. "Although my *daed* was afraid, at first, the world was pulling me away because I want to stay here. It's not the world pulling me here."

"I see. Is there a particular young man involved?"

Heat blazed a trail from Betsy's neck to her cheeks. "Um . . ."

"Never mind. It's not my place to pry."

"Thank you." Her friends dogged her like hounds, wanting to know who claimed her attention. Miriam had guessed it was Jacob, but promised to never tell.

They sat in silence, sipping lemonade. The hardest part was over, speaking to her parents about remaining in Florida. Church attendance would be simple. The Old Order church in Pinecraft had its own building, and attendance brimmed in the wintertime with an overflow church that met in a neighborhood home several blocks away. She believed she'd convinced them not to worry about her being so far from their Ohio home.

Aenti Chelle's stomach gurgled, upon which they both laughed.

Her *aenti* patted her belly. "I guess it's suppertime, and here I didn't plan a meal. Are your feet so sore they aren't up to making a trip to Emma's Pizza?"

"Maybe if we take the bicycles?"

Within five minutes, Betsy had found her change purse and her slip-on shoes, and redid her hair. She'd been all set to relax for the evening, but a restlessness inside made her want to *do* something. But she didn't want to be rude to *Aenti* Chelle.

Aenti might as well have been twenty and not almost forty as they rode side by side, taking a little footbridge across the tiny trickle from Phillippi Creek and into the heart of the neighborhood. The aroma of someone's supper drifted into the street as they passed rows of homes.

"The last planning meeting for the Haiti auction is tomorrow night," *Aenti* Chelle said as she pedaled along. "We're making fried pies to sell this year and it's only a week away."

"Oh, I'd love to help, if I may," said Betsy. "I'm a fairly good baker."

"I hear you're more than a fairly good baker. I've heard your pies are as good as the ones served at Yoder's Restaurant, if not better." Aunt Chelle gestured with her head. "Turn here, on Kaufman."

A glow lay ahead of them at the end of the street along with the traffic of Bahia Vista.

Betsy had already frequented Village Pizza by Emma with her friends. Her mouth watered at the prospect of a fresh hot slice of pizza, oozing with cheese. *Englisch* food or not, the small shop behind Big Olaf's kept up a brisk business.

"What flavors of fried pies will you sell?" Betsy asked.

"Apple, cherry, lemon, chocolate." Aunt Chelle crossed over to the opposite side of the street, and Betsy followed. Her feet didn't hurt as badly, and the bicycle ride had done her good.

They rolled to a stop by the pizza shop and found a nook to park the bicycles. A pair of grandmotherly-looking women, gray hair and dark dresses with black aprons, exited the pizza shop. Deep in conversation, and one of them hugged a two-liter bottle of a drink called Mountain Dew. Betsy tried not to stare. Old Order elderly women, older than her own *mammi*, drinking Mountain Dew?

"I would *love* a soda pop." Betsy tried not to lick her lips. She need not tell anyone of all the little indulgences adding up, and this during her first day of semi-independence.

"I'm not a fan. But get yourself one." Aunt Chelle nudged her as they walked toward the shop. Voices echoed off the building wall and parked vehicles as a family approached.

"See, Miss Bennett, Amish can have pizza too," a little girl's voice rang out.

Betsy froze. The Millers, complete with Jacob and his children, his grandparents, and the *Englisch* woman from the hospital.

The *Englisch* woman smiled as she pushed little Rebecca's wheelchair, negotiating the pavement. Betsy touched the back of her neck. Was it her imagination, or did she have hackles rising up? No, maybe it was only the winter breeze.

Their gazes met, and the *Englisch* woman nodded at her and kept her smile on her face, before turning her focus back to the children. "Maybe we can have pizza sometime."

So the woman's visit at the hospital wasn't a one-time occurrence. *Charity believeth the best*, or so the Scriptures said. Scriptures didn't say charity would be easy, especially where her feelings for Jacob Miller and his family were concerned.

Here, away from prying watchful eyes, it was easier to think of Jacob. The trouble was, did he think of her at all?

"Are you coming in, or do you want me to order for you while you visit with the Millers?" *Aenti* Chelle was saying.

"I'm coming in," Betsy replied as she cast a look over her shoulder. The family was heading for the open-air deck behind the pizza shop. They all had servings of ice cream in some form, bowl, cup, or cone.

She breathed in the aroma of melted cheese and willed her racing pulse to slow down. The tiny shop held a pizza oven behind the counter and a stack of boxes waited on a table in the back corner. Customers could wait on chairs in the front area across from a refrigerator that held all varieties and sizes of bottled soda pop and water.

The girl behind the counter looked very *Englisch* in her T-shirt and blue jeans. "Hi there. What would you like? Our special tonight is pepperoni, a dollar a slice. Our 20-ounce drinks are a dollar-fifty."

"The special sounds good to me," said Betsy, fishing coins and a bill from her purse. "One slice."

"For me as well," said Aunt Chelle.

The young lady took their money. "Help yourselves to the drinks from the fridge."

"You're Marian Fry's granddaughter, aren't you?" Aunt Chelle asked the young woman, who now was dishing up their pizza onto paper plates.

"Yes, Ma'am. I'm Tara Fry."

"You've grown up so fast. What are you doing now?"

"I'm here in Sarasota, winter break before I head back to Virginia for college." Tara's nimble fingers snatched some napkins from a dispenser. "Here you are. Enjoy."

"Thank you. Tell your grandmother hello for me—I'm Rochelle Keim. She used to be my teacher a long time ago in Ohio."

A college girl. Betsy picked up her plate of pizza, then pulled a bottle of soda pop from the glass-front refrigerator. Coca-Cola, something she'd never had until coming here to Florida.

Tara, the girl working in the pizza shop, was about her age, and she was going to college. She must belong to one of the more liberal Mennonite congregations because she didn't wear a head covering. Of course, she kept her hair pulled back and covered with netting while working with pizza.

Betsy mulled over the whole concept of liberal Mennonites, education, and pizza in an Amish village as they exited the pizza shop.

The Millers still congregated on the deck, but Jacob's grandparents had left. Zeke sat between Jacob and the *Englisch* woman on the deck's bench, with the woman's attention turned to Rebecca sitting in a wheelchair.

Of course, *Aenti* Chelle had to say hello, which she did, and Jacob was quick to introduce the *Englisch* woman, along with an explanation.

"Natalie Bennett. She volunteers at the hospital where Rebecca stayed," he said, as Natalie stood. She had the grace of a cat, her movements smooth as she shook hands with *Aenti* Chelle.

"Does your volunteer work bring you to Pinecraft as well?" Betsy stood as tall as she could, and Natalie merely blinked at the question.

"No, actually. I found Rebecca's doll in her hospital room after she'd been discharged, and then I tracked down the Millers to here." She folded her arms across her waist.

Betsy had the same hackles rising feeling she'd had moments before. Her aunt's expression bored into her. "That's good. I'm glad, for Rebecca's sake then, you found her doll."

"Me, too," said Natalie Bennett.

Betsy mentally chided herself. Natalie Bennett was no threat to whatever might happen between her and Jacob Miller. She needed only to bide her time. An *Englisch* woman, even with Amish roots, would not fit in their Plain world. She could visit, yes, but it would always be a foreign world to her.

8

Jacob's shirt collar couldn't feel any tighter than it did just then, with Natalie and Betsy facing each other, with him in the middle.

"My grandmother invited Miss Bennett to stay for supper in thanks, and she in turn, bought us dessert." He gestured to his bowl of mint chocolate chip.

Betsy nodded, then sat down beside her aunt and set her bottle of pop on the bench beside her. "Big Olaf's has the best ice cream. I try to eat as much of it as I can while I'm here in Pinecraft."

"That is the children's aim as well, I'm afraid." Jacob tousled Zeke's hair, his collar loosening fractions of an inch.

"Will . . . will your family be at the Haiti auction?" Betsy asked. "I'm going to be helping *Aenti* Chelle sell fried pies."

"We're going to try. It depends on how Rebecca does with her physical therapy." He didn't want to ask Henry for time off from work for her appointments, but Henry had offered him the option. There were plenty of volunteers, plenty of helpers, plenty of food being dropped off for the Miller family. The weight of it all made him want to retreat to a quiet place with just him and the children.

He listened to the children banter together and laugh, the first normal sounds in a while. Now *that* was an answer to prayer. Natalie ate another spoonful of her ice cream as she gazed across the side street at Yoder's market, closed for the night.

Betsy was interested in him, for certain. Something about her felt very safe. She'd be good to the children. If he asked to walk her to church, he knew she'd grant permission. She was a bit younger than him, not that it was a problem. A number of her friends had started to leave the circle of unattached women and join the ranks of the married.

On the other hand, literally on his other side, the unexpected and unimaginable idea of Natalie Bennett. He couldn't ignore the facts she was beautiful, she intrigued him. Over supper tonight he'd learned of Natalie's own Christian beliefs, not so different from his own. She had come to her faith as a young adult, not quite three years before.

No, it was unimaginable and foolhardy to even entertain thoughts of Natalie Bennett. Despite some of what they held in common, Natalie Bennett was definitely not Plain. He would pray she found the answers she sought and would be on her way to know her own family. He didn't need to deal with the obvious worldly pull of the woman, even though she professed Christian beliefs.

"So then, I made quick work of that delicious maple walnut ice cream so we could head back to his grandparents' house," Natalie said as she bent at the waist, feeling the pull in her hamstrings as she reached for her toes, her legs spread-eagle on the exercise room floor. "The word awkward doesn't even begin to cover it."

Grace chuckled from her place on the cushioned mat not far from Natalie. "You should have invited me on this little adventure of yours. That must have been a sight to see. The Amish woman jealous of you spending time with the Millers. The Amish strike me as so—so pious, and not given to typical human vices like jealousy."

"Ha." Natalie rose to a sitting position, her arms stretched over her head. "Amish are human, just like us. I admire their dedication, though."

"You mean, by wearing Plain dresses and head coverings?" Grace glanced at Natalie, who'd chosen her most comfortable leggings and tank top for practice today. "That, I can't imagine you wearing."

"No, I mean I admire their dedication to living Godly lives. It's a hard thing to do in this world we live in." Natalie leaned over her other leg, feeling the stretch. "It's hard to know how much compromise is too much, and what's not a big issue at all. Most of us who aren't Amish could argue all day about what's a compromise to our faith, and how 'separate' from the world we should be. For them, being separate comes from the inside as well as out."

"I'm still shaking my head over the pizza parlor and the ice cream shop."

"I know, the Amish like all kinds of good food, even not traditionally Amish food." Natalie stopped and inhaled deeply.

"You sound like an expert after just one afternoon and evening with the family."

"Nah, I'm happily surprised. I've heard about the no modern conveniences like electricity, living off the land, their generations-old farming traditions. It's just, I'm trying to wrap my mind around the whole thing. Jacob and his family aren't what I expected, at all." She ignored the recollection of the spark she'd seen in his blue eyes as he studied her face and hair. He probably didn't think she noticed. But she had. Her own stirring wasn't an unpleasant one.

"What are you going to do about Miss Jealous?" Grace asked.

"Nothing. Not that I could or would do anything, anyway. If Jacob's interested in her, I'm sure he'll pursue her. Doesn't a man do that? Obviously, he has once before, since he was married before." Ah, she was babbling now, all because some blue eyes rattled her insides. "Anyway, I'm taking Mom's quilt top and the Bible pages on Monday, when Rachel is going to help me begin to put the quilt together."

"So, they're going to help you search for your mother's family."

Natalie nodded. "In fact, Jacob already asked Betsy Yoder's parents if they knew of my mother, but the name is fairly common. They didn't."

"That would be funny if you and Miss Jealous were distant cousins, wouldn't it?"

"I don't know. And her name's Betsy."

Grace laughed. "So, what are your thoughts on Mr. Jacob?"

"I, um, I don't really have any."

"Uh-huh. So you say. What do you think Miss Betsy has to be jealous over?"

"Nothing, absolutely nothing."

"He must be something else."

"He's handsome. Think of Josh Lucas, with an Amish haircut and the beard." From the time she'd first seen Jacob, he'd reminded her of someone. While changing TV channels the other night, she'd seen the actor Josh Lucas and his image on screen made her pause.

"My, my, my. Those baby blues, be still my heart." Grace chuckled.

Oh, yes, those baby blues. Natalie swallowed hard. "I have *no* romantic notions about him. He might be handsome, but that's nothing to base a relationship on, especially someone who's probably my polar opposite. Our worlds are completely different."

"Handsome's a good place to start. At least the scenery's good while you're getting to know each other." Grace stood to her full height, arms over her head, and leaned to one side.

"Grace!" Natalie flopped on her back. She'd hoped to leave the *something* that she'd felt the other night way behind her. Step back and let Betsy Yoder have dibs on Jacob. They would be perfect together, of course. Surely, she could get a quilt sewn and search for her family without getting tangled. So far, she'd avoided getting tangled, with good reason.

Children's voices echoed in the hallway. *Thank you, Lord, for delivering me from Grace's interrogation. I don't need anyone. After Mom and Dad's fiasco of a marriage, and my own track record—*

She sat up, trying to focus her mind on the class to come. They needed her attention, not her being distracted.

"We'll chat more about this, I'm sure." Grace grinned as she headed toward the open door and the children.

First class of the new year, the advanced beginner aerial silks class. Eight girls and one boy, age ranging from nine to fourteen, entered the room. They all spoke at once, talking about the Christmas break and return to school and now classes, and they missed practicing, and did Ms. Bennett get anything cool for Christmas?

They were the reason she'd hauled herself up out of the blues, after the ankle and wrist surgeries, and she thanked God for the open door at the circus school every day.

"Okay, gang, let's warm up and stretch. Sami, set the timer for ten minutes, please." Natalie nodded at the girl on the edge of the line, who trotted off to the digital timer.

Their chatter went on for a few more minutes, in sharp contrast to the lilting accents of the Miller children. But the smiles were the same, the same hunger to learn.

She clapped, the noise echoing off the walls. "Okay, we'll never get warmed up at this rate. Let's work on our French climbs as much as we talk."

The chattering sound lowered, then gradually disappeared as the kids practiced their aerial moves several few feet above the crash mats below them, from one end of the practice room to the other.

If she couldn't continue her own aerial silks career, at least she could watch the sheer joy—and determination—on her students' faces as they learned the moves she once loved so much. An old pang of if-onlys swept through her. If only she hadn't fallen and blown her ankles, if only her body could take the stress of performing multiple shows per day, the constant training and striving to learn yet one more gravity-defying move with the aid of long strips of silk. But here she was, and God had taken care of her, even if that dream had died.

She bit her lip as the children continued to warm up. Funny, she thought she'd quit asking God "why" more than a year ago. *I won't ask why today, but be thankful for where I am right now.*

Natalie shoved her wistful thoughts to the side. Today wasn't about her. It was about these young ones, full of promise, most of them not knowing the depths of disappointment life could bring. Not just yet.

Maybe on Monday, she'd start a path to something new. A path to a family eluded her still. She'd never known traditional family before and while her parents were together, it all seemed to make sense. Now, adrift on some foreign sea she never imagined she'd travel, she longed for someone to share the journey with.

9

The chatter of children was absent when Rachel Miller opened the door to Natalie's knock on Monday morning.

"Come in, come in." The warm smell of citrus drifted past Rachel and outside. "Jacob has taken Rebecca to a doctor's appointment and Zeke is with a neighborhood friend. So it's only us women today."

Natalie nodded. "How is Rebecca doing?"

"Better, every day. It's hard to see her in pain. She's brave, though, and never complains." Rachel motioned Natalie into the living room as Natalie pulled the page of family names from her tote bag.

"I brought the list of names."

"Ah, good," Rachel said as Natalie waved the page in front of her. "I don't know how much we'll be able to discover, but we can put the word out with friends. Perhaps one of them knows your mother's family."

Natalie nodded and slung her bag onto her shoulder. "Unless they moved, or something."

"Even if they moved, we could still learn where they are." Rachel motioned toward the kitchen. "Come and have a cup of *kaffi* and some fresh marmalade cake. We can see what you have."

"What do you mean, if they moved you would still know?" Natalie followed Rachel and dared not protest the older woman's offer of food. She'd have to start working out an hour a day, just to keep pace with the goodies from the Millers' kitchen. She still had the leftovers of half a peach pie Rachel had sent home with her from her last visit.

"If they moved to another district, say, ours near Sugarcreek, our bishop would confirm where they'd come from and speak to their previous bishop." Rachel pulled a pair of cups down from the cupboard. "We verify where people have been. Unfortunately, some would like to join the Amish faith to hide from the law, or for their own illegal gains. So, we do 'check references,' as the *Englisch* would say."

"Ah, well, I guess it could be a good thing for me then." Natalie watched the older woman pour cups of coffee, then slice two pieces from a loaf and place them each on a small plate. She could almost smell the orange aroma from her seat at the table.

The kitchen wasn't much different from any other kitchen she'd seen. No wood stove, or anything like that. She stood to help Rachel carry the refreshments back to the table.

"How, if you don't mind me asking, can you have electricity here? Isn't that sort of, not allowed?"

Rachel gave her a slow smile. "Things are different here in Pinecraft. Those who come for the winter, or for vacation, are allowed since this is not their permanent home. We still keep things simple here." A knock sounded at the front door and Rachel glanced past Natalie. "Oh, this would be Imogene Brubaker. I asked her to join us this morning."

Rachel left Natalie in the kitchen and voices soon drifted into earshot. "Yes, you're right on time. The bread is still warm."

A woman followed Rachel into the kitchen. "Well, hello there, friend." She wore a head covering more like a head kerchief and had a long ponytail. The hem of her cape dress swished above a pair of clogs. A camera dangled from a strap around her neck.

"Um, hello."

"Imogene Brubaker." She extended her right hand. "You can call me Ima, or Gene, or Genie, or even 'hey you' if you forget."

The woman's firm handshake swallowed up Natalie's hand as they shook. "Natalie Bennett."

"So you're the one whose mother left the Order."

Natalie nodded. She couldn't help but grin at the older woman's friendly demeanor, as if Natalie were a long-lost friend who'd come to down, and they picked up their friendship right away.

"I asked Imogene to join us because she knows just about everything about everyone who's come through Pinecraft, who's related to whom." Rachel motioned for them to sit. "I'll get your glass of milk, Imogene, and your bread. You just take a seat by Miss Bennett."

"I used to be Amish," said Imogene. "I loved my family, and still do, but I couldn't take the legalism anymore. Lots of us former Amish don't or can't. But I still love God and worship Him."

"I see." Natalie hadn't run into such a colorful character in a while. "That's good. I didn't come into my faith until, well, a few years ago. I'm still figuring things out."

"Some of us take our entire lives to do so," said Imogene. "Oh goody, whole milk. Not the skim watered-down milk." She took a generous sip and then a nibble of the marmalade bread.

Natalie made her racing thoughts slow down as she picked up her slice of bread. Rachel slid a plate holding a slab of butter across the table. "Butter." Natalie put a swirl onto the bread and watched the creaminess melt into the bread.

The bite was like a taste of warm sunshine, with a tang of orange. "Mrs. Miller, this is delicious."

"It's one of Jacob's favorite things, so I try to have it around. My *kinner* Jacob may have grown up, but I still see the little boy he once was. Much like Zeke, except with the roundest blue eyes and not brown."

"Hannah had brown eyes," observed Imogene. "That's where Zeke got them from."

Hannah. So that was her name. "I see," was all Natalie said.

"It was sad, losing her and not seeing her face here in Pinecraft every winter." Imogene chased her bite of bread with another swallow of milk. "But I think Betsy Yoder wants to be the next Mrs. Miller."

"*Imogene Brubaker*." Rachel sounded a tad scolding.

Imogene hung her head. "Well, it's true, you know."

Natalie shifted on the wooden chair, no doubt handcrafted somewhere in the north, sturdy and strong. She took a sip of coffee, not minding the lack of cream and sugar, the strength of the brew yanking her focus from the conversation for a few seconds.

Rachel cleared her throat and reached for the paper with the family names. "Now, let's look at these names. I should probably write them down, so you can keep your paper." She passed the paper to Natalie.

"Well, it says my mother's name at the bottom, being the newborn, Katie Yoder. Her birth date was June 23, born to Samuel and Anna Yoder." She touched the page, wishing the names told her more. "Her name is next to a Eudora. I assume that's a sister."

Imogene sighed. "Common names, except for the Eudora. I know at least three Samuel Yoders in Ohio, not counting some in Pennsylvania."

Rachel picked up the paper and squinted at the bottom. "It looks like there may have been more on this page, but it was torn off."

"I wish there were more family names on that list," said Natalie "At least I'd have names of some aunts or uncles, or cousins."

"You should also prepare yourself for the possibility that Samuel and Anna Yoder might not wish to meet you, considering their daughter left the Order." Rachel shook her head.

"Oh, I hadn't thought about that." Natalie bit back more questions. "You're right. I suppose there's always a chance. But if I find them, I'll at least know who they are. And more about who I come from, if just a little." She took another bite of Rachel's bread, letting the sweetness melt onto her palate. But the bitter idea Rachel gave life to with her words just wouldn't leave.

"I'll write some letters and see what my cousins in Ohio might know." Rachel patted Natalie's hand. "I just didn't want you to be disappointed if we didn't hear anything."

"I have an idea." Imogene tapped the tabletop. "Are you up for a walk, Miss Natalie?"

"Sure." Natalie glanced at Rachel, who rose from her chair.

"You two go ahead and walk. Don't mind me." Rachel put her empty plate in the sink. "I might wander to the shuffleboard courts before lunch, we'll see."

"If I take you around and introduce you to some people, they can see you for themselves," Imogene said. "Maybe they'll know something. Or at least they'll remember you as my friend."

"All right then." Natalie finished off her coffee and the last two nibbles of bread.

Off they went into the winter sunshine, and Natalie saw possibilities despite Rachel's warning. They reached the light at Bahia Vista and waited for the light change. Imogene knew the pair of women on bicycles waiting to cross with them. They talked about who would be arriving on the next bus and who might be leaving, about the Haiti auction that weekend, and when the next singing would take place.

Then the light changed and the women crossed. Here in the snug neighborhood, Natalie was the bit of oddity. She didn't mind so much, and waited while Imogene kept talking to the ladies on bicycles. However, the more she looked, the more she saw what appeared to be *Englisch* mixed with the Amish. Or did they belong to a group of more liberal Mennonites? Some of them looked no different than Natalie, in regular street clothes.

Imogene waved as they rode off with a chime of a bicycle bell. "Those are the Bontrager sisters. Never married, and they own a quilt shop in Indiana. You ought to see what they've brought down for the Haiti benefit auction this weekend." They ambled along Kaufman Avenue, away from the traffic.

"Haiti benefit auction?"

"Every January we gather at the Sarasota Fairgrounds for a whole day of auctions and food vendors." Imogene squinted at one house as they approached. "It's a nonprofit group that raises all the money, and goes to help people in Haiti."

"What kinds of things do they auction off?"

"The men bring furniture they've made, and some sell farm equipment and different tools. Some people weave rugs." Imogene faced Natalie, a twinkle in her eye. "But for me, the best part is the food. A group of Mennonites from Mississippi is bringing about two hundred pounds of catfish to have a fish fry."

They passed Big Olaf's, which wasn't open yet, and Emma's Pizza. One preconception she'd recently had turned completely upside down was the Amish and Mennonite palate. She chuckled. "A fish fry."

"Is that funny to you?" Imogene's tone was gentle.

"No, not funny. I just didn't imagine the Amish and Mennonites eating such . . . I don't know. I used to think Amish food as more, like, I don't know . . . like shoo-fly pie." Natalie fumbled for the right words.

Imogene let loose with a laugh of her own. "As long as it's made with love and tastes good, we'll eat it. Pretty much. Although I can't say as I've ever heard of Amish sushi."

Natalie chuckled and nodded. "Wow, those people must have a lot of guests." One home had dozens of bicycles stuffed under the carport. Many of the bicycles were three-wheeled models with baskets on the back behind the seat.

"That's the Frys' house. They rent bicycles by the day, for five dollars each. It's a good way to get around. Of course, the wealthier families will bring down bicycles for the whole family to use during their visit."

"I can see it's a fast way to get around. I like to bicycle, too."

"I left my bicycle at the Millers'," said Imogene. "I wish I'd thought of riding it. Then you could have rented a bicycle from the Frys and we could ride around the neighborhood together. Have you seen the park yet?"

"No. I've only been to the Millers and to Big Olaf's."

"Well, we should go to the park. There's always something happening at the park." Imogene nodded and tugged on her camera strap.

"Do you live here year-round?"

"I do, except when I visit family in Pennsylvania, and then I'm not here. There aren't many of us who do live here year-round. You should come visit in the summer, too." Imogene paused at the edge of a driveway. "It's like what people call a ghost town."

"I've probably driven by the neighborhood for several years now, but I never really knew about it until I met the Millers." Natalie knew they were in the middle of a city of more than 50,000 people, but aside from the bustling traffic of Bahia Vista that bisected the village, the farther she walked with Imogene into the snug little blocks of streets, the more she felt as if she'd entered a sanctuary.

Some SUVs and sedans were tucked into driveways, along with bicycles lining carports. Palm trees and tropical plants like hibiscus made up the landscaping of some houses.

"It's a special place, Pinecraft," Imogene said. "We don't advertise, but people find us. Especially now that a documentary film crew came to visit a couple of winters ago."

Natalie nodded. Imogene placed her hand on Natalie's arm. A trio of Amish men were studying something in a nearby yard. "Hold on. I think that's Ike Wagler, visiting from Pennsylvania. He's my mother's cousin. He might know someone who can help you find Katie Yoder's family."

Imogene crossed the street, with Natalie following. The woman's enthusiasm made a hope take root and bloom inside Natalie. Then Imogene did something to make Natalie pause.

She lifted up her camera, murmured something to the trio of bearded men, and they laughed as she took their picture and approached them.

"Ah, Imogene, it's good to see you," said the man with the grayest and longest beard, as Natalie stepped up to join Imogene. "I'll have to tell Barbara I saw you. She'll be so pleased."

"When did you arrive?" Imogene's eyes sparkled.

"On the bus, Thursday."

"Where's Barbara?"

"She's at the church with the ladies, working on getting at least one more quilt put in before the auction." He gave an inquisitive glance in Natalie's direction.

"Oh, we'll have to see her and say hello." Imogene plucked at Natalie's arm. "This is my new friend, Natalie Bennett. She is searching for her grandparents who live in Ohio. Her mother, Katie Yoder, left the Order as a young adult."

"Hello," Natalie said. She immediately stood up straighter, wishing she looked a little plainer, if only it would encourage people to help her.

"Katie Yoder, huh?" Ike scratched his bearded chin. "That's a common name."

"I believe her parents' names are Samuel and Anna Yoder."

"It will be tough to find them, but not impossible." Ike looked at one of his friends. "You're from Holmes County. Do you know of a Samuel Yoder?"

The other man nodded. "At least three, just in Holmes County."

Maybe one of them was her grandfather. Natalie wanted to hug Imogene, just for this little bit of hope. "It's, it's very important for me to locate them, if I can," Natalie ventured to say. "I didn't even know about my mother's family until after she passed away last summer."

"Sad thing, when our children leave the Order," said the third man, who'd been silent until now. "Consequences always follow. Families splintered." He frowned, shaking his head.

Yes, talk about consequences. Natalie looked at Imogene. "Well, we can at least try, can't we?"

"And if someone can do it, it would be you, Imogene," said Ike.

"*Danke*, Cousin Ike." She gave them a wave as she continued along the street, Natalie keeping up with her long stride.

"Well, I think that's encouraging," said Natalie. "I feel like we're getting somewhere, a little bit."

"Here's another idea," Imogene kicked at a pebble. "You could always run an ad in *The Budget*."

"*The Budget*?"

"The Amish weekly newspaper. You could run it in the national edition and everyone can read it, everyone in every settlement."

"Newspaper?"

"The latest edition arrives on the Thursday bus. You'll have to meet it at the Mennonite Tourist Church parking lot around twelve-thirty. The church is a block over from the post office."

Natalie's head spun. Amish, fish fries, newspapers, and Amish riding on a bus. And Imogene, snapping a photo of Amish men—who didn't normally like their photos taken. One even smiled for the camera, although he didn't look at it directly.

Imogene kept tapping a button on the back of her camera as they walked along, studying her photos. "That's a good picture of Cousin Ike."

"You took their pictures." Unbelievable.

She nodded. "They let me." As if that explained everything.

One thing life had taught Natalie was learning to go with the flow. Sometimes she didn't like the way things flowed and had had more than several one-sided arguments with God about it. Times like this, though, it left her with a sense of astonishment.

"I always thought the Amish didn't like their photos taken."

"Not normally, but I never ask them to pose for me and I always take the photo quickly. And, they trust me." Imogene shrugged. "I'm a blogger. Families around the country like seeing their relatives and keeping up with them. Of course if I know someone truly objects to being photographed, I don't do it."

Natalie decided to switch gears. "You said you used to be Amish. Why did you leave? I know you said the legalism bothered you."

Imogene sighed. "I was tired, tired of conforming to things I didn't believe in my heart. I believed in God, but I was tired of a harsh bishop and always feeling like I was looking over my shoulder. Also, we were taught that wanting to read the Scriptures for ourselves was presumptuous and prideful. At least in my district, it was so. Some districts can be different. I always had many questions. And some people don't like it when you ask questions. That's the short version of my story. But I consider myself a Christian."

"So, you stay here."

"Yes, it's my home. I can't leave my roots, and these are still my people. I don't belong to the church, but I do believe in simple and Plain living." Imogene bit her lip. "Also, I feel like part of the reason I'm here is to help others, who start having questions no one wants to answer." A trio of young men hurried past. "Hello, Imogene!" one of them called out. One of them held a folded blanket and another a canvas tote bag.

"Hi, boys!" Imogene waved. "Heading for the beach?"

"Yah," the shortest one said.

"Don't forget to use sunblock." She smiled as they passed.

"I was wondering where the young people are," Natalie observed. "I've seen quite a few older people in the neighborhood."

"Ah, the kids, yes." Imogene motioned to the right. "This way, if we're headed to the park, which we are. The teens like to spend the day at the beach, playing volleyball and soaking up the sun, something they'd never get to do in Ohio. When the weather's good, they're working."

They ambled along the curving street until it dead-ended at a park, containing a sandy volleyball court, a wide expanse of lawn ending at the bank of a creek. A lineup of women in cape dresses stood along a waist-high fence, their backs to Natalie and Imogene.

"Shuffleboard court," Imogene said. "They have some mighty fierce games here, everyone vying for the top spot." Another cluster of men stood on one side of the lawn, engaged in an intense bocce match.

"I see."

"You can meet everyone and they can meet you, too." Imogene beamed. "Maybe, just maybe, someone will know your grandparents or—wouldn't it be wonderful if they were here, in Pinecraft, right now?"

"That would be too easy."

Imogene shrugged. "It could happen."

A small figure approached them at a run, dark hair bouncing, little arms pumping—Zeke. He slammed into Natalie, clamping his arms around her legs.

"Zeke." She hugged him back.

"Miss Natalie," he said in the funny little accent. "You came to my *haus*?"

"I did. Your *mammi* gave me some of her marmalade bread."

"It's very *gut*."

"Yes, it is. The best I've ever had."

"We're fishing, over there." Zeke pointed toward an inlet that snaked through the park. "With my friends, the Grabers."

Natalie looked up to see an Amish man striding toward them. He looked anything but pleased. "Did you tell them you were running over here?"

Zeke said nothing, but tugged on Natalie's hand.

"Well, if the boy's been fishing, we ought to go see what he's all excited about," said Imogene, following behind Natalie. "Hello, Earnest, we've collected Zeke for you."

"I'm sorry he ran off," Natalie said to the man with the dark beard.

"It's not your fault." His voice was warm. "Come, Ezekiel, James wants to show you the fish he just pulled in."

"I like to fish," Zeke said as he skipped along. His young little friend scampered up and the two of them chattered like a pair of squirrels.

"Stuart Graber," the man said, shaking hands with Natalie. "You must be the circus lady Zeke has been telling us about."

"Yes, sir."

Imogene then launched into an explanation about Natalie, her mother, the Yoders, and Ohio. Mr. Graber nodded.

"Well, I certainly hope you find them."

"Thank you." Natalie smiled at Mr. Graber and Imogene. These were truly remarkable people. She wasn't one of them, yet they were doing what they could to help her, stranger though she may be. She tried to remember the last time she'd felt so . . . at home. And couldn't.

10

Jacob stared out the van window as the street signs flew past them. He could see how having a vehicle would speed things along, especially in a city the size of Sarasota. In Ohio, a van picked him up at the end of his driveway every morning for a ride to the cabinet factory; today, Henry's generous offer to take Rebecca and him to her appointment was easy enough to accept.

However, the traffic whizzing by reminded him of their own speed. Part of him more than once had wished to own a car, a Mustang in candy apple red. He'd put such wishes to rest long ago and instead, had been baptized into the *Ordnung*, married Hannah, and taken the job at the cabinet shop. But the other day he'd heard the roar of a similar vehicle, and the memory came back.

He glanced at his daughter, who was buckled into the seat behind him. She'd managed to maneuver herself so her casted leg lay stretched out on the seat. She'd also fallen asleep.

Poor little *kind*. She'd cried during the exam when the orthopedic doctor explained one more time the cast was not coming off anytime soon. Next step, if x-ray results permitted, she'd be moved to a removable cast. But that was weeks away.

She needed the comfort of a *mamm*, her own *mamm*, and that was not to be.

Gotte, *I'm doing my best. If I could take her pain, I would.*

The older his children got, the more he knew there were some pains he couldn't carry. Also, he was still learning to bear his own burdens.

"Next traffic light, Kaufman," announced Henry Hostetler. "If it's all right with you, I'll stop at Big Olaf's. Maybe a small cup of ice cream will set things right with your young one."

"Maybe." He should have had someone else take them. But Henry had insisted, saying their supplies for the new roofing job weren't coming in until tomorrow, so him keeping busy was far better than sitting at home bemoaning the slow delivery of supplies.

Jacob was accustomed to pitching in and giving a hand where needed. But this, being on the receiving end constantly, was tiring to him. He refused to chalk it up to pride, but there it was. *Gotte* forgive him, but he was a proud man, able to give, reluctant to receive.

"Will Zeke be starting school here in Pinecraft?"

"Yes, but I don't think he'll want to go. My *mammi* is going to help Rebecca with her lessons at home for now, but Zeke will start school here in Pinecraft, at the Mennonite school." Which was another bit of news he had to break to his son. If only he could help Zeke out of his shell.

Hannah had been concerned as well, since Rebecca did most of the talking for both of them. Zeke had started his first year of school back in Ohio and Jacob wanted to minimize the interruption of Florida.

Ever since late December, they'd had one interruption after the other, ever since the accident. He glanced back at Rebecca again, who yawned and stirred.

"My leg hurts, *Daed*."

"Ice cream, Miss Rebecca?" Henry looked into the rearview mirror.

She shook her head. "No thank you, Mr. Hostetler."

The girl really was tired, refusing ice cream. "We can just go home, Henry," Jacob said.

Instead of turning left at the light for Big Olaf's, Henry nodded and took a right, heading for the Millers' home.

Home. It had always been his grandparents' winter home, now their full-time residence. Now it was partly his home, too. Henry stopped the van behind a familiar-looking sedan. Natalie's.

"Oh, before I forget, your first paycheck." Henry pulled his wallet from his back pocket, opened it, and took out a folded piece of paper. "I'll be here at seven-thirty tomorrow to pick you up."

"Thank you." Jacob received the check without looking at it. Next thing, to open a bank account while he was here. "All right, Rebecca, let's get your chair out, then get you tucked back in bed." He exited the van and set up the folding wheelchair. Amazing, how quickly he could do it now, almost second nature.

Rebecca put her arms around his neck as he scooped her from the back seat of the van and deposited her onto the wheelchair's seat. "Ow." She bit her lip. The therapist had warned she might have some extra soreness, but it was important for Rebecca to continue her range of motion as much as she could.

"Miss Natalie's car is here." It was the first time all day Rebecca sounded happy about something. "I wonder if she brought more oranges."

"We'll find out soon enough." Jacob paused at the curb. "Thank you, again, Henry. I'll see you in the morning."

"Bright and early, early and bright." Henry waved before climbing into his van.

Jacob tried not to jostle the wheelchair too much as he wrangled it up the drive, then around the rear bumper of Natalie's car, and up the sidewalk.

His grandmother opened the front door. "I thought I heard a vehicle out front. How did our Rebecca do?"

"According to the therapist, she did well." He smiled down at his daughter.

"It hurt."

"Next week, crutches."

Mammi held the door open, and Jacob maneuvered the wheelchair into the living room. Just when he thought he'd figured out how best to get Rebecca around in the contraption without bumping into things, or catching on a bit of sidewalk or other tiny yet aggravating obstacle, he'd realized how this was beyond his skill level.

He nearly dumped Rebecca onto the hardwood floor. "*Daed*!" She gripped the armrests of the wheelchair and braced herself with her good leg.

"Sorry." Once clearing the final hurdle, he stopped her at the hospital bed. Really, the monstrosity didn't belong in the living room and he should have told his grandparents to refuse the delivery. There was a phone number, somewhere, for the medical equipment company. He'd have to borrow Henry's phone tomorrow and ask them to pick the thing up.

"Tomorrow," he announced as he deposited Rebecca onto her bed, "we will send the bed back. Do you think you can stay in your bed here?"

"I think so."

He tried not to let his gaze wander toward the kitchen, but it slid there anyway.

"Natalie is out walking with Imogene," *Mammi* announced. "Imogene is trying to help her find her family."

"They're in Pinecraft?" The words sounded almost silly to his ears.

"Now, wouldn't that be providential?" His grandmother helped Rebecca adjust the quilt over her bare, uncasted leg. "I was thinking Imogene might know someone who knows her family."

"She definitely seems to know everyone in the village." The idea of interviewing so many people made his brain tired. Asking the same questions, over and over. Better her than him. "I do hope she can find them."

"Next week, we're going to quilt. Or, rather, she is, but she doesn't know it yet." *Mammi* motioned to the kitchen. "Lunch is almost ready, for whoever wants it."

Jacob followed his grandmother, feeling thirteen instead of thirty-one. Ah, to be young again when things were much simpler. But then, his young ones hadn't had things very simply for the last nearly two years.

If you follow the immediate path in front of you, things can be simple again.

Grief wasn't a simple addition to life, no matter how much they spoke about it, adding sweet Scriptures to help deaden the pain. Only, the bitterness remained underneath. To speak of questioning *Gotte's wille* bordered on blasphemy. To question if Hannah's virtues had been enough to see her through to an eternal reward, well, he knew he wasn't supposed to wonder about such things. His own threat to leave years ago, echoed in his ears.

"Why obey Gotte *if there is no guarantee it will be good enough to please Him?"* He hushed his thoughts and focused on lunch instead, and realized his stomach growled.

Simple sandwiches, fresh lemonade, sliced and salted garden vegetables made up their lunch spread. Fresh vegetables, and not from a jar full of what his sister-in-law had put up from the summer before, as they would be eating if they were in Ohio right now. The colorful produce came from only a block over at Yoder's market. He let himself smile at this luxury in the winter.

A ruckus in the living room followed by voices made Jacob turned in the direction of the noises. Words like "fish" and "alligator" and "Natalie" followed by a stream of Pennsylvania Dutch drifted into the kitchen. Then came laughter.

Zeke bounded into the kitchen. "*Daed*, I went to the park and went fishing with the Grabers and we saw an alligator and Miss Natalie and she said she would help me get the fish ready to eat." All of this came in Dutch, with Zeke holding a string of fish, the tail of the lowest fish dragging on *Mammi's* kitchen floor.

Then Natalie rounded the corner. Her eyes widened and she stopped short. "Jacob." She smiled, her cheeks flushed. Then she cast a glance at Zeke. "We'll have to see if your great-grandmother has a fillet knife we can use. But outside. And, of course, if it's okay with your father." She turned her focus back to Jacob. "Unless you'd rather do it?"

She was talking to him.

"Oh, I've never filleted a fish before," he admitted. "Just, ah, take care with the knife."

"Of course, we will."

"Yes, *Daed*, we will." Zeke beamed.

Imogene joined them for lunch, and spent the time telling them all about who was supposed to be arriving on the bus tomorrow and Thursday. She heard there was going to be a concert on Friday night at the park, but didn't see the point if it was the night before the Haiti auction, maybe no one would come, although couldn't even a few people make a joyful noise?

"I thought your *daadi* would be here by now," *Mammi* said during a lull in the conversation, while Imogene snacked on some sliced tomatoes.

"There were a bunch of men playing bocce. It looked like a pretty intense game." Natalie wiped her mouth with a napkin. "I think I saw him there when Imogene and I arrived at the park."

His grandmother nodded. "I try not to wonder when he's out and about during lunchtime. Some days, I'm just not up to it."

"*Mammi*, are you feeling well?" Jacob studied her face, wrinkled with years and her strong, but slim hands with their papery-thin skin.

"I'm fine. Some days eighty-five feels older than others." She smiled at him. "Don't you worry. Your grandfather and I will be keeping house here for years to come."

A knock sounded at the front door. *Mammi* waved Jacob back to a seated position. "I'll get the door."

They continued their meal until a cry made the hair on the back of Jacob's neck stand up.

"Jacob!"

Natalie knew grief, the kind of grief you prepared yourself for. She'd had months and months while Mom fought her last battle with cancer, then succumbed to the illness. Natalie thanked God for those precious times at her mother's bedside. Even though she knew grief would follow, she had the chance to say goodbye. Her only regret now, Mom hadn't ever told her about the other side of her family.

But if Mom had, maybe Natalie wouldn't be here now, sitting at a newspaper-covered picnic table in the Millers' backyard with little Zeke, while the rest of the house filled up with Amish and Mennonites of all kinds. Isaiah Miller had collapsed at Pinecraft Park this afternoon and no one could revive him.

"He's dead." Zeke sniffled and looked at the fish in front of him. "Just like *daadi*. And my *mamm*." At first, when he'd arrived back from the park, he'd begged Natalie to take him outside where they could see to cleaning the fish. And at first, Natalie had thought it would be a good distraction for the little guy.

The open windows released the sound of voices into the yard, some in hushed tones, others not quite so discreet.

"*Dropped dead, right at the end of the bocce match.*"

"*Heart attack,*" someone else said.

"*Did anyone call back to Ohio? The family still has a chance to board the bus.*"

"*The bus is already on its way here. They'll have to hire a van to get here if there's to be a funeral this week.*"

Natalie focused her attention back on Zeke. "Everything, everyone dies, Zeke. Sometimes we know when, and sometimes we don't."

"Did you know when your *maam* would die?"

"She was very sick, with cancer. So, yes, I knew it was coming."

"*Mammi* didn't know *daadi* was going to die today."

"No, she didn't." Natalie swallowed and brushed aside her own tears. She hadn't known the man well at all, but she was fond of Rachel, and the children—fond of them all, really. "We must pray for her and help her all we can."

The once-merry lunch provided the basis for a smorgasbord of food from neighbors, which was followed by more food from fellow mourners.

"I don't think I want to clean the fish now."

"You should," came Jacob's voice. "It would be wasteful not to."

Natalie looked over her shoulder at Jacob, his voice heavy with grief. His eyes were red as he gazed down at his son. She stood and moved closer to him, then placed her hand on his arm.

"Jacob, I am so sorry about your grandfather."

He studied her hand on his arm, then covered it with one of his own. Somehow, much of the air disappeared from the backyard as if a giant vacuum switched on. Natalie wanted to say more, but Jacob found his voice first. "There was nothing you or anyone could do. *Gotte* decided it was time for his days here to be ended."

She could feel strength in his warm hand, and tried to remove her hand from his arm. His own hand pressed harder. "He . . . he lived a full life, and I wish I'd had the chance to know him more."

One corner of Jacob's mouth drew up in half a smile. "He left this life as he wished. He never—" Jacob cleared his throat "—never wanted to grow old and be a burden to anyone."

"What hurts my heart is to think of your grandmother . . ."

A flash of color entering the backyard caught the corner of Natalie's vision.

"Jacob, I came as soon as I heard," said Betsy Yoder.

Natalie's hand felt cold when Jacob released it and turned to face Betsy. If she'd been working today, Natalie couldn't tell, from the young woman's fresh-looking apron and robin's egg blue cape dress. Her hair, smoothed back into its customary bun, didn't bear the signs of a woman cleaning houses.

Betsy only blinked, but studied Natalie's clothes. Capris and a t-shirt and flip-flops. She was nearly as covered up as Betsy, although her neckline was scooped wider than Betsy's narrow and high one.

Jacob nodded, then turned and ruffled Zeke's hair. "Now, let Natalie show you how to clean the fish. It will do my heart good tonight to eat something you caught for me."

Natalie wouldn't meet his eyes, but she knew he'd given her a long glance as he headed toward Betsy. She reminded herself once again she wouldn't put herself between Jacob and the most suitable choice of Betsy Yoder.

But he'd called her Natalie. She'd never heard her name roll off his tongue before.

Hold your horses, girl.

She swallowed hard and took her place at the table beside Zeke once again. "All right, you heard your *daed*—did I say that right?—Let's clean these fish."

"You sound funny trying to talk Plain." Zeke laughed for the first time since grief showed up at lunchtime.

Natalie let herself laugh. "Okay, I hope you're not squeamish, but now we need to cut its belly and take out the insides. We don't want to eat those parts."

Zeke shook his head. "No, we don't."

"Thank you for coming," Jacob told Betsy. He strode toward the back door of the house and paused at the back step.

"I know you'll have a lot of people coming through over the next few days, but seeing as I'm someone from home, your home, I wanted to make sure you know my family will be here for yours."

He pulled open the back door and regarded her with blue eyes, rimmed in red. "My *mammi* will appreciate that."

It was her turn to touch his arm. "I saw you, holding her hand." She regretted the words as soon as they darted from her mouth.

"It was nothing." He looked down at her hand, but made no move to touch it. Then he looked down at her face.

"She's not like us, Jacob. She's not Amish. She can't begin to understand how it is for us, what is required, what's expected."

"Some of her beliefs are very similar to ours."

"Her life is not simple and she is *not* Plain." Well, she might as well say it now as opposed to later, before she lost her nerve. "What do you think your family, and worse, the bishop would think if they'd seen you? Sarasota is very worldly. I've seen it firsthand. But I haven't forgotten who I am."

"Neither have I." He frowned. "You won't say anything, will you?"

"Of course, I won't. It's not my place. But surely, surely, Jacob, isn't there someone Amish who is more suitable? Someone who understands the great responsibility of raising your children in our ways. Someone like . . ."

"Someone like you?" The question hit her like a stray volleyball, skimming the net and smacking her in the face.

How close he'd been to the truth. Betsy sucked in a breath before replying. "No, I meant someone like Hannah."

"There will never be anyone like Hannah."

"No, she was practically perfect at everything she did." Betsy kicked a stone from the back step. Not like her, elbows and arms in the way all the time, a fair-to-middling seamstress, a bit distractible when it came to housework.

Jacob gently pushed her hand from his arm. "Elizabeth Yoder, you are kind and thoughtful and selfless. But I'm not ready to choose another wife yet. I know I have to, but like I tell my brother and the rest of my family, I still need time. I won't have a marriage of convenience to someone solely for the sake of my children. It wouldn't be fair to the woman, whoever she is."

She nodded, her cheeks seared as if she'd been in the sun all afternoon. "I understand."

"Let me have time." He drew in a deep breath. "Right now, I have to see to burying my *daadi*."

11

Grace let Natalie reschedule her Friday morning adult silks classes to attend Isaiah Miller's funeral. She wasn't immediate family, but all the same, she felt like she should be there.

Natalie wore a black skirt, calf-length, with a white blouse topped by a black bolero jacket, and her dark low-heeled sandals. It was the most conservative and appropriate clothing she could find in her wardrobe. She put up her hair in a simple French twist. It was as if summer had come to Sarasota for one day and the humid breeze kept her neck somewhat cool.

When her mother died, she'd worn a red silk Japanese tunic over black leggings for the private service. Mom's choice.

"Celebrate my life, not my passing. Wear something pretty and fun," Mom had told her during those final days, right before the pain was relieved only by keeping her unconscious.

At the cemetery, Natalie almost blended in among the dark clothing. She didn't venture close to the graveside, by the Millers, but instead she searched for a familiar face. There was only so much room in the Sunnyside Mennonite cemetery, which was the final earthly resting place for some of the Pinecraft Plain people.

There was Imogene in a black cape dress and carrying a gigantic parasol to block out the sun. Natalie ambled to her side.

"Why, hello, Natalie," Imogene whispered. "You're just in time. The bishop is going to read some Scriptures, some of Isaiah Miller's favorites."

"Good." A few glanced their way, but Natalie ignored the looks and strained to see the Millers.

"The whole family is here and just in time. Rented two vans and drivers." Imogene shifted the parasol so Natalie had her own patch of shade. "You'll come to the meal at the church, won't you?"

"I didn't bring anything. I would have, if I'd known, but I didn't have a way to reach them, and—"

"Never mind. You bring your sunshiny self and that'll be plenty."

Natalie nodded, and listened to the bishop speak. Pennsylvania Dutch, of course.

"He's reading from the book of John, chapter fourteen," said Imogene.

"Let not your hearts be troubled. Ye believe in God, believe also in me. In my father's house, there are many mansions. If it were not so, I would have told you. I go to prepare a place for you, that when I come again, I will receive you unto myself, that where I am you may also be," Natalie whispered. She'd clung to those words for comfort. *If it were not so, I would have told you.*

A permanent home, no more good-byes. No more parents leaving children, or worse, children leaving parents before their time was truly done. What a close call, for little Rebecca Miller. No more pain, or tears.

But Natalie wanted some of that here, some of home. It was one thing to think of eternal rest and those "blessed reunions" the bishop spoke of. However, what about now? These people seemed to have some of that, even in their grief.

Natalie wiped fresh tears from her eyes. She glanced at some nearby faces. She wasn't the only one in the group with stained cheeks.

Another reading, this one from the book of Psalms, or so Imogene told her.

Amid the head coverings and straw hats surrounding her, perhaps one of them knew her grandparents. When someone had arrived from Pinecraft Park that fateful lunchtime, bringing news of Isaiah Miller's collapse, Natalie's quest didn't seem as high a priority. For the Millers, anyway.

Even if her grandparents had known of her mother's illness, Natalie doubted they would have come to the funeral service for Kat Bennett last summer. They'd only known Katie Yoder, and she was dead to them before she physically passed away.

How could someone shun a loved one? How many of these around her had done the same? She couldn't fathom turning a shoulder, literally or figuratively, to her flesh and blood. Yet the people she now found herself immersed among might have done the same to some of their family members.

Someone, Imogene, if Natalie remembered correctly, had told her that shunning was supposed to be a way to encourage fellow Plain people to repent, to return to their faith and fellowship, to be restored.

The bishop's voice continued, Natalie understanding "Isaiah" and "Miller" easily enough. Then he punctuated his words with, "Ah-men."

"Amen," Natalie echoed with the others.

They made a silent procession back to their hired vehicles, some to their bicycles; others headed toward the nearest bus stop—again, Imogene offered an explanation.

"I have my car." Natalie gestured to where she'd parked along a side street. "Would you like to ride with me?"

Imogene nodded. "Thank you. I'm sure the van will seem less crowded without me and I'm not a fan of the city buses."

"So, you said the meal is at a church? One in Pinecraft, I assume?" Natalie popped the locks on the car.

"That's right. The spread is laid out at the Tourist Church. It's large enough and easy to get to for most of us. It's where the Pioneer Trails buses stop," Imogene explained. "Oh, but you've never been out to meet one of the buses yet, have you?"

"No, I haven't."

"For some of us, it's the highlight of our day. What a sight it is. I've seen everything from people to potted plants to caskets come off the buses. You have to come meet the bus sometime. Speaking of which, I picked up an extra copy of *The Budget* for you, so you can see our newspaper."

Natalie negotiated her car down the street, then headed in the direction of Pinecraft. "Well, thank you. I do need to write the ad Rachel and you and I were talking about, the other day . . ."

"Seems to me like there's been many days since then and now."

"It does." After Monday afternoon and helping Zeke clean his fish, she'd helped him clean up and bring the plateful of fillets into the house. She'd left without further explanation, but assuring a heartbroken Rebecca she'd be back soon.

The familiar city passed by the car windows, the trees dripping with Spanish moss, the rest of Sarasota going on with life as they knew it. Except for one Amish family, losing its patriarch.

"So, the Millers tell me you work for a circus?"

"I did—I teach at a circus school here in the city. I love working with the children—teaching acrobatics, juggling, but mostly aerial silks. I worked for a circus for many years, starting with my parents, but then I had to stop a few years ago."

"Ah, that's too bad."

"It was my ankles. I've had surgery, but they'll never be up to the rigors of regular performing." She could say it now almost glibly, whereas a few years ago she thought it was a death sentence.

"Sometimes the circus comes to Pinecraft and performs a few routines. Not the whole circus, of course. There's not enough room. But one year, we got to see a high-wire act. Nik Wallenda came." Imogene shook her head. "I don't know how he does it."

"Me either. I'd much rather be up there with silks to hold me." Natalie flipped the turn signal to head onto Bahia Vista. "I was just thinking. In a couple of months, one Saturday in April, we're having our spring exhibition at the school. It's our student show, and we faculty even get to perform. I can get you free tickets—and for anyone in Pinecraft who would like them."

"Oh, fun, fun." Imogene beamed. "I would love that."

"You just take the bus down Bahia Vista, it's as easy as pie to get there . . . now which street do I turn on? I see Yoder's coming up on the left."

"Take the light at Big Olaf's and head left, and then we'll take a quick right on the side street and come to the church parking lot from behind."

"All right." Natalie tried not to nibble her lower lip at the thought of seeing Jacob at the meal. A recollection from Monday drifted through her mind. Her words with Jacob, the touch of his hand. Was it her imagination, or had he felt *something* too? She tried to shrug it off. Sometimes attraction was natural. That didn't mean someone had to follow that attraction. No, it was impossible for the two of them.

Anyway, she wasn't looking for love, she was only looking for her family.

❧

Jacob sat with Rebecca and Zeke at one of the long tables set up at the Tourist Church. More food, more love and concern, poured out for the Miller family.

He'd eaten some meals since Monday, even managed to eat the fillets Natalie had helped Zeke prepare for cooking. Her help had been a good distraction, especially for Zeke. Aside from the fillets, though, he didn't really remember eating much else.

Death was a part of life; they all knew it, from losing Hannah and the children losing their infant brother at the same time. Times like this, though, gouged up those wounds afresh.

Ah, Lord, forgive me for mourning too long. If Hannah were here, she would know exactly what to say and do. Now his grandmother would know aloneness after more than sixty years of marriage.

Sixty years. There she sat, at the opposite end of the table. She caught his eye and gave him a slow smile and nod.

"Well, Jacob, I can't say but you still being here with your grandparents was a blessing in disguise," said Henry Hostetler, clad in white shirt and black trousers and suspenders today. "Do you think you'll be here much longer, or will you be leaving for Ohio soon?"

He felt his parents' eyes on him. They'd come for the funeral, of course. "Rebecca's still not ready to travel, not that far of a trip. I'll feel better once the neurologist clears her, especially from her brain injury."

"I wish you were coming with us, now," his mother interjected.

"By spring, *maam*, spring."

"Mr. Hostetler is right, though," his father said. "It makes the family feel better, knowing you're here with your grandmother. So, your work is going well?"

"It is." He glanced at Henry, who nodded.

"He's one of the best helpers I've ever had. In fact, I'm considering expanding the business and a good partner would definitely be a blessing."

"But it would mean . . ." Jacob began.

"It would be a permanent position," Henry said. "Year-round here, not just winter. I have plenty of work throughout the city."

"Son, I don't know if it's wise." His father frowned. "It's one thing to vacation here, yet another to live here all the time. No offense meant, Mr. Hostetler."

"None taken. It can be quite a culture shock if you're not used to it."

"Right now, my main concerns are taking care of Rebecca and providing for my family while I'm here. And, of course, being here for *Mammi*." Jacob could see both opposing sides. Florida, though, was only supposed to be a two-week vacation. Now here they were, going on five weeks away from Ohio and everything familiar. In a way, it was a good thing. But the cost pained him still.

He blinked when he saw a figure pass by the table. Then he blinked again, not quite sure of who he saw.

Natalie, wearing black and her hair up. He almost didn't recognize her, but she was one of the few women not wearing a head covering. She walked with Imogene, who stopped every few paces to say hello to someone and pull Natalie into the conversation.

He caught her eye, and she gave him a slight wave and a nod before she continued along. He hadn't noticed her at the service, but evidently she'd been there, judging by her respectful clothing. She stopped at his *mammi's* side. His *maami* stood to whisper something in her ear, at which Natalie smiled and said something in reply.

Her short black jacket covered a white shirt almost like a man's shirt with a straight hem and cuffed sleeves. She reached up and tucked some hair over one ear.

Hannah had wayward locks she had always tried to keep pinned into place, but a few refused to submit to the hairpins. She used to make the same gesture Natalie did now.

"*Daed*, I'm not feeling too good." Rebecca pulled on his sleeve. "My head hurts."

He tore his attention away from Natalie and touched Rebecca's forehead. "*Ach*, your forehead is warm." Then he touched her cheek. "I should get you home."

"Is everything all right?" his mother asked.

"Rebecca's not feeling well," Jacob replied. His mother was well-intentioned, of course, but he could take care of her fine. Most likely, the events of the week had caught up with her. Quite frankly, too, he was ready to be done with the crowd and be back at his grandmother's house, which had been invaded again, this time by the entire Miller clan. One of his other brothers had even borrowed a pop-up trailer from the Mullets, the Mennonite family who lived around the corner, and the trailer now sat in the side yard.

He wheeled Rebecca from the room, with Zeke following. "You can stay with your grandparents or cousins. There won't be anyone to play with at the house."

Zeke tugged on his sleeve. "I want to be with you, *Daed*."

"All right, then."

He angled the wheelchair over a low curb. It wouldn't take long, and they would be home after a short walk.

"Jacob."

Natalie had followed them from the building. She caught up with them within a few steps.

"Thank you for coming," he said. "I know my *mammi* appreciates it."

Natalie nodded. "It was a nice service, even though I couldn't understand some of it. I was with Imogene, and she helped with a bit of translation." She pulled some invisible hairs over one ear this time. *She's nervous*. A trio of Amish men chatted ten yards or so away, standing among a herd of bicycles. One glanced their direction, then back at his friend.

"Miss Natalie." Zeke gave her a hug, and she hugged him back. "Rebecca's sick."

"Oh, no." Natalie squatted beside Rebecca's wheelchair. "Jacob, she's burning up."

"My leg hurts."

"Yes, I'm taking her home for rest, and medication."

"Please, let me give you all a ride there. I'm ready to leave."

"But the dinner—"

"I've eaten already. I don't mind taking you."

"All right, then."

They followed her to her car, where they arranged Rebecca on the backseat, with Zeke beside her. Once inside and next to Natalie in the front seat, the car seemed much more confining than Henry's van.

Jacob found himself again on the receiving side of someone else's kindness. Natalie maneuvered along the side street, then back onto Bahia Vista. A few pedestrians in their Plain clothing waved. He didn't recognize them, but waved back.

What would people think, to see him riding alone with the *Englisch* woman? Betsy had peppered him with questions the other night. Her questions were reasonable, her heart open before him, even with her roundabout way of speaking. She said she understood he wouldn't marry someone for convenience. Maybe some could, but not him.

Betsy deserved to have someone love her. So did Natalie.

Natalie had never mentioned a boyfriend or any love interest, but then it had never come up in conversation with his family, and rightly so. Married men didn't discuss such things with unmarried—or married—women. But then, Jacob wasn't married. Not anymore.

"Will you be going to the Haiti auction this weekend?" Her question interrupted his thoughts.

"Probably. With most of the family in town, even unexpectedly, I'm sure they'll want to seize the chance to see friends while they can. No one will frown at them not staying home."

"I've heard I should bring my appetite." Natalie clicked on the turn signal. Yes, she did say their trip home would be much faster this way.

"True, very true."

"I want a soft pretzel and a chocolate fried pie," said Zeke from the back seat.

"We can do that. If Rebecca isn't feeling well tomorrow, I'll stay with her and you can go with *mammi*."

"I might even go, too." Natalie glanced at the rearview mirror and smiled.

12

Saturday silks classes ended at noon, and Natalie breezed through her paperwork. She had plenty of time to head to the Sarasota fairgrounds to the Haiti benefit auction. Her meager budget allowed her room for a good meal and some snacks, but probably not an auction item like an Amish-made quilt.

Still, it would be fun to watch. And anyway, she and Rachel Miller would soon begin working on her mother's unfinished quilt. So, that counted as Amish-made, since Natalie figured Rachel would end up doing a good deal of stitching.

Imogene promised to be at the auction, too, along with her camera. "You must come. Maybe we'll make some headway on finding your family."

No one had admitted to knowing her Yoder grandparents so far, but lately the village's attention was on the Millers and their latest bout with grief. Oh, to be part of a family who stretched beyond mere genetics. Grace, though her boss, was probably the closest almost-family Natalie had.

Thinking of her boss and friend, Natalie popped into Grace's office. "I'm through. Off to the Haiti auction."

"Do you have your prayer *kapp* and dress ready?"

"No, I hadn't thought about that."

"It's a joke, Nat." Grace smiled as she stood and stretched. "You're not seriously considering . . ."

Natalie shook her head. "No, not really. Finding my mother's family is plenty enough for me."

"The Amish are a tight group. I watched one of those 'out of Amish' shows. It seems like they can be pretty hateful to those who leave them. I can't imagine being treated like that by family, turning my back on them because I don't agree with their lifestyle."

"Not all of them are hateful, but no, I couldn't imagine family treating me like that, either. Imogene—a former Amish woman who lives in the village—said maybe my mom's family doesn't want me to find them, and not to be surprised if I don't hear anything. But the way they all take care of each other . . . it's true fellowship."

"You almost sound like you want to convert." Grace smiled. "My young queen of the aerial silks, trading her leotard and costumes for a Plain dress."

"I only want my family," Natalie managed to say. "Say, do you want to come with me to the auction? It's open to the public. I heard they have all kinds of things for sale—from farm equipment to furniture, handwoven rugs, even hand-pieced quilts."

"Well, I can't say I have much use for a hay baler, but the furniture part, and handmade quilts . . ." Grace paused for a moment. "Wait for me. I'll get my purse. It'll be fun."

Of course it would be. Anything with Grace was made fun just by the older woman being there, lending her warmth and laughter and hilarity to situations.

"Do you want to ride together, or follow me there?"

"We should probably take separate cars. I need to leave around three. Dog groomer's. Queso and Burrito's nails are sharp enough to leave marks."

In less than twenty minutes, with Grace following in her wake, Natalie made it to the Sarasota fairgrounds and waited in a stream of vehicles to park. She glanced in the mirror. Grace waved from her car. What would Grace think of this glimpse into a different world, far different from the colorful pageantry and performance of the circus?

A crowd surged around the main arena and large white rectangular tents dotted the yard of the outer fairgrounds. How could anyone locate friends in a crowd like this, unless they made plans to meet at a specific place?

"Look at that sea of white bonnets." Grace scanned the outer courtyard. "I've never seen anything like this before. Some of them are very, very different from the others. Look, that lady's head covering almost resembles a doily. She must be a more liberal one." She stepped over a curb, and Natalie led the way into the arena.

"Probably. I'm not sure." Natalie tried not to chuckle at her friend's observation.

First was the tool auction area, where a kaleidoscope of varying colors and lengths of beards lined the bleachers. Up for auction was a woodworking tool set, a perfect gift for a young man.

Natalie had heard that Jacob's primary occupation in Ohio was as a cabinet-maker. Did he miss it, now as he made the rounds with a Mennonite man named Henry who was a general contractor and fix-it guy?

"Nope, I've definitely never seen anything like this," Grace repeated. "But I'm not into the tool auction."

Natalie picked up a program at a nearby table. "It's time for some of the quilts to be auctioned off on the other side of the arena."

"Oh, can't wait to see them." Grace beamed. "I might even make a bid or two, myself."

Just past the tool auction area lay the main auction space. A long elevated stage ran the length of the building, flanked on one side by the bleachers and facing rows and rows of folding chairs. At the back of the arena stood a line of tables with signs above each labeled Registration, Pickup, and Information.

"I'm going to register for a number," Grace said, tugging on Natalie's arm. "I should if I'm going to bid."

Natalie laughed. "All right, then, let's go." She avoided the urge to scan the crowd for the Millers, for now. Maybe it was too early for Rachel to be in public. But then, she didn't know much about Amish funeral and grieving practices.

Right now, a quilt was being shown off by a pair of Amish or Mennonite women, Natalie couldn't discern. These ladies, however, didn't wear the more formal-looking aprons, so she guessed they were Mennonite. The quilt pattern, a vivid rose chain, had thousands of stitches covering the off-white surface of the quilt.

"Beautiful," Natalie said aloud.

"Ah, that it is," said a woman at her side. She wore a vivid burgundy cape dress under her black apron, fixed in place with straight pins. "I donated that one—I didn't make it, though. I bought it at an auction myself for nowhere near what it's really worth."

"I can't believe someone couldn't see its value."

"They probably did, but I knew had to buy it. Right now the bid is up to nine hundred dollars." The woman nodded. "That's a more fitting price, I think, and all that money will do someone some good."

"Here, I've got my number," Grace said as she approached, waving a card. "Oh, is this one of your Amish friends?"

"We just met," Natalie began.

"Anna Yoder," said the woman, shaking hands with Grace, and then with Natalie. "Is this the first time you've attended the auction?"

Anna Yoder. Her grandmother's name. Natalie's throat tightened. "Yes, for both of us," Natalie said.

"Well, I hope you enjoy it. The food is special, because it is made by women from all over the country, New Order, Old Order, and Mennonites visiting Pinecraft."

"We plan on it." Natalie smiled at Anna Yoder and a hope crept into her heart. "Anna, if you don't mind me asking, do you have any daughters?"

"Yah, why I have three daughters. Seven *kinner* altogether."

"Do, or did, you have a daughter named Katie?" She felt Grace's hand gripping hers.

"Why, yes." Anna paused. "Why do you ask?"

"My mother is . . . was . . . a Yoder, named Katie, who left her Order. I've been searching for her family."

"Oh, dear child, it couldn't be my Katie. She is married, named Katie Fry, lives two miles from my husband and I, and has four children of her own. It couldn't be the same Katie Yoder."

Natalie tried to shrug off the sting and disappointment. "No, it couldn't be."

"What happened to your *mudder*? Where is she?"

"She . . . she passed away last summer."

"*Ach*, I am sorry to hear that. Well, I will pray for you to find your *Mammi* Yoder."

"Thank you, Anna."

"*Ach*, there's my cousin, and I haven't seen her since last winter." Anna waved across the crowd. "*Gotte* bless both of you ladies."

"Thank you," Natalie repeated as Anna left them. She turned to face Grace. "Everyone is so kind." She blinked back tears, not expecting the surge of emotions that meeting Anna would bring.

Grace snorted. "I'm sure they have their bad days just like the rest of us." She slung her arm around Natalie's shoulders. "Chin up, hon. You'll find her. It might take time, but I'm sure it'll happen."

Natalie nodded. She shifted on her feet. *Us* and *them*, Grace had said. They were the outsiders, and she felt it acutely. Was it clothing, or mindset, or both?

"So, what's next?" Grace pointed at the program Natalie held. "More quilts, I hope?"

"If you want to hang out here and bid, that's fine with me." Natalie thumbed through the program's pages. "Okay, that was the 'Rose Garden' quilt. The next two are the 'Star of Bethlehem' and the 'Wedding Ring Rose.'"

"Well, I'm going for it." Grace studied the stage. "One of those two quilts will be *mine*."

Natalie tried not to laugh at her older friend's intensity and found herself studying the crowd. The more she saw the Amish and Mennonites of Pinecraft, she saw subtle differences in dresses and *kapps*. Anna Yoder's dark apron signified she was Old Order, likely from Pennsylvania. And the more liberal Mennonites didn't dress or look much different from Natalie. One neighbor of the Millers' two doors down wore her hair cropped short and also wore capris.

The next quilt came up for bid and the first bid was three hundred dollars out of the gate. Grace countered with her own bid of four hundred dollars, and off she went. An Amish man in the front row would raise his card, as did a woman seated halfway back in the bleachers.

"It's for a good cause," Grace said, waving her card for a six hundred dollar bid.

"Are you reminding yourself of that?" Natalie chuckled. Despite their nonaggressive and pacifist beliefs, the Amish and Mennonites were fierce bidders. Did the woman bidding on the quilt from the bleachers donate the quilt and wanted to make sure it went for a large donation?

The program proclaimed that last year's auction had raised more than one-quarter-million dollars at the one-day event, a testimony to what a varied group of people could accomplish when they set their minds and hearts to work together.

"Fourteen hundred? Do I hear fourteen hundred?" the auctioneer called into the microphone, his gaze drifting from the Amish man, to Grace, and then the Mennonite lady in the bleachers.

Grace frowned. "Todd would kill me if I spent that much on a quilt for the guest room, even for a good cause," she murmured to Natalie.

The star quilt auction closed to a round of applause.

"Next up, 'Wedding Ring Rose Quilt,' number one-three-three," said the auctioneer.

"Here we go, girlfriend, one more quilt coming up." Grace clutched her card.

A flurry of bids later, and the Wedding Ring Rose belonged to Grace, with a closing bid of nine hundred dollars. Cheeks flushed, Grace hugged Natalie.

"It's mine." She practically dragged Natalie over to the payment table.

"*Ach*," the woman behind the table said when she saw Natalie, "You're the Millers' friend. I saw you at the funeral earlier this week."

"Yes, I was there," Natalie said. "My heart goes out to them. The family has been through a lot."

"*Gotte* has His ways, but still, I pray they have peace for a good long time." The woman signed off on the auction item—the quilt was indeed won and paid for in full by Grace Montgomery.

"Me too."

"The Millers are here today, though." The woman wrote a receipt in her book.

"I haven't seen them yet, but I'll be sure to look for them." Natalie resisted a glance over her shoulder back at the crowd. No, she couldn't imagine them keeping little Zeke seated, watching quilts be auctioned one by one. He'd probably be somewhere outside among the tents.

The woman handed the receipt to Grace. "There. Present this when you pick up your quilt. You don't have to pick it up now, not if you're headed to the food tents. People can pick up their winnings when they leave the auction."

"Thank you, Ma'am," said Grace. "This will make a lovely addition to my guest room."

"That quilt was made in Shipshe," said the lady at the desk, as if guessing Natalie's thoughts.

"Shipshe?" Grace echoed.

"Shipshewana, Indiana. Made special for today." The woman's cheeks blushed red.

"Did you make it?" asked Natalie.

The woman's head bobbed. "Well, I helped. It's my pattern, actually."

Grace placed her hand on her heart. "Oh, well, it means so much more now that we've met one of its creators, Mrs. . . . ?"

"Byler. Stella Byler." The woman smiled. "I'm glad it's gone to someone who will love it."

A line had formed behind them, so Natalie nudged Grace. "Are you ready to go see the other tents?"

"Okay." They ambled off together, after saying goodbye to Mrs. Byler. "So, your Millers are here today. I hope I get to meet them."

"My Millers, huh?" Natalie stepped out of the arena, blinking at the sudden sunlight. "If they're here today, I'm sure it'll be at the food tents."

"You have a unique connection to the family, you know."

Natalie nodded. "I start working on the quilt top on Monday. I asked Rachel if it wasn't a good time, but she assured me that finishing this quilt with me was the best thing for her to do right now."

"Have you ever sewn anything before?"

"Just a minor repair or two on a costume, or sewing on a button, but nothing as large as a quilt. I hope I don't ruin it."

"Of course you won't, not with an expert overseeing the project."

"Thanks for the vote of confidence."

"Miss Natalie!" The perky voice of a child rang out among the crowd.

"That must be one of your fans." Grace pointed toward a cluster of people, heading in the same direction.

It was the Millers, with Rebecca on crutches and Zeke pelting in her direction.

And today, when Natalie's eyes met Jacob's, she could have sworn she saw a light go on in those blue eyes of his.

Jacob's palms felt as clammy and cold as the old root cellar in Ohio. Now, *this* wasn't supposed to happen. His mouth was parched, although he'd just sampled a piece of orange over at the produce tent.

It should be Betsy Yoder heading in their direction, making him all *naerfich* and jumbled inside, not the *Englisch* woman with Amish ties.

He felt his brother's eyes on him, listened to Katie greeting Natalie again.

An older woman was with Natalie, with a shade of platinum blonde hair. She was probably about his own mother's age, but didn't dress like a woman of that age.

Natalie introduced her. "This is Grace Montgomery, my boss and my friend."

"Nice to meet all of you," Mrs. Montgomery was saying. "Natalie has told me about you all." She leaned over. "And you must be Rebecca, one brave little girl."

Rebecca nodded, then glanced up at Jacob. "We have to stay in Pinecraft until I get better."

"How is she doing now?" asked Natalie. "The other day, she had a fever."

"It was gone the next morning," Jacob said, grateful his voice wasn't betraying him.

"That's good, very good."

"Will you have lunch with us?" Rebecca asked. "We're going to the food tent."

"I think we can do that."

So Jacob gathered the children, or attempted to, but Zeke stuck next to Natalie, holding her hand and telling her about more fish.

"Maybe we can go fishing sometime. I like it, but I haven't been in a long time," Natalie said.

Ephraim coughed where he stood at Jacob's elbow. "So how's Betsy?"

"Fine, I'm sure."

"She caused quite a ruckus with some of her family, staying here in Florida."

"I'm not surprised." They entered the tent, filled with the scent of pie and barbecue and freshly cooked pretzels. Jacob's stomach rumbled. "We've run into each other a few times. She's been a big help, after *Daadi's* death."

"Any news then?"

"No news." Jacob watched Natalie, talking to Grace and Zeke, then pointing at the menu for fried pies. He'd better intervene before Zeke got his way and had dessert before his lunch. He stepped away from Ephraim.

"I don't think your *daed* would want you to have a chocolate fried pie before you have your lunch," Natalie was saying. "Although a chocolate fried pie sounds super delicious."

"Natalie's right, son," Jacob said, resting his hand on Zeke's shoulder. "You can have either a barbecue sandwich or a catfish plate."

"Fish!" Zeke said.

"And then we'll come back for pies."

Natalie laughed and her eyes met his. The memory of the other night in the backyard came roaring back into his head as the group started moving again. And just like the other night, he saw Betsy in the corner of his eye. He glanced in her direction. She was busily folding fresh fried pies, crimping the edges of the dough semicircles.

After filling a tray with pies ready for the fryer, Betsy looked up and caught his glance, her cheeks blooming a shade of pink, her fresh complexion complementing her wide smile. Then she looked at who stood next to him, and her smile drifted away.

"No news, huh?" Ephraim whispered in his ear. "A lot has happened in a few weeks, and we need to talk."

"I don't think we do," he muttered back at his brother.

"You'd be better off talking to me than our father, or the bishop. People are giving you more leeway, especially after Rebecca's accident. But she's healing, and you need to get your family set straight again. And soon. Is Zeke even in school?"

"Not yet." He tugged at his collar.

"You know they have plenty of room for him at Sunnyside's Mennonite school."

"I know. I've been meaning to enroll him. I promise. I'll see about it first thing Monday." Of course, there were three physical therapy appointments for Rebecca next week, too. "It's just been easier, having him stay at home."

"Katie and I could always take him back to Ohio with us."

"No, but thank you." Ever since Hannah, he'd been ever vigilant about keeping the three of them together, as much as possible. Maybe it wasn't practical, but at least no one was questioning *that* decision he'd made.

Fortunately, the conversation drifted away from his unmarried state, for now. But they stood waiting for barbecue and fried catfish plates, they made an unlikely group with Natalie and her boss tacked onto their line.

"She's such a natural with children," he heard Grace telling Katie behind him. "I count it a blessing every day she's at my school. She helps those children do things acrobatically they never dreamed they could do. And with such confidence." Grace shot a grin at Jacob when he glanced over his shoulder.

"I never imagined aerial silks, or circus performing, could help a child in such a way," Katie said.

"It's amazing. Some children with discipline problems or academic issues, well, it can be the key to their learning. My husband and I founded the school, but I'm glad we have Natalie on our staff with us."

Yes, it was good to have Natalie with them, Jacob allowed himself to admit. If only for his children, he ought to thank *Gotte* for bringing her their way. As soon as Natalie found her family, she'd likely drift out of their lives. It was only appropriate, with him and the children heading back to Ohio.

Eight weeks. He gave them eight more weeks. Then, life could be normal again. As normal as it could get, anyway.

13

Betsy wiped her damp brow with the top of her arm. Nobody had told her how warm the food tent could get in January. But then, she'd never stood under a gigantic food tent before and helped fill hundreds of fried pies. The Ohio cooking team from her home district made them fresh, with a choice of fillings.

Fried pies were nice, but the next time she cooked a dessert, she wanted to try something a little different. Like cannolis or tiramisu, for example. Nobody ever heard of an Amish woman who could make delectable desserts worthy of a five-star restaurant.

Jacob passed by with his family, little Rebecca now hobbling along with crutches, easier to negotiate the grassy area outside than using a wheelchair. There were plenty of tables and chairs, if Rebecca needed a breather.

Natalie Bennett hovered along with the family, this time accompanied by an older *Englisch* woman who looked fancy, even in her simple outfit. Why didn't Natalie just go away somewhere, somewhere besides visiting among the Plain people? There was nothing wrong with Natalie searching for her family, but why latch onto the Millers?

Betsy bit her lip. The woman was a distraction to Jacob. She could tell. Ephraim spoke to him, but Jacob's focus kept drifting to Natalie, who was oblivious of the effect she was having on the poor man. If only she had whatever quality Natalie had, that would make Jacob follow her every gesture and listen to every word, even though he wasn't part of the conversation.

"Uh, Betsy, we need three blueberry and two lemon, not five chocolate pies." Vera Troyer pointed at the pies Betsy had just dropped into the bubbling fryer.

"Oh, no." She glanced at Vera, then toward the waiting customers who'd paid for the pies. "I'll remake them right away. I'm sorry."

"No worries." Vera smiled. "Chocolate pies are popular; they'll be purchased before they're cool."

Betsy blamed Natalie Bennett for her own distraction and messing up the order. So Natalie was looking for her Amish family. Betsy would do what she could to help Natalie in her mission. The sooner Natalie found her family, the sooner she could go on with her own life, apart from the Millers.

There they went, settling down at one of the long narrow tables lined with folding chairs. Her own stomach growled. The Stoltzfus family outside the other edge of the tent, were frying up hundreds of pounds of catfish, caught fresh in Mississippi and transported to Florida in time for the auction weekend.

"Are you all right?" Vera asked as she used the skimmer to pluck the fresh pies from the oil and put them on a rack to drain.

"I'm okay." Betsy snapped her attention back to the pies. There she went again, letting Natalie and the Millers drag her focus away. Vera's probing eyes didn't miss much, either.

"Huh." Vera smiled at a customer and handed them a plate of still-warm pies. "There you go, thank you very much."

Betsy stirred the apple filling, which didn't need any stirring at all. Vera might be one of her *Aenti* Chelle's older friends in the village, but Betsy didn't need any advice. Of course, she had a feeling she'd be getting some straightaway.

"It must be hard, being so far away from your family," Vera said.

"No, not most days. I do enjoy living with my *aenti*. Pinecraft is different, but I like it very much. We're very busy with the cleaning business, so I'm glad I can be a help to her."

"So, is there anyone back in Ohio? Do you have a young man?"

"No, there's no one." *Not in Ohio.* But she didn't tell Vera that.

"Oh, I know sometimes you'll wonder when it'll be your turn." Vera said. "I thought the same thing, myself. My time would never come. *Gotte* has His ways that we don't often understand. It's not always meant for us to understand."

"How old were you when you married?" Maybe she could take the focus off herself.

"Twenty-five. Not old, but not as young as some." Vera shook her head. "I think young women are in too much of a hurry now. Once your vows are taken, there's no going back to the life of not being the lady of the house, of not having as much responsibility. It's one thing to help your mother, quite another to be in charge of everything."

"*Ach*, I see. That's why I'm spending time in Florida right now."

"*Gut*." Vera studied the line, which had shortened. "Go, take a break and get a bite of lunch. I can fry and serve at the same time."

Released from her duties for the moment, Betsy fled in the direction of the food tables. She had ten dollars in her dress pocket and an appointment with a fried catfish plate.

So far, so good. Natalie smiled. Grace had toned down "spotlight Grace" for today, but she still held the group's attention as she told them stories of touring with the Ringling Brothers circus many years ago.

Natalie took another bite of delightful "cowboy stew," a combination of beans and seasoned meat, with a recipe known only by an Old Order Amish man named Henry. Reportedly, he made buckets and buckets of the stew every year for the auction. She could eat several bowls of the stuff, if she let herself. She followed the bite of stew with a nibble of cornbread.

She'd situated herself at the opposite end of the table from Jacob, which sat her away from the children, but closer to Katie and Jacob's brother Ephraim.

"Any news on your family?" asked Katie.

"Not yet," Natalie replied. "Imogene Brubaker suggested I write an ad for *The Budget,* which I've done, and it should run next week."

"Which edition?" Ephraim spoke to her directly for the first time.

"The national edition. I always thought my mother's family was from Ohio, like she said, but maybe they moved to Indiana or Ohio. Or, maybe somewhere else."

"That might be. But even still, someone may know where her family is even if they've moved. That's a good idea, running an ad in the national edition," said Ephraim. "It will receive much more exposure that way."

A rustle of fabric at her right elbow made her look up. Betsy Yoder stood by the table with a plate of food. "Is anyone sitting here in this seat?"

Natalie glanced at the empty chair next to her. "No, not at all."

Betsy set the plate down and pulled out the chair, then sat beside Natalie. "I know you're looking for your grandparents, and I want to help."

Now, *this* was something Natalie hadn't imagined happening. "We were just talking about it, so thank you. I took out an ad in *The Budget*."

"What did you write?" Betsy asked.

"I said, 'Searching for Samuel and Anna Yoder, possibly of Ohio, with a daughter named Katie. Please contact Natalie Bennett.' I gave her birth date and my phone number." Natalie shrugged. "So I hope someone, somewhere will call me. Of course, I've prepared myself for the possibility they might not want to meet me."

The admission, again made aloud, made her cheeks burn.

"I can't imagine someone not wanting to meet you," said Betsy. "You're—you're interesting, kind, and you were brought up well, and I know you are a Christian."

Natalie nodded. "But I'm not Amish. I'm not very Plain, either."

Katie spoke up. "*Ach*, Natalie, you aren't so much different from us on the inside. I can tell from the few conversations we've had, and how my *mammi* has spoken of you. I'm praying you have a fruitful quest."

"Me, too," said Betsy. "As a matter of fact, I'm going to call and leave a message for my father tonight, to see if he can call me on our district phone line. Maybe your *daadi* Samuel Yoder is a distant cousin of his. What if we're almost like, cousins?"

"Thank you, thank you very much. I appreciate it." She felt an urgency, a craving to find where she fit, when for years she hadn't known the place. Despite Katie's assurances otherwise, Natalie still felt as if she was on the outside looking in.

"Here's my phone number," Betsy said, holding out a business card. "Call me, so I'll have your number and we can keep in contact."

"All right, I'll call you." Natalie studied the card. *Cleaning With Chelle – Betsy Yoder, Associate.*

"Betsy Yoder, you have a *cell phone*?" Katie set down her fork and stared at the card in Natalie's hand.

"For work. *Aenti* Chelle has one, too. She uses it for her clients so they can reach her and leave messages. So that's why I have one." Betsy's chin stuck out.

"Does your mother know?" Ephraim asked.

"N—no. I don't use it to be frivolous or waste time. It helps me with my schedule, too."

Natalie felt sorry for the young Amish woman, almost squirming under the line of questioning.

"This is why we must be careful, coming to Pinecraft." Ephraim frowned. "I am glad we only visit during the winter for a few weeks."

Natalie opened her mouth, then decided against it. It wasn't her place to pick sides or voice an opinion. Such matters were the group's concern. She shifted on her folding chair. No, she didn't think she could be a part of this group.

Laughter echoed down the table in their direction.

"And that's when I knew, I wanted to spend a career as a trapeze artist, and not as a high-wire walker," said Grace. Always sure of herself, no matter what the occasion or setting.

Natalie nibbled the last bite of flaky catfish. *Lord, help me find my place. With or without my grandparents, with or without the family I've dreamed of having. Help Betsy, too. If she and Jacob are meant for each other, so be it. I won't stand in the way.*

14

Natalie's fingers ached from repeated jabs from the quilting needle, and she and Rachel had only spent two hours quilting after breakfast on Monday morning. "Remind me, Rachel, why I'm doing this."

"To finish what your mother started," was all Rachel told her.

"My fine motor skills have always been lacking." Natalie studied the row of tiny stitches she'd just completed. "I've always been more, uh, athletic and active instead of doing things like this fine work."

"Needlework plays an important role. Years ago, it was all women had, Plain or otherwise, before clothing stores sold everything. And not nearly as well crafted, in my opinion." Rachel worked her needle in a slow, yet steady, rhythm across the fabric.

The quilt top, once pieced and stitched together in a quilted sandwich of fabric and batting, would easily cover a queen-size bed. Maybe the pattern wasn't as intricate and well-stitched as the quilt now covering the bed in Grace's guest room, but Natalie imagined her mother cutting the blocks of cloth for the pattern and stitching them together, along with the ambitious appliques of roses and leaves and vines.

"I would have made a lousy pioneer," Natalie said. "I like conveniences such as pre-sewn clothing and bedding."

"Me too. Don't tell anyone, but Vera Byler has been sewing my dresses for years. I order them from her and she ships them to me. I can put in a quilts, no problem, but piecing shoulders and sleeves together." At that, Rachel chuckled at her own words. "When Isaiah and I . . ." Her voice trailed off.

"No, it's okay. When you and Isaiah what?"

"When we first moved here to Pinecraft, the streets weren't even paved. People thought we were crazy, spending winters here after our children grew up." Rachel sighed. "I never imagined . . ."

She fell silent, and Natalie stitched almost half of one side of a block before speaking. "I know, we never imagine people we love, leaving us before their time."

"Oh, it was his time. *Gotte* decided his days were finished on this earth." Rachel continued stitching. "I never imagined time passing so quickly. Seems we were just setting up house. Did you know, he helped build some of the houses in the neighborhood? Pinecraft may look like a hodgepodge of homes, but some of the original homes are still here."

"How did Zeke do, heading to school this morning?" She had to ask. Neither of the children, nor Jacob were there when she arrived midmorning. It was just Rachel, sipping a cup of coffee and eating a slice of toast alone.

"Ah, he cried over breakfast. But Jacob wouldn't back down, especially since he had to take Rebecca to her appointment this morning."

"It must be tough for Zeke, being far from home for so long, with so much focus put on Rebecca after the accident."

"He's a good boy," was all Rachel said. "His *daed* has done a good job teaching him. You've done him some good as well. Ever since meeting you, it seems he has come out of whatever shell he entered after his *mamm's* death. Always, 'Miss Natalie' this and that."

Natalie nodded. She'd grown to love the Miller children, much as it wasn't her place. Come spring, they'd be gone and she'd be here, with or without her own family.

"I'm going to miss them when they leave Sarasota," she said aloud.

"I am, too," said Rachel. "But there will be and always is much for me to do here. Same for you, I imagine?"

"Yes, my classes. I have a one o'clock adult class beginning today, plus three classes after three today." She certainly didn't suffer for lack of things to do.

"Promise me you'll come visit?"

"I will. I'd like that." Natalie kept stitching. *Ow*. There went the needle again, bypassing the leather finger guard Rachel had shown her how to use.

"There's talk, too, Rebecca can go to school with her brother, possibly starting next week," said Rachel. "I think it's a good idea. The child will only get bored around here and she can't get up and around and do housework. And the chatter! Much as I love them under my roof, I must admit the quiet this morning has been pleasant."

Except for Isaiah's place at the table being permanently vacant.

"I think she should be as mobile as she can, and do as much as she can." Natalie hoped she wasn't overstepping, giving her opinion. "From someone who's had surgery that interfered with mobility, I know. It was hard, and it hurt sometimes, but I did it, anyway."

They kept sewing in silence. By the time their allotted hours were completed, Rachel had finished half of one block, Natalie had outlined one rectangle of one block.

She surveyed her work after she tied off the knot. "Oh, Rachel. I'm so slow. I'll try to be faster next time."

"You're learning." Rachel moved closer and bent at the waist, inspecting her stitches. "Not bad. I don't think I'll have to rework more than half of these stitches."

"Oh, no, half?" But Natalie smiled when she saw a twinkle in Rachel's eye.

"See you on Thursday?"

"I'll be here."

She regretted leaving the older woman alone in the house. She knew how a gaping loneliness felt. Mother's big personality filled every space she entered, and even while fighting the illness that eventually claimed her life, that bigness had remained.

On Thursday, also, the national *Budget* would release. She would make sure she had her phone well charged and with her at all times. Surely, someone would remember a vivacious young Amish woman named Katie Yoder, who turned her back on all of them, just shy of her eighteenth birthday. A presence like hers would have left a void, just as it had last summer.

Please, Lord, let someone read my ad and remember Mom, someone who knows her parents.

Jacob hammered more nails into the shingles. Henry, not far away, was doing his own work on the opposite end of the roof, but using a pneumatic nailer. He zinged along, shooting nails into the shingles with a *pop, pop, pop.*

Jacob drew the line and kept use of his hand tools. He even learned to use the electric drill and the jigsaw. Of course, he used machines at the cabinet shop in Ohio, but here, he wanted to hang onto whatever Plain ways he could.

"Almost lunchtime," Henry announced. "Finish what you're working on and we'll break. A short break, though." He studied the clouds. "Chance of showers later in the afternoon and I want this roof done today."

"Yes, Henry." Jacob picked up his pace, hammering away. One more shingle strip and he'd be done. Henry disappeared over the roof's edge.

Sweat trickled down his back and neck. He mopped his brow once more before continuing with the last few nails. Sweating outside, in late January. It wouldn't happen in Ohio.

There. One last nail, and now for lunch.

He scurried down the ladder and joined Henry under a nearby tree, where Henry had unpacked a lunch from the massive cooler he kept in his van.

Henry prayed over the simple meal in their people's language.

They tore into the sandwiches of thickly sliced beef, two sandwiches apiece, along with containers of fresh fruit salad, small bags of chips, and a quart of sweet tea for each of them.

"Good food," Jacob said.

"My cousin Chelle packs a mighty good lunch."

"Well, thank her for me."

"I'll do that."

Jacob studied Henry's tropical print shirt topped by suspenders. Today's shirt was a flaming red color with bright flowers covering the fabric. On Sunday, he'd seen Henry, dressed like other Mennonite men, simple and Plain. He even wore the beard.

"Can I ask you a question, Henry?"

"You just did." The man chuckled. "But then, you're serious, so I should be. Ask away."

"How—how do you know what pleases *Gotte*? How can we be sure what we do is . . . enough?"

Henry grunted. "What do you mean by, enough?"

"There was a time, right after Hannah died, I had many questions. No one wanted to listen to them, and the questions I did ask, well, my father and others said I shouldn't ask them."

"Like what?"

"How can I be sure I'll see Hannah again, and our little Samuel? Questions like that, you never think you'll ask, not until you really want to know the answer. I was told, I would discover that one day. But, Henry, Hannah never did a wrong thing in her life. I knew her for most of it, knew her even better from our late teens on, especially after we began courting and were married. She never gossiped or lied, was the best wife and mother any man could want. She was quick to give to the needy, quick to forgive." The words tumbled out, words he'd locked up for a long time.

Henry took something from his pocket and held it up. "A penny. President Lincoln on one side, the Lincoln Memorial on the other."

Jacob couldn't comprehend what his questions had to do with a penny. "Yes, two different sides."

"The way I see it, God's nature is like two sides of one coin. You see the God of justice on one side. This is our holy God. He hates sin and evil. This is God our judge, the judge we will all stand before one day. Even Hannah, with all her earthly works. As the Scriptures say, 'All we like sheep have gone astray, and the Lord laid on him the iniquity of us all,' and 'There is no one righteous, no not one.' Essentially, sinners in front of a holy God are doomed, especially if it means all of us.

Even Hannah." Henry flipped the coin in the air and showed the opposite side.

"See, this is what I mean. If Hannah served *Gotte* with all her heart and it wasn't enough, then all her goodness was for—for nothing." Jacob shook his head. "*Nein*, I'm not turning away, or thinking of it." He tossed his hat on the ground. "That's just a hat, a hat I wear because I am Amish. Does it make me closer to *Gotte*? I don't think so. Not anymore."

"That is the saying of a wise man," said Henry. He snapped his suspenders and tapped his shirt with his free hand. "This doesn't make me holy or unholy, but what's in here." He laid his hand over his heart and held up the coin again.

"Now, let me tell you about the other side of the coin, what protects us from His wrath, which is God's love. 'Beloved, let us love one another, for love is of God and everyone who loves is born of God. He that loveth not knoweth not God, for God is love.' And then there's also, 'Behold, what manner of love the father has given unto us, that we should be called the sons of God.' And my favorite, 'For God so loved the world, that He gave his only begotten son, that whosoever believeth in him should not perish but have everlasting life.'

'For if you confess with your mouth the Lord Jesus and believe in your heart that God has raised him from the dead, you will be saved. And, the wages of sin is death, but the gift of God is eternal life.'"

Eternal life, a gift. Jacob looked at his cast-off hat on the ground.

"Eternal life . . . I've always heard it's presumptuous to believe my salvation is secure. That it's prideful to think so."

"No, not prideful, it is something it took me a long time to learn. I'm not better than anyone else. Every day I get up in the morning is another day to serve my Lord and my fellow man, a chance for me to 'work out my own salvation with fear and trembling.'

Oh, my brother Jacob, it's not presumption to me to know where I'll be once I leave this life. It is God's great gift of grace. We are all capable of sin and we all sin, but God makes a way for us to be free and to know in our hearts . . ." Henry pressed his palm on Jacob's chest, ". . . to know in your heart you, and Hannah, and all who call upon God's saving grace, are saved. Not that we don't face obstacles in this life. It is a sin-weary world we live in. But we know God's mercy new, every morning."

It was a lot to take in. He hadn't heard anything quite like it before. He knew about praying for forgiveness from sin, but didn't know the joyous relief Henry had, it even now shone in his older friend's eyes. But then Henry wasn't Amish. He couldn't know.

"I . . . I almost left the *Ordnung*, not long after we buried Hannah and Samuel." His own confession sounded horrific to him. He glanced around. It wasn't like there was anyone listening, anyone who would tell his father or worse, the bishop. He respected their bishop, but then he was the same man who had given stern warnings to those visiting Florida, to beware of the ways of the world prone to creep in, should someone not be vigilant.

"Why would you leave?"

"The same reason I told you. Why try, if it is pointless? Just like casting off my hat, it does not change me or make me who I am." Jacob sighed, then took a long drink of sweet tea. "But I couldn't do that to my children, couldn't remove them from where we were, everything familiar. How could I explain shunning to them? So, I stayed."

"Ah, that's understandable. Many things we do for the sake of our children. So how is your Rebecca, healing up?"

"*Yah*, better all the time. The orthopedist wants us to wait until her cast is off before giving her more physical therapy. The first sessions were helping us with her wheelchair, how to get her in and out of bed. Then, training with crutches." Good thing the visits were getting fewer.

"And Zeke?"

"He's in school, and Rebecca is now, too. She couldn't sit home with my *mammi* all day and I want her to keep up with her studies too, and keep a routine."

"Good, good." Henry appeared as if he wanted to say something more, but held back and instead chomped down the last few bites of his sandwich.

"What is it?" He worried he wasn't doing a good job. Roofing, general construction, some of it was new to him. He hoped Henry wasn't going to be replacing him.

"I want to let you know I've been working on something to help you and your family with bills, and such."

"Now, Henry—"

The man silenced him by raising one hand. "Nope, I know that your district has helped with Rebecca's medical bills—I can't imagine how much it has all cost."

"Far more than my family's property is worth." He'd seen the bills, tens of thousands upon tens of thousands. The price of healing shouldn't be so high.

"And now, with your grandfather's passing, I know your family here in general has had extra expenses."

"We're managing, thanks to your job, and *mammi's* church." Jacob picked up his hat and put it back on. "So, what were you planning?"

"A fish fry and a singing at the park on Saturday night. The Mullets from Indiana are coming, plus the Schrock family, Mennonites from Kentucky—and they play bluegrass and gospel. People can come and buy a plate to take home, or eat at the park and listen to the music. And all the money raised will go to your family."

Jacob was grateful he was sitting down. "For my family? For us?" He was accustomed to how the district pitched in and all helped each other, in good times and bad. But he wasn't part of this community.

"Yes, for you." Henry put the cover back on the cooler. "This is Pinecraft. We help take care of each other, too. Now, back to work before the rain comes."

15

Jacob was dreaming. He knew it was a dream, because Hannah was still alive and they were walking together in a park, lush and green. He'd had this dream before, for many nights and many months since Hannah had died. The dream had disappeared as time went on and hadn't come for several months.

This time, the dream was a bit different. There was a nearby volleyball court, shuffleboard court, and pavilion—like Pinecraft Park, along with its swings for the children. But not Pinecraft Park. He couldn't see the end of the path they walked together.

"How are the *kinner*?" she asked in her soft, gentle voice.

"Zeke is speaking English better and better every day. Rebecca is healing from her injuries. I was afraid, more than once, we were going to lose her."

"*Nein*, it's not her time yet," Hannah said, facing him. She wore her wedding dress, the dress they had laid her to rest in. "Not for a long, long time. I'm glad Zeke is coming out of his shell, like a little turtle." She laughed, a joyful sound to Jacob's ears.

"How do you know about Rebecca?"

"*Ach*, the things I know now, I didn't know then." Hannah beamed. "I can't explain it, but there are things now I just *know.*"

"I want you back, here and now, with me." He tried to reach for her hand, but it was like running his hand through rushing water, getting pushed back.

"*Nein*, you wouldn't wish that for me. Not if you'd seen what I have." Her face glowed as if reflecting the sun.

"If not for the children, I would be with you," he admitted. When would they come to the end of the park? Or had they made an infinite lap, in this his dream?

"Don't say that. Our days together have all been written and are over. Our time together is done." Hannah stopped short. Her words snapped at him, then softened as she continued. "I can tell you this: you have a purpose not yet fulfilled, Jacob Miller. You will live to fulfill that purpose and beyond, and will die full of years, with more *kinner* to join Rebecca and Zeke."

"More children?"

They began walking again, and this time Jacob could see the edge of the park and the first few homes of the neighborhood.

"More children." She beamed at him again.

"That means . . ."

"You will find love again." Hannah looked toward a figure waiting at the edge of the park. Jacob followed her gaze.

It was a man who appeared familiar, but Jacob knew he'd never seen him before. Or had he? He tried to remember how he must know this man.

"I'm coming, Samuel—" Hannah called out.

"*Samuel*?" Jacob echoed.

"He begged to see his *daed*." Hannah smiled at him until the light grew too strong for his eyes, and he closed them against its brightness.

He woke, finding himself in *Mammi* Rachel's house, with moonlight painting a light wash on the covers. Somehow, he knew he'd never dream about Hannah again.

The cuckoo clock in the living room chirped three o'clock. Not quite time to get up, a little time left for more sleep.

Of course, he'd dreamed about Hannah. After the deep discussion between him and Henry in the afternoon, how could he not? Dreams usually meant indigestion, a meal, the mind's flight of fancy while he slept. *Ach*, how he wish he knew if the dream were real. His eyelids felt heavy again.

As Jacob drifted off again, this time with no dreams, he silently prayed *Gotte* would show him the way. He'd been clinging to the hope *Gotte* would have paved a more distinct path than the one he walked.

"Go, take a walk around the block and stretch your legs," Rachel said to Natalie about noontime on Saturday. "We've worked hard this morning."

Natalie nodded. Her quilt, now in a frame, took up a good part of the Millers' living room while they worked on it. Two weeks' worth of work so far and maybe one-fourth of the quilt had been stitched. Rachel was a patient and able teacher, insisting that Natalie work on the bulk of the quilt herself. Natalie had a sneaking suspicion Rachel sewed on days Natalie didn't come.

Today Rachel had banished Jacob and the children from the house, insisting the three of them head to the park and meet up with other friends in town from Ohio. Natalie missed them, but understood the need to be able to work without the younger ones underfoot. Or, the more very real distraction of Jacob. Maybe he'd run into Betsy at the park, too.

The thought rankled her, and it shouldn't.

She glanced at her phone on the lamp table. A little more than a week now and her ad had appeared in *The Budget*. They'd gotten everything right, of course, including her phone number. But her phone remained silent except for calls from Grace and a friend or two from church, and a text message from her father with a photo of his young family and him at Sea World San Diego.

No one called about Katie Yoder. She knew most Amish had access to phone shanties and made calls when they needed to. Maybe Katie's family didn't think it was a necessity to call. Maybe they didn't want to call her.

"I'll be back in half an hour or so, then," she told Rachel.

"*Gut*. Perhaps you could bring us back some pizza from Emma's? Pepperoni, or plain cheese."

"All right, then." She tried to mask her near double take at Rachel's request. Pizza. Well, why not? She supposed even an Amish woman might want the Pinecraft equivalent of takeout.

Rachel approached, counting some bills. "Here."

"Oh, no. please, let me. You've helped me so much, let me do something for you."

The older woman slowly tucked the cash back into her apron pocket. "Next time, it will be my turn."

Natalie went out into the sunshiny early February day. Pinecraft, she realized, was best seen on foot or by bicycle. She crossed Bahia Vista, passed the pizza parlor, intending to stop on the way back.

A familiar figure with a digital camera slung around her neck greeted her as she passed the outdoor sitting area. "Natalie."

"Imogene." She'd seen the woman talking with a pair of older women and had only planned to wave and keep walking.

"Come over, meet the Lapp sisters. They just arrived Thursday from Pennsylvania." The pair of Old Order women bobbed their heads in unison. "Clara and Estelle, this is my friend Natalie Bennett. Her grandparents are Samuel and Anna Yoder, from Ohio."

"It's nice to meet you, ladies." Natalie shook hands with them, and received more nods, but this time with a pair of smiles. One of the women clutched a two-liter bottle of Coca-Cola under one arm.

"How is it that you're not Amish? Are you Mennonite?" asked one of the sisters.

"No, I'm neither." She explained about her search and they both um'ed and ah'ed in response.

"Your poor mother, doing such a thing to her parents." The other sister made a tsk-ing noise.

"I'd still like to meet them. I have no other family, save my father, and he lives in California." Natalie didn't bother to explain the family dynamics.

"Natalie is a good, Christian woman," said Imogene. "I hope she finds them."

The sisters went along their way and rounded the corner to Big Olaf's. A sweet tooth knew no age limits.

"I've been thinking," Imogene said as she and Natalie walked along. "You forgot one thing in your ad, one important thing that could help in your search."

"Which is?"

"A post office box, here, in Pinecraft. If your mother's family was Old Order, which I'm betting they are, only I don't bet, they likely would be extremely reluctant to make a phone call to a stranger about such a vital matter. It would be impersonal." Imogene paused. "*Ach*, one moment. I must get this photo. Look at the colors of the dresses as they flap in the breeze."

Imogene pointed to a side yard of a residence, with a white picket fence and laundry hung out to dry, a palette of jewel-toned cape dresses of varying sizes. The colors made a striking contrast to the white of the house and the green of the yard.

"Got it." She showed Natalie the shot on her camera.

"It's gorgeous. You have an artist's eye, Imogene. I can picture the photo framed and hanging in someone's laundry room above the washing machine."

"Thank you." Imogene started her ambling pace again. "But as I was saying, maybe you should rent a post office box, and run another ad in *The Budget* for two more weeks. Sometimes it takes readers a while to catch up on the issues."

"What, there's a post office here?"

"I'm surprised you didn't see it already. C'mon, we need to cut through the side street and head toward the Tourist Church."

They came upon a snug square building. Sure enough, it even had a sign for Pinecraft with its own zip code. "What a cute building." A pair of cars occupied one of several parking spots; two bicycles were chained to posts outside.

One entire outside wall sported a bulletin board, with tacked-on written and typed pieces of paper with various messages, advertising everything from drivers to rental property to items for sale.

A child's shoe hung from a string with a note attached: "Found at Siesta Key Beach."

A larger piece of paper caught Natalie's attention, and she read it aloud.

"Fish fry benefit for the Miller family, Saturday, Pinecraft Park. Eight dollars a plate, catfish, hush puppies, corn on the cob, potato salad, and roll. From 5 until ? Music in the pavilion by the Mullet and Stoltzfus families. Bring your own lawn chairs.

Oh, is this our Miller family? I didn't know about this. It's tonight."

"Maybe they didn't say anything, thinking it would appear as if they were asking for your donation."

"Maybe. But I'll come. I'd love to hear some live music and help them, too." Natalie knew the family's medical bills had to be astronomical, with the combination of Rebecca's head injury and her broken leg with surgery. And, the physical therapy and follow-up appointments.

"All right, let's see about your P.O. box, plus sending another ad to *The Budget.*" It took only a few moments for Natalie to open her post office box and compose another ad similar to the first one.

She hadn't thought about the family being reluctant to call. But then, she was a stranger to them. They likely didn't know she existed. "I can only hope this will help."

"This time, I know it will." Imogene smiled at her and gave a firm nod.

Once back home, Natalie pulled out the box from her father. She'd left her mother's cape dress and prayer covering inside after she'd pulled out the quilt top. The quilt top? It had been easier to deal with. Simply begin working on it, with Rachel's help.

And what a quilt it was going to be. She planned to treasure it, forever, and hang onto the memory of her mother with its stitches. But the clothing? She tried to imagine her mother in the dress, a much younger version of her mother, anyway, yet couldn't.

Natalie set the box on the bed and pulled out the dress. Hand-stitched. She held it up to her. She was a few inches taller than her mother, but the length was forgiving. Hems were easy to fix, compared to quilting.

She slipped out of her work clothes and pulled the dress over her head. Nope, no curves visible in this. Which was fine with her, but she didn't think a dress like this was meant to flatter.

She ought to look up the word, *flatter*, to see what it meant. The round neckline was higher than she was accustomed to, but not strangling by any means. Just plain, simple.

Natalie stepped in front of her dresser. If she walked through Pinecraft right now, she'd look much like the other women did. Except her hair fell past her shoulders, not quite halfway between her shoulders and her waist. Didn't Rachel and Katie swoop it up behind in a bun or knot of some kind?

With the help of a scrunchie, Natalie made a makeshift bun with her hair. Now, for the *kapp*. She placed it over the bun and tried to make it look not lopsided.

The look was complete.

Her neck felt cool, with her hair up. Sometimes she wore a ponytail, especially when working out, but to dress this way all the time . . . It definitely felt cooler to wear the dress than capris, or shorts.

Natalie stood sideways, trying to catch a side view of her hair, but was unsuccessful. She found a hand mirror in a drawer and used it instead. She knew the women wore head coverings because of what the Bible said in Corinthians somewhere about a woman's hair being her glory.

Natalie had never been a hat or cap person. She removed the prayer covering gently and set it on the dresser, then shrugged out of the dress.

Was this for her, or wasn't it? If her grandparents contacted her, should she wear this out of respect for them? But then, she wasn't Amish, or even Mennonite.

What would Jacob think of the dress?

She scratched that last thought, and got back into her regular clothing. She hung her mother's dress in her closet, beside the skirts and blouses that made up her Sunday wardrobe.

16

Pinecraft Park brimmed with Amish and Mennonites from every order and district. Rows of prayer coverings glowed white in the remainder of the sunlight as their wearers stood in line for the fried fish supper. February had come with a balmy night, and Natalie left her jacket at home in faith the warm breeze would continue. She found a place to park her car in a small lot at the south end of the pavilion.

A line of bicycles had formed not far from an enormous fryer, with Henry Hostetler at the controls, and Betsy Yoder piling food inside Styrofoam containers with fold-down lids. Another woman next to Betsy was taking cash and making change. Those with to-go orders pedaled off on bicycles or walked from the park. The rest of the crowd busied themselves with finding a place to sit in the park's pavilion before the music began.

In this crowd, much like at the Haiti auction, the attire varied from cape dress to capris, to blue jeans, to the rare shorts outfit. Natalie smiled at Imogene, who took photos of the hodgepodge lineup, and then hopped out of line to get a close-up shot of Henry. Today his tropical print shirt was a vivid turquoise, in contrast to his black trousers and suspenders.

"Catfish?" Henry asked when Natalie reached the fryer. "We've got fresh hush puppies, too."

"And potato salad," said Betsy.

"I'll have some of everything," said Natalie. "It looks delicious. I can never eat enough fish."

"You should come fishing with us sometime," the woman standing beside Betsy said. "I'm Rochelle Keim, but you can call me Chelle. My great-nephew has a boat."

"Natalie Bennett. I'd love to go fishing. I haven't gone in ages." Not since her father's last trip east, right before he remarried.

"I've been hearing good things about you from the Millers." Chelle accepted the cash Natalie offered, then gave her change.

"Oh, I see." She didn't want to squirm. "Well, they are a terrific family. Rachel has been especially helpful to me in finishing my mother's quilt."

"Well, it sounds like you've done a world of good for them, too."

Betsy smacked a dollop of potato salad in the food tray with a bit of force, then folded down the container lid. The tab broke and the lid sprang up. "*Ach*, let me get a fresh container."

"Don't worry about it," said Natalie. "I'm staying here to eat and to listen to the music. I don't have far to carry it. It was nice meeting you, Chelle."

"Same here." Chelle smiled. "Imogene, you should come fishing, too, sometime."

Henry muttered where he stood at the grill, something about a boat being overrun with womenfolk.

"Ah, Henry, you know you don't mind," Chelle chided, but she grinned at the older man.

"I would *love* to come fishing. Unless I get seasick." Imogene pointed at the tray. "Can I have double hush puppies and no potato salad?"

"I don't see why not." Henry grunted and scooped some fresh fish from the fryer, laying them on a metal rack to drain before Betsy swooped them up into a food container.

Imogene and Natalie strolled from the food line, laughing.

"Henry seems like a growler, but he's really not." Imogene led the way to their chairs, already waiting for them in the pavilion.

"No, I can see that. And it's sweet and kind, what he's doing for the Millers." Natalie smiled, her stomach grumbling at the aroma of the freshly fried fish fillets with all the trimmings. Betsy had snapped the lid to her container, and Natalie hadn't missed the reaction to Chelle bringing up the Miller family.

She wanted to take Betsy aside and assure her she was *no* threat to any type of relationship between her and Jacob. Would that type of confrontation be expected or approved in their circle? Anyway, it would at least clear things between her and Betsy. She liked the younger woman and wished Betsy would relax more around her.

A quartet of bearded musicians took the small platform in the pavilion and began tuning instruments. Banjo, accordion, a pair of acoustic guitars. And a washboard. Natalie glanced at Imogene.

"A washboard, imagine that," Imogene mumbled around a bite of food. "I'm ready to hear whatever sounds it makes."

Natalie shook her head. "I saw one on a show once, it was more for keeping time than anything."

"That, and giving a little homespun flavor." Imogene tore into a hush puppy.

"Good food, great company, a beautiful evening," Natalie observed.

"Simple, but perfect."

"That it is." The warm breeze teased the ends of Natalie's hair and she released a contented sigh. Her life hadn't been terribly complicated up until now, but moments like this were ones she wanted to write on the calendar and always remember. Even with the uncertainty of her family's whereabouts, she knew she was exactly where she was meant to be at this given moment. Especially since opening that box at Christmas time.

Thank You, Lord. She didn't know what tomorrow held, but tonight promised plenty of joy, laughter, and fun.

A familiar-looking troupe in two cape dresses and aprons, two sets of suspenders, and one beard walked onto the pavilion's pavement. The Millers. Rachel looked efficient and proper as always, herding Zeke in the right direction, with Jacob giving Rebecca protective glances as she maneuvered with her crutches. He carried a folded lawn chair under each arm.

Zeke broke from the group. "Miss Natalie, Imogene!" He skidded to a stop in front of them, nearly colliding with their knees and almost sending their fish suppers airborne.

"Zeke." Natalie grinned. The little boy threw his arms around her neck, and she hugged him with her free arm.

"I *missed* you." His brown eyes were round as little marbles. "I have to go to school every day, but I want to stay home and watch you sew."

"Well, I've missed you, too." Natalie glanced up to see Jacob approaching. "But, of course, you should be in school. Maybe there will be one day, like now, when I can see you when there's no school."

"Come, Zeke," Jacob said. "We need to get our suppers." His blue eyes glowed in the twilight and Natalie couldn't help but smile up at him. Zeke gave Natalie one more hug, then scurried back toward his father. She glimpsed a flash of smile in her direction before Jacob turned away with Zeke.

"He likes you. I can tell."

When had Imogene's voice reached such a pitch? For some reason, her voice boomed louder among the group gathered in clusters to hear the music.

"Zeke stole my heart from the first time I saw him." Was it not quite two months ago when she'd walked into the hospital on Christmas night?

"I wasn't talking about young Zeke." Imogene gave her a sideways glance. "I was talking about his father."

"Oh, well, um . . ." Natalie grasped for words, but found she was mumbling instead. "He's Amish. Aren't Amish supposed to be nice to people?"

"Not that nice, normally." Imogene waved her fork.

"But . . ." Her cheeks flamed.

"So, you like him too, then."

"I didn't mean—"

"Well, you've obviously considered it. And you're glowing like a candle right now."

Natalie placed her fork on her plate, now balanced on her knees, and touched her flaming cheeks. Not her and Jacob. No.

"Imogene, you're awfully sweet, but I'm here because of my family, and Rachel's helping me with the quilt."

"Huh." Imogene nodded. "I suppose you're right."

Natalie took a bite of catfish and let the breaded seasonings dance on her taste buds for a few moments. "What about you, do you have a family?" She realized she didn't know much about Imogene other than she was a fixture in the village and loved photographs which she sold in a Sarasota art gallery.

"Of course, I do. Everyone has a family." Her eyes sparkled. "We all come from somewhere."

"No." Natalie had to laugh. "I mean, a husband, children, or anyone here in the village?"

"A husband? Oh, no. I never married." Imogene shrugged. "And that means no children, of course. But I have cousins who come to visit Pinecraft sometimes. I enjoy seeing their children and grandchildren."

"Do you ever feel alone?"

Imogene shrugged. "Sometimes, I do. But then, I start counting my blessings and I see how many people God has blessed my life with. There are people I help, the discouraged and those who feel they've lost their way. As if they're all alone, too."

Natalie nodded. It was easy enough to slip into the muddy pit of loneliness and turn inward. She'd done so for a few years, especially since leaving the circus.

"I understand. When I was on the road, with the circus, it was easy to be caught in the moment and not think about being alone. City after city, we'd travel. I loved it. And then . . ." She reached for her foam cup of iced tea and took a swig through the straw.

"And then?"

"I got hurt, needed surgery, and the doctor told me my performing career was over. It slowed me down long enough to visit church with my friend Grace. I blamed God for a long time, but finally realized it wasn't His fault. He was more concerned with my heart than my physical body. It was the true priority. Still, sometimes though, I'd love to be out there again, under the lights . . ."

"I love watching the circus. It's amazing how everyone does their tricks."

"We have our spring exhibition coming in about eight weeks. The students get to show their skills and the instructors take a turn. It's open to the public, and we're raising funds for our scholarship program and equipment."

"Ooh, I would love to come."

"Well, I'll make sure you get a ticket." She smiled at Imogene. Maybe the woman was what some would call an "odd duck," but she was truthful, kind, and sweet, all earmarks of a faithful friend.

"So," Natalie continued, "the people you help. Do they live here in Pinecraft, or are they just passing through?"

"Some are on vacation and some just pass through." Imogene looked thoughtful. "Sometimes former Amish will know about Pinecraft and come down here, thinking they can do whatever they want and it won't matter. But that's not true. Even in this more liberal environment, we don't forget who we are."

Natalie nodded. "Yes, I've noticed that."

"I might not be Amish anymore, but I still think of myself as Plain." Imogene shifted her chair closer. "It is heartbreaking, so heartbreaking, to hear of those who want to leave the Amish, or the Mennonites, and leave God behind, too. Legalism hurts more than it helps. I try to explain this to as many as I can, and tell them not to leave God behind, but in the end, the decision is up to them."

Natalie tried to imagine leaving behind everyone she'd ever known, cared for, loved, all because she couldn't measure up or didn't want to live by those regulations.

"Now, some leave for education." Imogene popped the last hush puppy in her mouth and chewed.

"I could understand that," Natalie said. "No formal schooling past eighth grade." Her own mother had homeschooled her while they were on the road, and in the end, Natalie ended up getting her GED at sixteen and then began to perform full-time.

"Good evening, we are the Stoltzfus cousins and we are from Ohio," said the oldest man of the quartet, standing on a makeshift stage.

"Good evening," some in the crowd chorused back.

The music began, a sweet cacophony of amateur, yet earnest playing. Now *this* was what Natalie had come to hear. Some of the songs she'd never heard before, and after the first two were completed, the little band had warmed up to become quite a talented group.

"Let's have some help from the rest of you. If you could join in with us, better yet, come stand with us," said the oldest gentleman. "That way we can all hear each other and blend. You, sir, there in the second row. I can hear you fine from here. Would you join with us, please?"

A familiar form shifted to a standing position, shoulders lowered. "I can't say as I'm a good singer, but I do enjoy singing."

Jacob. Natalie glanced at Imogene, whose eyes twinkled. Imogene said something in Pennsylvania Dutch, then chuckled at the sight of Jacob taking his place beside the washboard player.

He should have assembled the family in the back row. But then, he'd have to hear the children talk about how they want to see everything better, and of course Henry had somehow finagled things so he, *Mammi*, and the children had nearly front row seats to hear the musicians. *Mammi* beamed as he stood and moved to the front of the pavilion.

The old man with the washboard grinned at him. "Never played a washboard before, have you?"

"Can't say as I have." And he wasn't planning to start now, but he didn't say that aloud.

"You just sing along and we'll be fine here."

They began a familiar Amish song, in Pennsylvania Dutch. One big difference, though: Jacob had never heard the sound of musical instruments accompanying such a traditional song. Faster, too, than the usual slow and methodical sounds. The tune almost made him pause, but then he hadn't been pulled from the group to stand there staring at the musicians.

He tried to forget he was in the pavilion in Pinecraft Park, at a fundraiser and singing to help his family. *His* family. He thanked God for the provision. For one of the first times since arriving in Florida, he didn't feel the struggle against his surroundings or his circumstances.

Rebecca gravely injured, yet now healing. The family delayed in Florida for months, but God had given him a job. His financial obligations had soared, far more than at any time in his life, but with the help of friends like Henry and his home district, this mountain would be removed.

He sang the words of thanksgiving, pouring out from his insides. He dared not glance at the group assembled in the pavilion, but instead pretended no one but him and the four other singers were present.

But one glance betrayed him.

He saw Natalie sitting beside Imogene, not far from the edge of the pavilion. She was smiling, the same smile she'd worn the day she walked into the hospital room, but this smile had another ingredient he hadn't seen before.

Well, he hadn't seen it before, except when as a young man, gazing across the room to see Hannah smiling at him at a Sunday night singing.

His voice wavered, and he coughed. His fellow singers gave him quizzical looks, and washboard-man clapped him on the back.

"Don't forget to breathe," he said. "I know this is a faster tempo than you're used to."

Ach, breathing wasn't the problem. The guitar and banjo players ended with a flourish, punctuated by the applause of those in the pavilion.

"Thank you, thank you, sir," said washboard-man.

"You're welcome." He sat down quickly, before his eyes played traitors again and sought out Natalie.

Of course, he'd seen Betsy while she helped serve the food plates. Bouncing from one to the other was getting a bit short of ridiculous to him. Natalie, while kind and helpful, had never shown him any inclination she would be anything more than a friend of the family.

Although he still remembered their encounter in the backyard, the night that *Daadi* had passed on. It was as if she offered her strength, comfort, and support to him. Like a friend.

But friends didn't clasp hands, not like they had in the backyard. He didn't have female "friends," either, like some *Englisch* men were wont to have. Even his own sister-in-law was not a friend; she was his brother's wife and part of the family, but not a "friend."

The thoughts chased themselves around his mind while he ate what was left of his fish supper and listened to the music.

Yet another highlight of the contrast between groups in Pinecraft. It was entirely permissible to listen to such music, but all those instruments would never show up at a singing back in Ohio.

He rolled along aboard a boat on a sea called Compromise, and it was all he could do right now to prevent slipping into the waves and getting pulled under. Musical instruments, Mennonites and Amish blending together, and now an *Englisch* female "friend." His *daadi* would know what to say, how to advise. His grandparents had lived here year-round for many years, yet unwavering in their Plain ways.

He settled back onto his lawn chair beside *Mammi*, who was tapping her foot to the sound of the accordion. Evil? No, he couldn't think such a thing.

"Enjoy the night, Jacob." The touch of *Mammi's* hand patting his own was feathery soft. "Stop thinking so much, and just enjoy the evening. Follow the children's example."

Zeke clapped, Rebecca hummed, out of tune, but she hummed anyway. Sure, stop thinking so much.

It was Natalie's fault, of course. If he hadn't seen her, he wouldn't have been yanked from his reverie of thankfulness. But instead, a lovely smile had tripped him up and reminded him of why he was here.

But he should be thankful, he reminded himself. Tonight was for his family, for Rebecca, whom some of the older ladies fussed over during an intermission. Someone said something about dessert. Dessert?

"I made some pies," a voice said above his shoulder. "I thought I'd let you know."

Betsy.

"Th—thank you. Thank you very much for telling me." He nodded.

"I made apple and cherry and lemon meringue—with lemons from the village." She beamed. "What kind would you like?"

"Apple, please." He moved to rise from his chair, but she tapped his shoulder.

"No, I'll bring it to you. I don't mind."

Of course, she didn't mind. He didn't object as she turned away with a swish of long skirt, then padded away on the concrete in the direction of the nearest picnic table.

17

Rebecca wished she could skip, but she was stuck with the cast on her leg. She was good with the crutches and could almost beat Zeke in a race to the corner.

She liked school at Sunnyside Mennonite Church well enough; the other girls and boys were nice. She had never attended school with Mennonites before, but she didn't see much of a difference besides some of the clothes they wore. Some spoke her language; some spoke English only.

She squinted at *Mammi's* cuckoo clock. Natalie would be here soon. One day, she would know how to juggle like Natalie and do backflips. Maybe one day, she might wear those shortened pants, like Natalie wore. Capris, she called them.

Today was Saturday, a fishing day, and they were going out on a boat with Mennonite Henry's nephew, Steven. He liked to take people on fishing trips, especially Plain people like them who'd never seen the ocean before.

She wasn't sure if she should be scared or not. Everything was so different here from Ohio, she didn't know if being excited would be better.

"Whatever are you bouncing on your crutches for?" *Mammi* asked.

"We're going fishing. Me, Miss Natalie, Zeke, and *Daed*."

"I believe Chelle and her niece are going, too."

"Betsy." Rebecca tried not to frown. She liked Betsy, but Betsy made her feel like her collar was too tight, studying her as if she were a flower whose stem could break. Natalie never made her feel like that. Natalie made her feel like she could fly, even with a cast on her leg.

Her *daed* entered the living room. "Rebecca, sit down, please."

She obeyed immediately. "Did we get sunscreen? I don't want to get sunburned."

"We have sunscreen. But you're not going fishing."

The words hit her, almost as hard as the car had in December. She still remembered the bang and then the pain when she closed her eyes.

"Not going?" Her heart hurt. If Betsy was going, she'd be hovering between her and *Daed*.

"You're staying with *Mammi*. We can't risk you having a seizure if we're out on the boat."

"But I haven't had a headache in a long time. I feel good, *Daed*."

"That may be, but I'd feel safer with you at home today. Maybe, if the doctor gives permission before we leave Florida, we can go for a boat ride."

Tears stuck little knives into her eyes. It wasn't *fair*. She hung her head low. "Yes, *Daed*." Of course, he was trying to think of her, but still. Dumb old headaches. She should have never told anyone about them.

But her Dad, and Natalie, and Betsy all on one boat? How she wished she could be there, to help him stay away from Betsy.

Natalie found an ancient floppy hat with a wide brim, with ribbon ties that made a gigantic bow under her chin. It was Mom's, and she'd worn it during her chemotherapy after she lost her hair. They'd joked about the enormity of the hat after Mom bought it at an upscale boutique, and took turns pretending to be Scarlett O'Hara at a picnic.

She drove to the marina, where she met Henry and his van full of Amish, including Jacob and Zeke. No Rebecca, she discovered as they all hopped from the van. And Betsy was along, plus her Aunt Chelle, the friendly Mennonite woman she'd met at the park last weekend.

"Howdy, how-do," said Henry, clicking the lock on the van. A wheeled cooler was at his feet. "Steven should be around here somewhere."

"He worked so hard for his boat," said Chelle. "I can't believe he's only twenty-two years old and already has his own business."

A young man, tanned and wearing a white T-shirt and cotton plaid shorts, waved at them from a floating pier. "Over here, you guys!"

What a sight they made, with two women in cape dresses, Natalie in her long denim shorts and sneakers, along with an Amish man with his little boy, in trousers and suspenders. Henry rounded out the group, toting the cooler behind him. Today his tropical print shirt was a peppy lemon yellow, covered with blue hibiscus blooms.

"All right," said young Steven as they reached the boat and began clambering onto the deck. "I have life vests, which I insist on if you can't swim, and especially if you haven't been out on the water. The water should be good today, low waves, but you never know."

He grinned at Zeke and tousled the little boy's hair. It almost resembled his own sandy blond flyaway locks.

"Doesn't your mother tell you to get a haircut?" Chelle asked.

"Every time I see her." He shrugged. "I've been busy."

"That you have," Henry said. "I could take care of it for you, ten minutes tops with my set of clippers."

"No thanks, Uncle Henry." The young man grinned, a dimple appearing in one cheek.

He made sure they all took their seats before starting the engine. Natalie soaked in the sunshine. Dad had taken her fishing a few times as a child. She'd loved it then. She loved it now. There was something relaxing about casting a line, then waiting, followed by the adrenaline rush of a fish on the end of the line.

She found herself leaning back on one of the seats facing the center of the boat, with Zeke on one side of her and Chelle on the other. Henry and Jacob faced them, with Betsy taking up the end. The younger woman had strapped on a life vest and clutched the edge of the seat.

Away they surged, away from the floating pier and into the tiny harbor area. The breeze tugged at Natalie's hat, but the tie held fast.

"This is my second time going fishing," Zeke said above the whir of the motor.

"Right, you did a good job catching fish the last time."

"Well, my friend's dad caught most of them. Mine were too small." He ducked his head low.

"Sometimes they are too small, and you have to throw them back, so they can grow bigger."

"I don't want to catch little fish, anyway." Zeke squinted at the cloudless sky. "I want to catch a shark."

This made Natalie burst out laughing. "Well, maybe you'll get one on the hook." Although she was sure a rod and reel battle wasn't what any of them really wanted. They bumped along gently on the waves, with an occasional splash over the sides of the boat.

"So how long have you lived in Sarasota?" Chelle asked her over the roar of the engine and rushing of water.

"About five years total, three years full-time." She held memories of wintering in Florida until the injury. "I love the climate, the beach, and I love my work at the circus school."

"I understand you're looking for your mother's family, that she was once Amish."

"Yes, that's true." She told Chelle of her and Imogene's plan to advertise in *The Budget*, but so far not hearing anything.

"So, have you ever considered becoming Amish yourself?"

"Not really. I did try on my mother's cape dress and *kapp* she left for me." She recalled the sensation of wearing the dress and seeing herself in the mirror. "It felt . . . different. I don't know."

"Becoming Amish, or even Mennonite, is more than changing your wardrobe." Chelle paused as they bounced over a harsh wave. "Have you studied about the Anabaptist faith at all?"

"Yes, I have. I've learned that the majority of my beliefs are quite similar." She glanced at Chelle's cape dress, a shade of lavender. It was pretty, but it wasn't something she could imagine herself wearing on a regular basis. Plus, the long-held belief among some of the Amish that one could never be entirely sure if they were truly "saved" or not. To assume so would be presumption, to some.

"Good to hear. I think, sometimes, it's easier to focus on how we are different from each other, than on how we're alike."

"I agree."

The boat's motor grew quieter and then the boat decelerated.

"We're about to the fishing spot," Steven's voice rang out. "I've caught all kinds of good ones here, often mullet."

"Mullet, that's funny." Zeke giggled. "I know a Mr. Mullet."

Chelle clutched the cushion they sat on. "I've not been fishing in so long. I kept promising Steven I would go on his boat, so finally, here I am."

"I'll be happy if we catch enough for a good meal," Natalie said.

"Me too." Zeke hopped to his feet. "Do you have any fishing poles for boys?"

Steven left the front of the boat. "I think I have one just right for you." He moved to the rear of the boat and cast the anchor over the side. "There. Now we can bob here and fish without drifting."

Natalie managed to bait her own hook and remembered how to cast the line. It all came back to her. The boat gently swayed underneath her feet.

"You know how to do this." Jacob's voice at her shoulder almost made her jump.

She nodded. "It's been a while, but I remember."

"This is my first time fishing."

"It requires patience and plenty of bait." She felt a tug on the line; it was only the wave, teasing the weight holding the line under water. The boat jerked and she would have lost her balance, if not for Jacob taking hold of her elbow.

"Thanks." She turned and looked up at him. Too close. Way too close. While the Amish didn't seem to be an overly affectionate people, parents were loving toward their children. Yet she hadn't seen any public displays of affection. Did they know about personal space? Of course, there were eight of them stuffed onto a fifteen-foot boat. Plenty of room to sit, but in certain circumstances this could mean tight quarters. Like now.

"Well, we don't want you ending up in the water."

"No." She swallowed hard and yanked her focus back to her line.

She heard Chelle and Betsy talking about how to cast a line, with Chelle casting and Betsy watching.

"I think I'll do like Betsy and just watch for now." Jacob took the seat nearest to where Natalie stood.

She clutched the fishing rod, and Imogene's words came back to her. *He likes you*. She liked him, too.

Silly woman. Just enjoy the day, because days like this don't come around often. She was part of the group, this hodgepodge posse of would-be fishermen. Steven was the professional among them, and she imagined Henry did his fair share of angling, judging by the way he cast his line where he stood, a few feet away.

Zeke said something about having prize ribbons for whoever caught the first fish, the biggest fish, and the most fish. Of course, he kept insisting he'd reel in a shark.

"What would we do with a shark, my son?" Jacob asked.

"Eat it." Natalie felt a tug on her line. "Shark steaks are quite tasty. You could have grilled shark, fried shark, shark tacos . . ." Her line whined. Yep. Something had snagged the bait.

Her pole arched toward the water and she pulled back, cranking the reel. Steven was at her side in a flash.

"You've got it, come on, hang onto it."

Natalie gritted her teeth, pulled. A dark shape darted back and forth under the water. Steven grabbed a wide net.

She could do this. The reel threatened to snap back and unravel with the force of the fish pulling against her. Another crank brought the fish closer to the surface. She took a step back.

"Grab her shoulders." Steven stepped closer to the side of the boat. He'd spoken to Jacob.

Her shoulders immediately felt like she'd been clamped by two hands of iron. The support helped and she tried not to think about Jacob's nearness as she pulled on the fish.

"A little more. This guy's a fighter." Steven leaned over with the net.

"Go, Miss Natalie!" Zeke cheered.

The line fell limp as Steven pulled the fish over the side. It flopped in protest onto the boat's deck. It was a good-size red snapper, plenty for a meal for a family and then some.

"Well done." Jacob patted her shoulders.

Steven grabbed a hook and pulled the fish up. "Here, let's see what he weighs." The fish pulled down on the weight. "He's a good five pounds."

She'd never hauled in a fish so large before. "Wow." She reached for him.

"Let me take your picture." Steven held up his phone and snapped a shot of Natalie, holding the fish by the gills.

She then realized the fish still had the hook caught in its mouth, so he helped her unhook the future supper and stick him into a cooler.

Then Chelle and Betsy began calling out. Chelle's turn came next, with a similar haul.

Henry grunted as Steven tossed Chelle's fish into the fish cooler. "The ladies are beating us."

"Here. You might as well have a turn." Natalie held out the fishing pole to Jacob. He accepted it from her.

"I'll see if I can outdo you, then."

Feisty, huh? She laughed at his challenge. "We'll just have to see how that goes, won't we?"

Henry, whose line lay dormant in the water, helped Jacob bait his hook. Natalie turned away for a moment, her throat parched. Henry had mentioned his cooler contained plenty of water and sandwiches for them all.

A whiz of line, then came a searing pain in Natalie's hand. She screamed and grabbed at the source of the pain, as the line grew taut.

"Jacob, what have you done?" asked Henry.

Natalie sank to the deck, gasping. She couldn't look at her palm.

~

His pride and haughtiness had caused Natalie's injury. Jacob cast down the pole and moved to Natalie's side. She gritted her teeth as she stumbled toward the nearest seat.

"I'm sorry." He knelt down, the others in his periphery.

"What did you do, *Daed*?" Zeke's voice sounded small, dismayed.

"The hook . . . it's in my palm." Natalie allowed him to take her hand.

Gently, so gently, he opened her palm. The hook had gone in just below her thumb, in the fatter part of her palm. No blood evident, but he imagined it would bleed once they got the hook out.

"I'll get some tools." Steven scampered toward the driver's seat of the boat and soon returned with a metal box.

He'd hurt Natalie. He could see the tears in her eyes. Yes, hand injuries were painful with all the nerve endings.

"I'll get this out. Don't worry."

"Oh, I know you will," she told him. Her hand, soft, delicate, but strong. He held it with his hands as he looked at the hook.

"Wire cutters." Steven handed him the cutters.

"Okay, I'll cut the main part of the hook first, then see about the rest of it. Although you'll likely need to see a doctor after this."

"I know. Just . . . get . . . it . . . out. Please." She bit her lip.

"It's going to hurt." He couldn't say sorry enough. He could see the barbed end of the hook, just underneath her skin. Maybe if he could cut through and cut off the barb . . .

"Tell you what. I nearly cut off a finger once, with a band saw."

"You did?" She was humoring him, he could tell.

"I was new, maybe my third week on the job. Wasn't paying attention." He used an alcohol pad on a small knife. "Looked the other way for a second."

"That would do it," Natalie said.

It was as if only the two of them were on the boat, him telling her about his own foolish injury, while preparing to cut the hook from her hand. Steven was a silent helper, giving him tools and such from the first aid kit.

"Well, I know you didn't mean to do this," Natalie said.

"No." He cut into the skin and she winced. A quick snip cut the end off the hook. Then with another movement, Jacob pulled the long part of the hook from her palm.

"Ow—" She clamped her free hand over her mouth, then winced again and gasped when he poured antibiotic solution all over her palm. Steven was quick to clamp a sterile gauze pad on the injury.

"Now, we'll wrap this up." Jacob nodded his thanks to Steven. "You'll be all set. But what can I do, to make this up to you?"

Natalie shook her head. He quite liked the look of the big hat on her head. "Just catch plenty of fish, and warn me before you cast next time." Her eyes twinkled at him.

"Fair enough, then." Jacob smiled at her before he stood. He dared not look at Betsy, a few paces away at the rear of the boat. He hadn't intended on catching anything besides fish today. Instead, he'd caught Natalie. Literally.

Not good, not good, reason screamed inside him. *You're on the Gulf of Mexico, but you're playing with fire out here.*

18

The day moved past as the sun arced above them in the sky. Betsy had had fun enough, catching three good fish. Aunt Chelle had caught two. But the biggest news was Jacob "catching" Natalie, as Zeke called it. The little boy thought it was funny, but the meaning wasn't lost on Betsy. What a waste of time. She could have worked this morning instead of following Aunt Chelle's lead.

Another life lesson, she reflected as they said good-bye to Natalie at the marina and headed home with Henry's help, who dropped them off first.

Once back at Aunt Chelle's, settled on the lanai with a fresh glass of sweet tea, Betsy observed her sunburned nose. She should have worn a hat like Natalie's that blocked out the sun. She'd forgotten to apply more sunscreen, so this is what it got her. A stinging nose to match her stinging heart.

"Oh, Betsy." Aunt Chelle sighed as she sat down in the chaise beside Betsy's. "I couldn't help but notice, today . . ."

"Jacob and the *Englisch* woman." Betsy sighed. "I wish I could understand. What does she have I don't?"

"Nothing, nothing at all. There is a verse from Proverbs which says one of the things too difficult to understand is the way of a man with a maiden. Somehow, there is something that makes someone else more . . . appealing . . . than another."

Betsy sighed again. "I was hoping, the longer they were here, and I was here . . . maybe there'd be a chance. I had to stay, I had to try, and wait."

"I know." Chelle set her glass on an end table. "That was obvious to me from the start. You've given up a lot to stay here past winter season. I was afraid Pinecraft would end up . . . boring you, now that the visitors are sporadic. Most of your friends are back home now."

Betsy nodded. "They are. And I spoke with my *mamm* the other afternoon. She told me they'd wire me money for a bus ticket, should I want to go home now."

"There's no shame in that. I know I've enjoyed having you here, but you should pray about what to do."

"Thanks, Aunt Chelle." Betsy tried to find the right words, but they wouldn't come. There was no way to stop what might be happening between Natalie and Jacob. No way she could see.

Yet for the couple to be together, they would both have to make big compromises to their way of life. Betsy couldn't see either of them budging. She knew she wouldn't want to be a position like that herself, ever. Choosing between her Order and love? She wouldn't.

"What do you mean, Rebecca's *gone*?" Natalie could hear a frantic tone across the phone line. Somehow, little Zeke had found her number and managed to use someone's phone. She had no idea how he'd managed it. Kids were smart like that, though.

"She's gone," he sobbed. "We got home and she's gone."

"How are you calling me? I didn't think your grandmother had a phone."

"*Daed* has a phone, for when he works for Henry."

Jacob Miller, with a cell phone? She tried to wrap her mind around that one.

"*Mammi* said she went to lie down and tucked Rebecca in, but when she got up, Rebecca was *gone*."

"I'll be right there." She'd doctored her hand and planned to call her physician first thing Monday morning for an appointment. No way would she dampen their fishing trip by having them return to shore early. Instead, she'd let Jacob bandage her hand and contented herself with watching the rest of them fish, and handing out water and sandwiches as the day went on.

But now, Rebecca missing? Where could a girl on crutches go? Surely not far.

Natalie grabbed her purse and keys, trying not to favor her right hand, but wincing anyway.

She arrived in Pinecraft in record time, after sneaking through at least one yellow light on the way. A cluster of people had gathered in the Millers' front yard. She pulled as close to the edge of the lawn as possible without driving onto the grass. On this side of the street, there was no sidewalk to contend with.

Zeke came running to her, full tilt. She braced herself for the impact. "You came," he said as he hurtled into her knees.

"Of course, I did." She scanned the crowd as she leaned to hug him, then stood upright again. There was Rachel, standing on the front steps, shaking her head and gesturing, wringing her hands.

Jacob was nowhere to be seen. Of course, he was probably out looking for Rebecca.

A few steps brought her to Rachel, with Zeke scurrying along beside her. "Rachel, Zeke called me. What can I do to help?"

"Pray, Natalie. Pray. Ask *Gotte* to help us find her." Rachel shook her head. "I can't think of where she would have gone. Jacob said Rebecca was disappointed she didn't get to go fishing today. He didn't think it was wise to take her far from shore, in case something happened."

"That makes sense to me. How long has she been gone?"

"I laid down after lunch, then woke up at two o'clock and realized the house was empty." Rachel's voice trembled. "*Gotte,* watch over our little lamb."

A stray little lamb, at that. "Do you think she might have gone to the park?"

Rachel shrugged, raised her hands. "The whole village has started to look for her. We've called the authorities, but we're still searching."

"I'll start looking, too. What color dress was she wearing?"

"Pink. Her new pink one I bought for her last week. She's getting taller."

"Okay." Of course, they likely didn't have a photograph of her. "I'll have my phone on, just in case."

Rachel nodded. "I'll make sure someone calls you if she is found."

Another woman approached. "I made some fresh lemonade for the searchers."

"How sweet of you, Vera. Thank you." Rachel motioned over her shoulder. "Right in the kitchen, on the counter will be fine."

Zeke kept his hand clamped to Natalie's. She paused. "Rachel, may I take Zeke with me?"

She nodded. "Yes. Be careful."

Natalie gave the older woman a wave. Surely, Rebecca would likely be with a friend, or someone surely must have seen her.

"I hope we find her." Zeke trotted along beside her, and she slowed her pace. "I hope she's not dead."

"Oh, I don't think so. She might have found a friend at the park." She figured she would head across Bahia Vista, into the heart of the main part of the village. How far could a child get on crutches? They weren't the most comfortable way to get around, but if Rebecca was desperate enough, they likely wouldn't stop a determined little girl.

"We always watch for the light." Zeke stopped at the busy street corner. "That's where Rebecca was hit by the car." He pointed diagonally across the intersection in front of Big Olaf's Creamery.

"Yes, we do." She recalled them mentioning where the accident took place. "Let's start with Yoder's Market. Maybe she went to the market there to, uh, look around."

"I like Yoder's Market. They sell whoopie pies."

She'd never been inside the market before. Maybe one of the searchers had already gone through the store and asked employees if they'd seen Rebecca. But this would be a good distraction for Zeke and give him something to do besides worry.

They entered the market and Natalie inhaled the aroma of bread and muffins. Fresh produce lined one wall, open to the outdoors. Three aproned workers bustled around the store, assisting customers.

Funny how the world kept going when your world suddenly went off-tilt. Everyone else went about their ordinary business as usual. Natalie knew the sensation well of wanting the rest of the world to feel something—to have a clue her world was *not* right. Maybe Zeke did, too. The little guy had

had his world upended, and then some. She prayed today's encounter would have a happy ending.

"Maybe this lady has seen her," Natalie said as they approached the closest employee to them. "Excuse me?"

"Yes, how may I help you?" The woman's expression turned quizzical as she took in the sight of Natalie's *Englisch* clothing alongside Zeke's trousers and suspenders and light blue shirt.

"Have you seen a little girl, about eight years old, on crutches, her leg in a cast? She's wearing a pink cape dress."

"She's my sister," Zeke said.

"No, I'm afraid I haven't," the woman said, shaking her head. "Someone else came by about twenty minutes ago, asking about her as well."

"Okay. Well, if she should happen by, please have someone call my cell number." Natalie fumbled for a pen and scrap of paper from her purse, trying not to wince as she wrote the number.

"I most certainly will."

"Thank you." She glanced around for Zeke. He was standing at the bakery display and the stacks of packaged whoopie pies, freshly made banana breads, pumpkin, and zucchini bread. There was even a red velvet whoopie pie.

She pulled a bill from her wallet. "Go ahead, pick one out. You said you like whoopie pies."

"But my supper?"

"That's hours away. You need to keep your strength up." She nudged his shoulder.

"Keep my strength up?"

"I'm joking. But what kind do you like?"

"Chocolate, with the marshmallow filling."

"Okay, then. Pick the one you want."

He beamed, pulling a package of chocolate pies from the display, and walked solemnly to the register. "We pay here."

"You're quite right." She paid for the whoopie pies and off they went into the sunshine. For a few seconds, worry had fled.

Did the Amish worry, like the rest of the world did? Rachel was worried; Natalie could tell by the wringing of her hands, the furrow in her brow. Surely they must. Emotions like that were common to everyone. Just like grief.

But when the outcome wasn't what they hoped, how could they chalk it up to what they called *Gotte's wille*? God's will wasn't for children to be separated from parents so soon. Rebecca missing?

They walked along, Zeke chomping down on a whoopie pie and Natalie scanning the yards. Maybe she'd wandered over to a friend's house. They ambled closer to Pinecraft Park, where anyone and everyone spent time.

It would be in the winter, but not now, not when most of the winter crowd had returned to the north and left the year-round residents to rattle around a mostly-quiet neighborhood.

"There's no kids here," Zeke observed. Chocolate ringed his lips.

A quartet of men were playing bocce, and a trio of ladies were playing shuffleboard, not nearly the same crowd as in the height of the winter season.

She saw Jacob and Henry talking to a family next to the jungle gym.

"There's my *daed*." Zeke rubbed his mouth with the back of his hand.

"I suppose it won't hurt to find out where they've searched and who they've talked to already." Natalie headed in their direction. Zeke didn't break away to run for his father, but kept next to her.

It wasn't the first time she'd felt the maternal nudge. She'd wanted a family, to marry, to settle down at some point, but the road didn't lend itself to that and she didn't want to raise her children in the same way. Now that she'd been "home," such as it was, well, it had been difficult to insert herself into a life where everyone else knew their place.

Zeke wasn't her little boy, but the feel of his small hand in hers made her want to protect him, no matter what the cost. Even Rebecca, wherever she'd gone off to, had taken up residence in a corner of her heart.

This wasn't good. One day, they'd all be gone, back to their very real life in Ohio, and she'd be here again. Alone.

She forced a smile at Jacob. "Hello, we've been out searching for Rebecca, too. I thought a whoopie pie might help take his mind off his worries."

Jacob's brow furrowed, his blue eyes darkened. "Your supper will be ruined. And we're having fish." He flicked a glance from Zeke to Natalie, then back to his son.

"Entirely my fault," Natalie admitted. Henry was still talking to the family. "We stopped by Yoder's Market and I asked about Rebecca."

"She would never go in a store by herself."

"Maybe not, but she probably feels safe and secure here, much as she did on your property back . . . back home." Natalie choked out the words. "If I were a child, a yummy-smelling store with whoopie pies would be one of the first places I would want to visit."

She shrugged off the sting of his tone. Of course, it wasn't the fact Zeke had practically inhaled the package of whoopie pies and allegedly "ruined his supper." Jacob was worried, maybe a little scared, although he'd probably never admit it.

"Someone said she was upset about not being able to go fishing today." Natalie scanned the banks of the creek running through the park. "Do you think she might have tried to fish here, on her own?"

"She knows nothing about fishing." Jacob's reply came out clipped.

"She's smart. She could figure something out." Natalie headed toward the creek bank. "So no one's seen her?"

Henry joined them at the water's edge. "Someone said they saw a girl in a pink dress, heading for the park, but she was walking with a family so they didn't think anything of it."

Natalie exchanged a glance with Jacob. Who else knew her in the village who was a full-time resident? The winter traffic had trickled off and now the year-round folks were dealing with the ghost town Pinecraft was during the spring and summer months.

"We should check the creek banks." Jacob cleared his throat.

"I'm going to check the creek area," Henry said. "There's a tiny inlet near Schrock that has a footbridge crossing it."

"Call me if you find her." Natalie raised her phone. "I can send you my number."

"Please, do." Henry gave her his number, and she punched in the digits.

"There." She smiled at him, then found one of her hands claimed by Zeke.

Jacob had already begun walking off, muttering in Pennsylvania Dutch. She'd be muttering too, if it was her child.

Zeke regarded the water, his brown eyes full of emotion. "Rebecca can't swim."

"No, but I'm sure she's careful." Of course, it would be easy enough to slip into the water of Phillippi Creek. The waterway snaked past the park. To the northeast lay Bahia Vista. They headed away from the busy street.

It should be easy enough to see a bright pink dress against the green, grassy edges of the creek.

Natalie stopped short. Were there alligators in the creek? She dared not ask the question aloud, even to the breeze. Zeke didn't need to be worried any more than he already was.

"I still think she went fishing," Natalie said. "Maybe she borrowed a pole, or found one somehow. I don't know."

"The water looks deep." Zeke frowned as they ambled along, away from the pavilion and the shuffleboard courts. They crossed a small boat landing, the creek's water lapping not far from where they walked.

"I'm not sure." She couldn't quite make out the bottom and didn't care to try. Her phone chimed on her hip. Henry. She pushed the talk button.

"Did you find her?" she asked.

"No, but I did find a family, the Frys, who traded her the use of a kid's fishing pole and bait for a sack of fresh grapefruit. What about you?"

"Nothing so far. Say, how deep is this creek?"

"Not more than five feet in the middle, I'd venture to guess."

"Ah, okay."

Zeke chose that moment to pull away from Natalie. "I see a little boat!"

"I'll call you if I find her," Natalie said.

They left the area of the boat ramp and continued downstream, taking a narrow path through the woods, still keeping parallel to the water.

"Zeke, stop, wait for me." Natalie tried to keep a quaver from her voice. Water in Florida nearly always meant gators. And now, as they were headed away from a main area frequented by humans, it wouldn't surprise her at all to see one of the creatures. She'd seen them in the canal not far from Grace's home, drifting like piles of wood. Only the wood had eyes that moved and ended in rows of teeth.

"There's the boat." He pointed to a small flat-bottomed boat, shorter than a canoe, drifting on the water. Something pink peeked from the top.

"Rebecca!" Natalie called, charging toward the creek bank. She skidded to a stop when she saw a dark mottled shape in the water, not a dozen feet from the opposite side of the creek.

"Rebecca's in the boat?"

"I think so, Zeke." Natalie grabbed her phone and dialed Henry.

"Did you find her?" he asked, without preliminaries.

"She's in a boat here on the creek, stuck by some alligators." Natalie glanced over her shoulder. "Go past the boat landing and take the path."

"I know right where you are."

Natalie ended the call. "Rebecca, if you can hear me, wave your hand."

She heard the sound of sobbing, and a slim hand emerged over the edge of the boat. "Natalie . . . *Daed*!"

"*Daed's* on the way," Zeke called out. "And Mr. Hostetler."

Then another alligator emerged from the grass on the other side of the creek. It appeared not to care much about the boat, mere feet away, where it was stuck in the crook of a bent log. The animal slipped into the cool waters of the creek, and disappeared.

The crashing of brush in the woods behind them made Natalie look over her shoulder again. "She's over here. In the boat."

Both Henry and Jacob joined them at the creek bank.

"People take this path to see the toothy scaled fellers, safely, of course," said Henry. "I'm not going to ask how your daughter found herself a rowboat and got stuck."

"How can we get her over to this side?" Jacob paced the creek bank. "There must be something handy we can use to pull the boat in this direction."

"I can look for a long stick," Zeke offered.

"You'll stay right with Natalie," Jacob said.

"Yes, *Daed*." He hung his head.

"Rebecca, do you have a rope in the boat?" Henry called out.

"Yes," came her thin voice.

"Get the rope, and sit up slowly," Henry said. "What I want you to do is throw the end of the rope toward us, as hard as you can. Don't worry if it hits the water, we'll grab it somehow and pull you to shore."

"Okay." Rebecca sat up in the boat, her face wet with tears and smudged with dirt, her hair fuzzy from working its way out of a braid. She clutched the rope with her right hand, bit her lip, and threw. It splashed into the water, not six feet from their side of the creek.

Jacob plunged into the water, sinking up to his chest, his teeth gritted. Natalie tried not to scream as the dozing alligator began to move, slowly, silently in their direction. Henry followed Jacob, and grabbed onto the back of Jacob's suspenders as he clung to the end of the rope.

Together, the men pulled the boat free of the log, away from the curious alligator. Natalie sank to the creek bank. Her pulse hammered in her chest.

Zeke clung to her. "I thought the alligator wanted to eat *Daed*."

"I think he just wanted to be left alone."

With the small rowboat, minus oars, now half on the creek bank, Jacob lost no time in scooping up Rebecca in his arms.

He muttered a stream of Pennsylvania Dutch, some of it terse and some of it soft, and Henry laid his hand on Jacob's shoulder.

"She's had a good scare and a sharp lesson from this, I think."

Rebecca was sobbing, murmuring back to her father. "Miss Natalie found me." She reached in Natalie's direction, and Jacob set her on the ground. She hobbled to Natalie, and threw her arms around Natalie's neck.

"I was so scared. I wanted to fish, so I got some fishing things, and borrowed the rowboat. Nobody came for it, but then I lost the oars and got stuck. Then I saw the alligators and got scared, so I laid down in the boat so they couldn't see me. I yelled, but nobody heard me." The words poured out, punctuated with hiccups. "And I knew I couldn't get my cast wet."

"Well, you're safe now." Natalie glanced up to see Jacob looking down at them. "You had us all scared. There are people all over the village, searching for you."

"I—I'm sorry." Rebecca hung her head.

"Thank you," Jacob said. He touched Natalie's shoulder, his hand still wet from the creek.

"Of course," Natalie said. She nodded at him, seeing tears in his eyes. "I—I love your children, Jacob."

"I know you do." He touched her cheek with his thumb.

Henry cleared his throat, and Jacob lowered his hand. Natalie's face burned.

Today could have ended much, much worse. They fetched Rebecca's crutches as well as her catch of fish and her equipment from the boat.

"I'll see who owns the boat," Henry said. "They shouldn't have left it lying around."

Jacob nodded. "Rebecca should have known better as well to use something that didn't belong to her." He carried her to the edge of the woods. When Rebecca started to open her mouth, he continued with, "I don't care if you planned to bring it back."

"Wait here," Henry said as he walked away. "I'll borrow a golf cart to get us all back to the house."

More murmurings between father and daughter in their language, but Natalie didn't need an interpreter to know that Rebecca was in a heap of trouble. Then, in English, they talked about replacing the oars she'd lost in the creek.

Henry returned with a golf cart a scant ten minutes later. Zeke asked to sit on the front seat, which left the back seat for Jacob, Rebecca, and Natalie.

Natalie didn't realize until they took their seats how cozy the cushion was. Jacob put his arm behind them to help prop Rebecca up. It felt warm and family-like.

Henry dropped them off at the house, with cheers and cries of relief, and a sheepish-looking Rebecca was bundled into the house and straight to the bathroom where Rachel would help the little girl clean up.

The crowd dispersed, not a few of them with questions in their eyes about Natalie, with Zeke clinging to her hand like a lifeline.

"You're staying for supper," Jacob said. His tone surprised her; he was making a statement, not asking her.

"Well yes, I guess I am. If you insist."

"I insist."

19

Rebecca fell asleep over her supper plate, her nose and cheeks tinted red from her nap in the sun that afternoon. Jacob laid his fork on the table.

"I should put her in bed," he said to *Mammi* and Natalie. She was a bit hard to lift, especially with the weight of her cast.

"*Daed*, I'm sorry," she murmured as he lifted her from the chair.

"Time to sleep now." He voice caught at the recollection of her little form inside the rowboat. "We'll talk more tomorrow."

"Do I have to go to the doctor?"

"Yes, in the morning." It was another follow-up with the neurologist and a stop at the physical therapist's office; two appointments in one morning. He wondered what the therapist would say at the idea of Rebecca crossing a busy street, making it all the way to the park, and negotiating a boat, all while wearing a cast and walking with crutches.

He laid her on her bed, tucking the blankets around her. They'd missed their Bible lesson tonight, with all the goings-on. Perhaps tomorrow night's time would be best devoted to keeping out of trouble and being obedient.

When he emerged from the room, closing the door behind him, he reentered the kitchen to find *Mammi* had cleared the table and Natalie was pouring *kaffi*. The young woman's presence in the kitchen was both natural and unsettling. He could have never imagined this at their first meeting on Christmas night, months ago.

She poured him a cup without asking how he drank it. *Mammi* glanced from Natalie, then to him, but said nothing. Her raised eyebrows said enough.

He should give his grandmother an explanation, but not tonight. He settled back to his chair and picked up his cup of coffee.

"I'm thankful to God that today ended as it did," said *Mammi*. She moved to the sink and turned on the hot water.

"I can do the dishes, Rachel," Natalie said.

"No, sit, sit." *Mammi* waved Natalie away. "I heard you had an encounter with a fish hook. You were also a big help today already."

"Zeke was the one who found the boat." Natalie poured herself a cup of coffee and took her place at the end of the table. Zeke had already fallen asleep, the events of the day having worn him out.

"I have a feeling our time here is coming to an end, before too long," Jacob heard himself announce. "With what happened today, Rebecca's shown how strong she is. Truly, she would have never done anything like this back home."

"Home." *Mammi* stacked the silverware and cups into the soapy water. Tonight they'd eaten on paper plates, something they never did in Ohio. "I keep reminding myself you're not here permanently."

"The neurologist was pleased with her progress, and probably will be more so once he hears how much she's done."

Jacob sipped the strong coffee. He glanced at Natalie, whose expression he couldn't quite discern.

Natalie nodded. "She definitely got where she wanted to go. I'm sure her physical therapist will be happy."

"I'm sure." Jacob shook his head. "She would have never run off and done something like this at home. Sometimes I wonder, what am I going to do?" He found himself surprisingly relaxed in Natalie's presence, his words pouring out to her and his grandmother.

"You will do like your father did, and his father before him." *Mammi* wiped her hands on a dishtowel and joined them at the table. "You will find wise counsel and you will raise both Rebecca and her brother according to the Scriptures."

"The Scriptures don't talk about seven-year-olds who leave the house without permission, alone, crossing a busy street . . ." Every horrible possibility flashed through Jacob's mind. "All that, in a cast and on crutches."

"Foolishness is bound in the heart of a child, but the rod of correction will drive it out," *Mammi* quoted.

"I think she's received plenty of rod today, with that alligator scare," Jacob said. He recalled plenty of spankings as a youngster and the ones he'd given to his own were sparse.

"See how she is in the morning," said *Mammi.*

"I can't believe she did all this, too. Her walking cast comes off for good next week." Jacob looked at the wall calendar. "Sometimes it feels like we've always been here. Maybe the city's been a worse influence than I imagined."

"Well, I've grown used to all of you being here," *Mammi* said. "Those *kinner* can get into plenty of trouble in Ohio."

Jacob nodded. "True." He glanced at Natalie, who'd remained silent during the exchange. "So, how comes the quilt?" He'd rather discuss something else besides wayward children.

"It's turning out more beautiful than I imagined." Natalie studied her coffee cup.

"The quilt should be finished soon," *Mammi* said.

"Who knows? Maybe I'll start another quilt one day, this time starting from the very beginning." Natalie smiled at his grandmother.

"You purchase the fabric, and I'll help you get started." *Mammi's* face brightened. "I'm not sure what I'll do with all my extra time, once the family has gone. I'm sure I will find something to keep myself occupied."

Once she was left with an empty house, and reminders of her life with *Daadi*, is what she really meant. "Us being here has been a blessing in disguise, I think," Jacob managed to say. "I know the rest of the family wouldn't have wanted you to be here alone, so soon."

"I know." *Mammi* rinsed the silverware, setting it into the dish drainer. "But going to Ohio is out of the question. Pinecraft is my home, has been for years. I'll have to adjust to life without my Isaiah. *Gotte* will help me."

Gotte would have to help with adjusting—all of them.

"You're finished," Rachel announced. She watched as Natalie tied off the last stitch of the quilt binding.

"You know, I could have sewn this binding on with an electric machine." Natalie thought she'd tease the older woman, just a little.

"Nonsense. What you do on future quilts is your business, but this one is special." Rachel ran her wrinkled hands over the fabric. "You did well. Your mother, or her family at least, would be proud."

"Thank you." Natalie surveyed the finished quilt, more than large enough to cover her double bed. She hadn't thought about what do with it yet. It didn't really match her bedroom décor. But she could change all that. "I'm not sure what I'm going to do with it."

"Use it, put it on a rack so your guests can see what you have done, or you could donate it to charity." Rachel paused. "Although, you probably ought not to donate this one."

"I don't think I could." It was one of the last ties to her mother. "I'm happy I was able to finish what she started."

Someone banged on the front door, so Rachel rose to answer it, leaving Natalie to study the tiny stitches. Truthfully, Rachel had completed a chunk of the work. She'd have given up on it, if left to quilt the top on her own. It helped to have the older woman's supervision and stitching.

"I heard someone was finishing her first quilt." It was Imogene. "I should get some pictures of you with it."

"Oh, okay." Natalie raised her hands to smooth her hair. "I just tied the last thread a few minutes ago."

Imogene raised her camera and snapped a few shots. "It's pretty. Do you mind if I post the pictures online?"

"Not at all," Natalie said.

"All those online shenanigans." Rachel eased back down onto her chair. "I don't know about that. I like keeping in touch with family like I hear some do online with that 'e-mail,' but I've heard of places called web sites—practically the devil's playground."

"You're right, there's plenty of evil to be found online," Natalie said. "Plenty of good, too."

"Well, I'd rather keep away from all of it."

Imogene nodded. "I like writing about Pinecraft. People like to hear about us." But Natalie noticed none of her photo shots included Rachel.

"It's a special place." Natalie tapped the quilt top. "Ladies, I would like to do something to celebrate finishing my quilt. Lunch at Yoder's, my treat?"

"Well, I don't know . . ." Rachel sounded doubtful.

"Come with us," Imogene said. "You never know who you'll run into."

"Or, if you'd rather go to Emma's Pizza, we can do that instead," Natalie offered. Maybe Rachel didn't like crowds.

They ended up taking the walk to the pizza shop, with Rachel encountering several friends along the way. Natalie was used to the stroll by now. If you hurried through the neighborhood, you might miss someone. Friends were full of questions about Rebecca, how she fared after her scare with the boat and the alligator, and what *would kinner* find to get into next?

A few year-round residents were out and about as well, and the older woman was beaming by the time they reached the pizza shop.

"I don't think I've ever had her pizza," Rachel observed as they entered the snug restaurant, which only had outdoor seating.

"Never had her pizza?" Imogene echoed. "It's good, very good."

"It's a pretty enough day for us to eat outside, too," Natalie said as she surveyed the menu. "Should we order a whole pizza? If we don't eat it all, Jacob and the children will probably eat the rest."

"Sweet of you, to think of them," Rachel said. "Many a time I wish you were Amish, or Mennonite, at the very least."

Natalie waited to respond until after the woman at the counter took their order for a large pepperoni pizza. "Oh, really? Please, pick out whatever you ladies would like to drink."

"Yes, I do." Rachel ambled over to the glass-doored case that contained soft drinks of all brands. "I think I'll have a root beer. You know, I always used to think it had 'beer' in it, from the name. It took a lot of convincing to make me believe otherwise." She chuckled at herself.

"Let's get a table outside." Natalie knew the older woman had plenty of energy, but she didn't want to overtire her. "I'll see about the pizza in a few minutes."

They went back into the sunshine, and Imogene paused. "I'm going to head to the post office to check my mail, if you don't mind. I'll be right back. I think the mail has come already for the day."

Natalie realized she ought to check her mailbox as well. It had become a daily practice for her. "I'll wait until after lunch, unless you don't mind checking for me."

"I can ask the postmistress."

"Thank you," Natalie said, as Imogene headed off, away from the outdoor patio. She turned to face Rachel. "So, sometimes you wish I were Amish, or Mennonite."

"I see how Jacob looks at you. He cares for you, but there is that barrier."

Natalie nodded. "If I said I didn't care for him, I'd be lying. But, I'm not Amish. My mother was, and she left. I can't imagine someone like her being meek, wearing a cape dress and head covering, living on a farm, or working in a quilt shop. Her personality seemed too—too big. I'm not sure if that's the right word."

"We all make our own choices." Rachel popped the top of her soda can. "Her choices aren't yours. Besides, meek doesn't mean weak, either. I submitted to Isaiah for years, but he never treated me as though I were lesser than him. I was his helpmate, and he the provider. Amish marriages aren't perfect, either."

"I don't know how much I could change myself for someone else, either."

"*Ach*, I think he cares for you just the way you are." Rachel sighed. "Sometimes, though, there are compromises people can make. How do some people say it? Meeting in the middle?"

"Here's your pizza," the woman from the pizza shop said as she approached their table. The scent of melted cheese drifted on the breeze.

"Thanks," Natalie said. Rachel doled out a plate for each of them. Time to change the subject. She had no idea how she and Jacob could meet in the middle, or what the possibility meant for either of them. Did he even want to?

Then, there were the children. Her and Jacob's choices would affect them as well. She didn't want to cause any more disturbance to their innocent lives than they'd already endured.

Imogene stepped onto the raised patio. "No mail, not for either one of us."

"Maybe another day." Natalie heart sank just a little as she tapped the pizza box. "But the pizza's here."

Rachel asked the blessing before she picking up her slice of pizza. "I'm hungry. Quilting has definitely worked up my appetite"

Natalie watched the steam rise from her pizza. "I have something for you both. Next weekend at the circus school we have our annual exhibition. I have free tickets for everyone who would like to come."

"Oh, the circus!" Imogene took a bite of pizza. "Ow, hot. I love the watching the circus."

"Well, this is our spring fundraiser. Tickets are free, and donations are accepted. But I wanted you to know about it. You can see my students do their routines. And me, too." Natalie opened her purse. "Here's enough tickets for you, Jacob, and the children."

"Thank you, thank you," Rachel said.

"And Miss Imogene, here is a bundle of free tickets for you," Natalie said. "Give them to whomever you think will enjoy them. Make sure Henry Hostetler gets a few, also. I like him."

"He's quite the character, as Isaiah used to say." Rachel nibbled at her pizza. "He's been a blessing to our family, for sure."

"Yes, he has." Natalie closed her purse. "I hope you can all come. I don't know if there's anything going on in the village that day."

"We might be having a haystack supper the same evening," Imogene said. "But if the performance is at 2:00, we'll be back in plenty of time. And people will be hungry again."

"Good." A thrill went through Natalie, at the idea of "her" Pinecraft people getting to peek into her world, especially Jacob and the children.

20

Jacob had never been to a circus and found his excitement matching Rebecca's and Zeke's. Their seats were reserved, a few rows up from the center ring. A perfect view of the sights they would soon see.

"Will they have elephants, *Daed*?" Zeke asked. He sucked in his first taste of cotton candy.

"No, no elephants. This is at the school where Miss Natalie teaches, so all we'll see performing are children, some probably just a little older than you." He opened the program, scanning the events included in the "Semiannual Pathway to the Stars Circus School Exhibition."

The last part of the show included "teacher demonstrations." He'd get to see Natalie perform, at last. Not juggling, but doing the aerial silks. He'd never asked about her teaching, or about aerial silks. He'd tried to imagine what they were, but then noticed some long filmy cloth strips stretching from the floor all the way to the ceiling at least fifty feet above them, or so he guessed.

A number of Pinecraft villagers occupied the bleachers, as Natalie had distributed free tickets far and wide throughout the neighborhood, with Imogene's help. Henry sat in the row behind him, having served as chauffer and toting half a dozen residents to the event.

From the first acrobatic trio to the high-wire act performed by the older teenagers—dressed in spangled costumes he'd *never* allow one of his children to wear—Jacob's attention drifted from his children's faces to the performance floor.

Zeke gasped as a boy, perhaps twelve or thirteen years old, crossed a high wire at one end of the ring. A net was strung below him, of course. Jacob glanced at his son, whose brown eyes were round in his face.

At last, the lights fell low again and the spotlight focused on Grace Montgomery, dressed in the tuxedo and top hat of a ringmaster—or ring mistress, as she called herself.

"Our final performances today are demonstrations from our faculty who work with the children, teaching them what you've seen this afternoon. Most of our staff are former circus performers themselves. One of our acrobatics instructors is a former Olympic gymnast." Grace paused to allow a ripple of applause echo inside the arena.

"First up is Natalie Bennett, an aerial silks artist. Her parents were the world renowned Flying Bennetts who thrilled audiences everywhere with their feats above the ring for over two decades with Circus du Monde. Natalie traveled her own path, away from the trapeze where she enjoyed an aerial silks career for nearly a decade herself, beginning at the ripe young age of 16. And now, watch as Natalie performs 'Delights in the Air' over sixty feet above the ground, without a net. Accompanying music is Ravel's *Bolero*."

No net. *Mammi* gripped his hand. She must have noticed it, too.

"No net?" she whispered.

The sound of a horn solo wove a tune as the spotlight illuminated Natalie, posed at the bottom of a pair of sheer silks stretched to the ceiling high above. She reached one arm high above her, striking a pose on one leg, then shifted her weight to the other, acknowledging the crowd.

Jacob had watched Natalie's students perform using the silks earlier, but that didn't quite prepare him for the sight of her in full costume. From here, he could see her make-up, eyes that looked dusky as a model's, her full lips red and lined.

Her dark hair, braided, had a spangled pink fabric woven through its length. The braid bounced against her bare back and the spangled pink matched her costume. The higher she climbed, the more instruments joined in as the tune intensified.

Spangled pink ribbons of fabric covered Natalie from hip to ankle, but little else. Her top had long sheer sleeves, but evidently someone had forgotten to attach the bottom half of her shirt. Somehow it stuck to her ribcage without sliding up.

Natalie wrapped one foot and ankle with one silk, then did the same with the other and began slinking her way up the silks. Then she stopped about twenty feet above the ground, performing a split between the two lengths of silk, her back arched, her hands clutching silks above her head.

"Here, brought these so some of the oldsters can see the shows better." Henry tapped him on the shoulder with something hard. Binoculars.

Jacob nodded. In slow motion, he took them from Henry, held them up to his eyes.

Looking at Natalie Bennett through his own eyes had turned his mouth into sandpaper. Looking at her magnified through binoculars made his breath catch.

The fluttery pink fabric accentuated her curves, offering a flash of muscular leg. Her back arched, her head upside down, belly exposed to the ceiling. Oh, Natalie Bennett was definitely a woman. Not that he hadn't noticed before. But here, with her wearing sheer frothy fabric, sparkles, and her flash of smile at the audience . . .

"Here." Jacob jerked the binoculars from his face and reached back to Henry. He imagined all that pink in his arms, and all it concealed.

Gotte *forgive me.*

Yet another reminder of being married and all that he'd lost. Hannah, his wife, mother of his children, chaste and sweet. But they'd enjoyed their marriage bed, something he would admit to no one, nor would she. As a man, he missed that part of married life, the complete giving of himself physically to his wife, and she to him. *Gotte* had created a masterpiece when He formed woman. Like the one now who soared dozens of feet from the ground above him and the crowd.

A man's thoughts could take on a hundred lives and he dared not imagine one with Natalie, with her curves and legs and sweet smile.

One thing he knew for sure now: his time in Sarasota was done. Rebecca was ready to make the trip home. Even if it took three days. He'd already planned to hire a van. This was it. He'd stepped over a line with Natalie, even in his mind, an impossible line they could never cross.

Natalie did more aerial flips, including her final move with a crescendo of drums and wailing trumpets of the music. She tumbled down the length of the silks as her legs were unwrapped, stopping before she hit the floor at the bottom. Gasps went up from the crowd.

The music stopped, and she freed her feet from the silks, standing and waving on solid ground at the audience. Many rose to their feet, some whistled and called, applauding. Jacob clapped, trying to get the sight of her out of his mind.

"*Daed,* she can fly," Rebecca said on his other side. "I want to learn to fly, too."

Oh, no, she wouldn't. Jacob held his tongue while Grace thanked Natalie and the demonstrations continued.

After the show ended, Jacob tried to flee to Henry's van, but the crowd blocked him. The cape dresses and suspenders made way for pink froth.

"Miss Natalie, you sparkle." Rebecca hopped on one foot and threw herself into Natalie's arms.

"Only in the ring." Natalie stood, releasing Rebecca from her embrace. Something glittered at her navel, a fake diamond bauble. Stuck-on? Jacob tried not to stare at it, or at the curve of her hip. But she caught him looking and clamped her arms around her waist. Her face flushed and she looked down.

"You scared me," Zeke said at Jacob's side. "I was scared you would fall."

"Oh, I'm sorry." Natalie stepped closer. "I would never want to scare you. I've done this many, many times and only fell once."

"I can see your legs," Zeke said.

"I just wanted to say thanks for coming, before you all left." Natalie kept her arms around her waist. Now Jacob tried not to stare at the pink and sparkle covering her chest. Her neck now bloomed red as her cheeks.

"Thank you for inviting us," said *Mammi* at last. "I know the *kinner* enjoyed watching the students perform."

"I, uh, I should get back to the dressing room and get this gunk off my face, and change." Natalie raised her hand and gestured at her made-up eyes. "My pores are screaming for relief."

After a few more greetings and an exclamation from Imogene over Natalie's costume, or lack thereof, Natalie padded off on bare feet toward an exit. But her presence stayed with Jacob, like the spicy floral scent of her perfume.

Natalie's skin felt free of the performance makeup and she studied her natural features in the mirror. Much better. She wore a bit of makeup on occasion, but nothing like what she used to wear for circus performances. Circus makeup always had to be dramatic, vivid, so people in the back row could see her features.

On days like today, it reminded her of what felt like another life.

The parents had all picked up their children from a small party held after the show. The group had taken in just over several thousand dollars in donations, which would help finance one child's tuition for the scholarship program.

"Every year I say, this is going to be it," Grace said in the doorway of the locker room. She tossed her top hat onto the vanity counter and sank onto a nearby chair.

"Ha. It's in your blood too much to stop, even if you have to experience it through others." Natalie glanced sideways.

"You were magnificent, breathtaking." Grace beamed.

"I'm going to pay for it in the morning, if not tonight." She rotated her ankles. Maybe the stiffness wouldn't set in tonight.

"Make sure you ice, elevate. Take Monday off if you need to."

"Tomorrow's Sunday, a day of rest anyhow. I'll be fine." At the moment, however, her ankles were low on her priority list.

Grace left the locker room when the office phone began to ring. "I'd better see who that is."

Natalie released a pent-up breath and looked in the mirror again, this time unweaving the pink sparkled ribbon from her hair. She'd felt an awareness with Jacob this afternoon and it was all the stupid costume's fault. Really, it was more modest than many costumes she'd seen. More modest than bathing suits at Siesta Key Beach.

When the spotlight was on, she didn't individualize the crowd, or think of who might be in it. There was just the silk, and the music.

But when she'd approached the group of Plain people, she realized she was still an outsider. An outsider under Jacob's careful scrutiny. No, he didn't leer at her, or ogle. But she'd seen a dusky look in his blue eyes she hadn't noticed before, the look of a man appreciating the physical qualities of a woman

She felt like she owed him and his family an apology.

This performance had shown her the differences between her and the Millers, and the other Plain people, were too much to overcome. Worse, she didn't blame her mother's family for not writing, or calling.

Her heart ached a little, though. Part of her, the longer she'd been around the people of the village, believed she might have a place with them, somewhere, somehow.

With Jacob, and the children.

"No, it's not your place," she said aloud to the figure in the mirror as she brushed her hair.

Lord, I've been fooling myself. Or have I? If there's a compromise, a good compromise, I don't see it.

"And she was practically *naked*," Vesta Fry, a new acquaintance of Betsy's, said as they sat outside Big Olaf's and ate their ice cream cones on Monday after work.

She'd heard about the circus, but had been too busy with her schedule to attend. Natalie Bennett's performance, along with the others, were all thoroughly discussed and marveled over. The woman was fearless, wrapping her body in fabric and flipping and turning in the air.

"Naked? I'm sure she had a costume on of some kind, don't all circus performers?" Betsy licked her cone, vanilla bean, her favorite.

"You could see her midriff, her bare legs, her, ah, bosoms covered in pink sparkles, practically *everything*."

"But Vesta, she's not Plain. Some of us know her."

"Huh. Well, I can't say as her grandparents would want to meet her, Christian though she says she is. Someone should warn them, whoever they are."

Betsy sat up straighter. "What do you mean, whoever they are? Do you know Samuel and Anna Yoder?"

"No, I'm not saying that. I have no idea who they are, or where they are."

"Okay then. Did—did you see the Millers there?" Of course, Betsy had to ask. She supposed she could have cleared her schedule to be there, but work was busy, she was banking her money, and she would have preferred a more traditional way to spend time with Jacob. Such as a picnic in Pinecraft Park. As if that would happen.

"Yes, even Rachel. I heard Jacob could barely keep himself from staring at Natalie, the way she was dressed."

Betsy sucked in a breath. The conversation had turned uglier by the minute, starting with Vesta using the word *naked*. True, Jacob had this, this *thing* about Natalie. The circus probably went a long way toward showing him just how unsuitable someone like Natalie Bennett was to a Plain family.

Despite her smug thoughts, realizing her position might have improved as a result of the circus, Betsy wouldn't delve further into gossip.

"Really, Vesta. Natalie hasn't been shunned by anyone. We should leave her alone, because, well, she's really a nice woman and she's been good to the Millers." No need holding her to a standard she never claimed to own.

A faint hope began to grow inside Betsy.

21

Jacob smelled a spicy perfume as he entered the house. His *mammi* and Natalie were busy rolling up the quilt she'd worked so hard on. Fitting, that they should have closure now.

Natalie bloomed a shade of red when she looked at him. "Hello."

"Hello."

Rachel's eyebrows shot up, but all she said was, "I must go check on the bread." She disappeared into the kitchen.

"I'm sorry, Jacob."

"For what?"

"My appearance at the circus. I didn't intend to make anyone uncomfortable. I didn't even think about my costume."

"Don't worry about it. You're—you're . . ." A knot lodged in his throat, a fresh recollection striking his mind of Natalie dangling like forbidden fruit in the air.

"I'm not Plain. I know. But, I—"

"You are a beautiful woman, something I noticed from the start." He realized that somehow, the distance had closed between them. He allowed himself to reach out and touch the dark long silken strands hanging past her shoulders.

"Jacob, you and the children, you both mean a great deal to me." She caught his hand between her own, and he could feel the scar on her palm from the fishing trip. The simple gesture made it harder for him to breathe.

"You've come to mean a lot to us, too." He clasped her hands, strong between his larger ones.

A pounding sounded at the front door.

The moment broken, he released Natalie's hands. It was probably the driver he'd hired, confirming they were leaving and how much baggage they would be bringing to Ohio.

"If you want to talk to me later, I'll—I'll be at Siesta Key Beach tonight, before sunset." She cast a glance at her quilt.

Betsy would always remember this afternoon, how Jacob found her in the park. She was on a bench, watching the creek drift by, already missing the last of her friends who'd returned to points north. It was a balmy afternoon, with a light breeze teasing at the ends of the Spanish moss in the treetops above her.

Jacob stopped at the bench, but didn't sit down. "I came to say goodbye, Betsy."

She knew the words were coming—the moment had arrived. "So, you're going, then?"

"Wednesday morning. I hired a driver who has a van large enough for Rebecca to be comfortable." Jacob looked past her shoulder at the people enjoying a spring walk at the park. "The doctor said she's well enough to travel."

It was happening fast, too fast. Aloud, she said, "This place is a ghost town now. But I'll stop by to see your *mammi* and say hello when I can."

"So, you're planning to stay?" Jacob asked.

"Unless I have a reason to go back to Ohio?" One last time, she'd put her heart out there. She knew what had happened at the circus. Natalie, dressed like a woman of the night and made up worse, had pranced and exposed herself to everyone. It was one thing to watch a circus performance with people you didn't know dressed that way, but someone you did know? Someone who was searching for a Plain family? It didn't make sense to Betsy.

She knew Jacob's answer from his hesitation.

"Not from me," he said. "Betsy, I can't make myself love you."

"But . . . but I love you." She risked the words. "Maybe love could come in time?"

"I don't want to take the chance. I told you before, you deserve someone who will love you with his whole heart. I know . . . I once knew what it was like."

"But the *kinner* need—"

"*Gotte* knows what my children need and will send it at the right time. We are doing fine as we are. No, it's not traditional. But I can wait." He swallowed hard. "I have to."

Betsy nodded. "I see. And what about Natalie? You have feelings for her, then?"

"I do." He spoke the words slowly. "But that has nothing to do with you."

So this was how it felt, to have one's heart splintered. As long as she thought she had a chance, well, she'd been prepared to be there until Jacob realized how perfect the two of them could be together.

"Well, I guess there's nothing else then, is there?"

"No, there's not."

"Goodbye, Betsy."

"Goodbye, Jacob." She climbed on her bike and sped off before he could walk away. Only then did her tears begin.

They didn't stop, even after she got home to Aunt Chelle's. She didn't care who saw her.

The sun was sinking to the horizon by the time Jacob stepped off the bus near Siesta Key beach and caught up with Natalie, right where she told him she'd be. Rebecca and Zeke were fast asleep in their beds back at the house, with them needing a good night's rest before they began their trek back to Ohio.

The day visitors to the beach had all but disappeared. Natalie was facing the waves, her shoulders drooping. Evidently, she knew. Someone had told her.

"Natalie."

She turned to face him. "I said goodbye to the children this afternoon, before you got home from work." Even with the twilight, he could still see redness around her eyes.

"I know. Zeke cried over his supper." He hesitated, recalling the sight of Zeke staring at his supper plate, sniffling. "I had to come find you, and tell you goodbye in person, and thank you for everything you've done for my family. The children will miss you."

"And I'll miss them too." She shrugged. "Maybe, when I head up to Ohio, Lord willing, and my grandparents contact me, I'll stop by."

"Maybe," he said. Although part of him didn't think it was such a good idea.

"I—I'm going to miss you, too, Jacob." She looked down, speaking the words as if to the sand, white as flour.

"Oh, Natalie." He pulled her into his arms. Her body felt lithe and strong. Hannah had been slim, but she'd never felt as strong as Natalie did.

"Don't leave me," Natalie whispered. Her heart thudded and he could feel the sensation in his own chest. "Please, Jacob."

He allowed himself to cover her mouth with his. Kissing Natalie Bennett was as sweet and wild as he'd imagined. She molded against him perfectly. He ran his fingers through the length of her hair, down her back, and then pulled her more tightly against him. She snaked her arms around his neck.

"Don't leave me," she repeated, her voice husky. "Give us a chance."

He moved to kiss her again, recalling the fluttery pink of her costume. "A kiss, to remember me by." What was he doing? *A kiss, to remember me by?* It was better they strike each other from their memories and move on, to things as they should be. Yet the kiss deepened, hinting at all the passion he'd give her. Her response showed she could give him plenty in return.

"Don't go."

"This is wrong, so wrong." He muttered the words into her floral-scented hair. He spoke the truth, he knew.

"Why is it wrong?"

"Ever since the day of the circus, I haven't been able to stop thinking about you." He released her slightly, but held her against him. "There are times, I think maybe we could make something work. With *Gotte's* help."

"I'm ready to build a life with you, Jacob. We can figure this out. I know it would be difficult, for both of us. Can't Henry, or the bishops here, think of something?"

"But we're too different. Our worlds are too different. You can't give up what you have for me and I can't walk away from everything for you."

"You had a choice to marry someone you didn't feel anything for. Betsy was ready, waiting. Waiting for you. It's been obvious to everyone she's the logical choice, the uncomplicated choice. But will you even give me a chance? Don't deny you feel nothing, otherwise you wouldn't have broken a rule somewhere, by meeting me here. And who says we can't find someplace in the middle?" He tried to step back, but her strong, slim hands held tight. She wrapped her arms around him this time.

"It's too much to ask." He ground out the words, pulling away from her. Desire, the God-given desire of a man for a woman, screamed through all his nerve endings with Natalie's nearness. This hadn't happened since Hannah. Surely, though, feelings like this were only a sign of his corruption, of all the compromises he'd made since being in Florida. So perhaps the feeling wasn't from *Gotte* after all. Which meant this was all wrong.

Perhaps he was one step away from compromise and eventual damnation.

He had to think of his *kinner*, like he had before.

He left Natalie standing by a dune, with tears on her face.

22

Jacob had all but forgotten the chill of winter, but it lingered even in the early Ohio spring.

"Ah, it's a warm one today," Ephraim said, then gave a chirrup to his horse. "Nothing like Florida, though."

"No. Nothing like it." Jacob looked out at the fields, passing them by slowly. The first new shoots had already come up after the last frost. He yawned.

"Was a long trip, even in a van." Ephraim glanced at the children in the back of the buggy. "Your littlest one is out."

Jacob laughed, for the first time in days. "He can sleep anywhere, I think. But it will be good to have him back among everything familiar. Rebecca, too."

"I'm not tired, *Daed*," came Rebecca's voice from beside Zeke.

"I have a feeling you're more tired than you think. I know I am." But there was a lot to do today, upon returning to the house. Airing it out. Unloading their bags from the buggy. Seeing what needed washing.

With his house closed up for these months, who knows what needed tending to?

"Katie's been through the house," Ephraim said as if knowing Jacob's direction of thought. "She figured it needed 'freshening,' as she put it."

"I'm very grateful. Please, thank her for me."

"Thank her at supper. You know you're welcome tonight."

"*Gut*, we'll be there." Supper at his brother's was usually about five-thirty and Katie's cooking never disappointed.

They rolled on in silence for a time, and Jacob closed his eyes and listened to the familiar clop of horse's hooves on asphalt, the squeak of harness and creak of wheels. Now, those were sounds he'd missed while in Florida, with the only buggy in miles being a prop outside Yoder's restaurant.

Ephraim broke the silence. "Something's different about you, brother."

Jacob opened his eyes, squinting at the morning light. He shrugged. "Florida was different, very different. But you know that already."

"Did it change you?"

"My daughter nearly died after being struck by a car, our *daadi* passed on, I had to uproot my family for months. Yes, I think it did." He didn't mention a certain former circus star who'd nearly succeeded in laying claim to his heart with barely any effort on her part. Jacob struck the thought of Natalie Bennett away. Surely, as his family and others had suggested, there was someone else more suitable. Even someone else besides Betsy.

If anything, Natalie had helped open his heart, just a little, and open his mind to the idea there was a possibility for love after Hannah. For that, he would always be grateful.

"I had a lot of questions, Ephraim. Talking to Henry Hostetler helped."

"Your Mennonite boss."

"Yes, the same. He became a good friend while I was there. You know about the fish fry he sponsored?"

"I heard about it. But, Jacob, why question? Why not just accept?"

"Too late for that. I've accepted, but I still want answers."

"And Henry gave you some."

"He did." The memory of that conversation sprang up and filled him with warmth. "I know I'm going to see Hannah again one day. I know her faith saved her and not her works."

"Ah." Ephraim reined in the horse and turned onto the lane that led to their homes. "Careful where you tread, *bruder*."

"I am." He decided to drop the matter. He didn't care for a debate about doctrine. What mattered most right now was getting settled inside the house again, and figuring out what next, beginning tomorrow. Maybe he'd get his position back at the cabinet shop. They'd held it as long as they could, but he had no promise of what he would return to.

Ephraim pulled the horse to a stop not far from the kitchen door. Jacob's home was newer than Ephraim's, having been built on the Miller property before he married Hannah. Ephraim, having been married first, had his house built first.

"Home again, children." Jacob put on his best smile as he looked back at them. Zeke stretched and yawned while Rebecca clasped her hands.

"You're right, I am tired, *Daed*." She gave a little sigh.

They had the children unbundled and their bags and suitcases standing in the kitchen.

"I'll see you at supper, then?" Ephraim asked.

"We'll be there around five-thirty," replied Jacob, rubbing his chin.

Ephraim left them, and the children ran off toward their rooms. He'd call them back for their bags soon, but he too felt the urge to do a walk-through.

The atmosphere of the kitchen hit him like a board swung by a distracted carpenter. If it was barren without Hannah these long, long months, it was desolate now. The scent of cleaner and bleach met his nostrils at the sink and countertop.

Jacob went to the stove, where the teakettle waited for him. He ought to heat water for coffee, or something. He missed the warmth of *Mammi's* Florida kitchen with its accents of tropical color and the perpetual scent of something baking. He missed the laughter around the supper table.

They laughed around supper tables in Ohio, too, but under his parents' and brother's scrutiny, he was reminded of his shortcomings as a father. It would be worse, now that he'd returned to Ohio without a wife. Without Betsy. *Mammi*, the whole time he'd been in Florida with the children, had never once nudged him about his unmarried state.

"*Daed*, I will get your bag for you," Zeke said at his elbow. The boy had grown taller in these last few months. Still with big brown eyes and now a warm glow to his skin from hours outside with his Florida friends.

"Thank you, son."

"When . . . when will we go back to Florida?"

"Probably next Christmas."

"That's a long time from now."

"Oh, about eight months."

Zeke sighed. "I wonder if Miss Natalie will forget me." The boy's English skills had improved dramatically in the space of a season.

"No, I am sure she will never forget you." He wondered which of the children would bring Natalie up first. Not surprising, it was Zeke, although he was the quiet one between the two of them. He was the one who'd latched onto her the quickest.

He'd seen something in Natalie, just like they all had. Zeke picked up the handle to Jacob's suitcase and pulled it into place. He dragged it along behind him from the room.

The morning sun provided enough light for the kitchen, but Jacob turned on the light overhead with a flip of the switch. Nope. Battery dead.

"My room is too dark," announced Rebecca as she entered the kitchen.

This was the price they were paying, and would continue to pay, for being Amish. He had never missed what he didn't have, including electricity at the flip of a switch. The propane tank was full, so they'd have hot water for cooking and baths.

"Ah, well, I'll work on that. Is it too cold in the house for you?"

"No, *Daed*, it's fine." She yawned. "You're right. I *am* tired."

"You can nap. I'll wake you for lunch."

"Okay, *Daed.*" She crossed the room, with only a slight limp, and wrapped her arms around him. "*Danke.*"

"For what?" He placed a kiss on the top of her forehead.

"Being a good *daed*. I am thankful for you."

"That's good to hear."

She looked at her suitcase.

"Don't worry, I'll take care of it. Go sleep."

Inside of ten minutes, he could hear a soft snore coming from the direction of the sitting room, their one large soft chair adequate enough sleeping room for Rebecca. No one ever slept in the sitting room, but Jacob didn't care.

Sometimes it was better to pick and choose your battles about what was right and wrong. They'd all been through a lot, especially recently.

"You're getting skinny," Grace said. "Here, eat. A protein bar. A bag of chocolates. Or find a bacon cheeseburger. Something. You can't lose muscle mass. It's unhealthy."

Natalie shrugged. "I'm not hungry." She stared at the computer screen, trying to focus.

"Honey, you don't have to be hungry to eat chocolate. Every woman knows that."

Natalie had to chuckle at that. "I know." She wasn't *that* skinny. Her mind crept back for the thousandth time, to her last encounter with Jacob. The memory of the kiss still woke her up at night, breathless.

She thought his beard would have been rough, but it wasn't. The way he'd kissed her was a gentle kiss, sweet at first. But the next one progressed and had promised more, much more, and had left her pulse roaring in her ears.

No, it wasn't a mere physical attraction between them. There'd once been a trapeze artist she'd toured with. Physical attraction was nothing to base a relationship on. She knew from past unfortunate experience. Yet, it was another life, someone else, and wasn't her anymore.

But with the Millers and Jacob, she'd more than had fun. It was more than the novelty of seeing into a lifestyle she'd only heard about. It was their acceptance of her, *Englisch* ways and all, acceptance as a fellow believer. She found how much she had in common with them. They weren't as legalistic as she'd thought.

Maybe she didn't have full acceptance, as she'd never been baptized into their faith, although she'd been baptized at her own church. But still, all she'd felt from them was love.

And the children. She, Zeke, Rebecca, plus the addition of Jacob had added up to more than just four people. It was the prospect of fitting into a family as if the hole Hannah had left behind was just her size.

"You're quieter than usual." Grace's voice snatched her away from her thoughts. "What are you looking at?"

"Job openings." Natalie's shoulders slumped. What was wrong with her? Ever since Jacob had left a week ago . . .

"What?"

"I'm sorry. This is terrible and unprofessional. You've been so good to me. I'm not really looking. Right now, I just feel like getting—away. Somewhere, anywhere."

"If you need a vacation, you should take one. You never ask for time off. Go to your dad's in California."

Natalie tried not to snort. "We haven't spoken since right after New Year's."

"Give him a chance."

"It's Jacob."

Grace yanked up a chair. "I know he and the children left. I also know something was going on with you two. Was it *verboten* love?"

"Yes. No. I don't know." Natalie shook her head. "Right before he left, I asked him to stay in Florida. For me. For *us*."

"Oh, honey. That's a big step, for a man to uproot his entire family practically halfway across the country."

"I know. But he had a job here, and I know Grandma Rachel is lonely without Isaiah. And Jacob is supposed to remarry, especially for his children's sake."

"And you were ready to apply for the job?"

Natalie nodded. "I feel so . . . alone . . . since they've been gone."

"What about your volunteer work? I notice you haven't mentioned the hospital since February or so."

And volunteering was what got her into this mess in the first place. She'd crossed a line a long time ago, made it personal. Not like any of it mattered now.

"I should get in touch with the hospital auxiliary group. They haven't called in a while," Natalie admitted.

"Good idea. And you should visit Rachel." Grace blocked Natalie's view of the monitor with her hand. "Go, find something to do, someone to help. I did offer you chocolate therapy."

"Thank you, Grace." She scurried from the office.

Seven days made one week, but it might as well have been a century. Every day since opening the post office box, she had stopped by the little building to check if there was any word about her mother's family. Except for the last week.

Grace was right. She should check on Rachel, as well. The woman had her community and her own people to help watch over her, but Natalie couldn't help but wonder how she was getting along in a now-empty house.

As if her car knew the way on its own, she found herself turning onto the street for the Pinecraft post office. The afternoon was a sleepy one; the streets of Pinecraft were vacant.

She checked her post office box.

An envelope.

Fingers trembling, Natalie fished it out.

"I thought that was something you'd be looking for," said the postmistress, a sweet Amish lady, yet another in the village familiar with Natalie's story.

Neat flowing script gave a return address in Ohio. The same handwriting had directed this envelope all the way to her:

Miss Natalie Bennett

P.O. Box 149

Pinecraft, FL

"Yes, yes, it is." Her voice trembled worse than her hands, and she flew outside into the sunlight

She didn't trust herself to drive, but instead leaned against the driver's door. The envelope opened easily enough and a short note was enclosed inside, in the same precise lettering.

Dear Miss Bennett –

I am Anna Yoder, wife of Samuel Yoder, and I once had a daughter named Katie. I read your advertisements in The Budget, *and I believe I am the person you seek. I am most commonly known as JoAnna because of my cousin Anna also marrying a Yoder first.*

I understand you have been searching for me for some time. If you are ever in the Holmes County, Ohio area, my door is open to you.

Respectfully,

Mrs. Samuel (JoAnna) Yoder

Her grandmother was alive. Grandma. *Mammi.* Natalie hugged the letter to her chest and choked back a sob. No, it wasn't an enthusiastic letter, by any means, but JoAnna, or Anna, had said her door would be open.

No mention of what had happened to Samuel, or if he was still alive, or if he was against (or for) the idea of meeting Natalie.

Her knees shook. She read the letter again. She had to tell Rachel, to find Imogene—both instrumental in helping her in this search.

She had a grandmother who would at least see her if she was in the area. Hadn't Grace said something about her taking some time off, a vacation? She never took time off.

Natalie carefully backed out of the space and drove to the Millers' home. The sky looked bluer, the palm trees more joyful, the yellowy-orange of the grapefruit more vivid.

She parked at the familiar home and scurried to the front door, then knocked.

A smile appeared on Rachel's face when she opened the door. "Natalie, please come in for a moment. I'm about to go to a friend's house for supper."

"All right. I won't be long. I wanted to let you know that I received a letter from my grandmother today, JoAnna Yoder, of Holmes County, Ohio."

"Oh, wonderful news for you."

Natalie handed Rachel the short note, and the older woman scanned it. "Oh, she must be happy to hear from you. You're going to Ohio, aren't you?"

"I was thinking about it . . ."

"I would go. Her home is open to you."

"I—I feel like I have a family. I don't know why she took so long to write, but I'm glad she did."

"You must let Imogene know. Every time I've seen her in the last week, she's asked about you."

"I . . . I've been busy with class, and the quilt is finished."

"And, Jacob is gone."

Natalie swallowed hard. "Yes, I . . . I miss him, and the children."

"I think you should know something. My family lives but one county over from your grandmother, in Tuscarawas County, not far from the Sugarcreek area." Rachel adjusted her *kapp* and gave Natalie a pointed look.

"I didn't know that. I'm not big on Ohio geography."

"Well," Rachel said as she picked up her house key, "if you go to Ohio, you must let me know. I have some of the children's things to return to them. Clothing, before it's outgrown."

"I . . . I'm not sure if I should—"

"Humor an old woman. We Amish honor our elders and listen to them." Rachel poked Natalie's shoulder.

"Yes, ma'am. I'll let you know when I go. Maybe you'd like to ride along with me?"

"Oh, no. Not at all."

Natalie followed Rachel back into the sunshine. "You're sure?"

"Pinecraft is my home. I don't need to travel hither and yon."

"Well, *if* I go to Ohio, I will make sure I deliver whatever it is the children have left behind."

23

Betsy Yoder has stayed in Florida," someone said at the Sunday after-service meal, plenty loud enough for Jacob to hear at the men's table.

"How are you holding up, Nora?" another female voice asked. "Surely she will see the sense in returning to Ohio."

"I am fine, fine," said Nora Yoder.

Jacob tried not to lean closer to the women's table so he could hear more. He'd hurt Betsy, but he'd tried to tell her before. And this time, when leaving, he knew he'd sent a clear message: they were not to be.

So far, no one had tried to nudge anyone in his direction, not counting the new family that had moved to the district with a daughter of marrying age. He'd seen the young lady at the church meeting. It was hard not to notice her, with a similar lithe figure to Natalie's and hair the same shade of brown, almost familiar brown eyes.

But no, she wasn't Natalie.

"I had my hopes," continued Mrs. Yoder. "But, things don't happen as we expect or hope. *Gotte's wille* be done. Betsy is insisting on remaining with her *Aenti* Chelle."

"It's a shame," one voice whispered. Jacob wanted to turn around to find the voice's owner, but he dared not. "I know she had her heart set on Jacob Miller."

"*Ach*, Jacob Miller," Betsy's mother murmured. "I don't know if I would wish my daughter to become a mother straightaway after saying her wedding vows."

"He needs to find someone, soon," continued the whisperer. "It's not the right order of things. Those children need a *mamm* and a proper bringing up. Katie has her own brood to watch over."

"And Katie is happy to help her *bruder*-in-law as long as she is needed," Katie said, loud enough for almost everyone to hear.

At that, the group of biddies hunkered down and began eating their meals, and Jacob frowned. Gotte, *I'm not trying to be obstinate here and only please myself.*

Why then, the indecision?

He took another bite of pie. Because he didn't want to go through losing someone again. You never knew when someone's days on earth "were complete" and you'd be left putting your world back together again.

He thought of *Mammi* Rachel, facing life without *Daadi* in Florida. The house must feel so empty now. He understood that feeling.

While every inch of his home in Ohio was as familiar to him as his own hands, Pinecraft had been a distraction. In some ways, it had helped ease the pain to be in strange surroundings.

No fresh reminders of what he'd lost. Unlike the last several nights as he tried to sleep, covered in a quilt he and Hannah had received as a wedding gift. All throughout the house, wherever he stepped, simple handwoven rugs covered parts of the hardwood floors. The utensils by the stove—Hannah had had her favorites.

Enough.

He made himself stop pacing the floor in his mind.

"Are you back at the cabinet shop, Jacob?" he heard the bishop asking.

"*Yah*, Bishop Graber. Part-time to start, which will change, I hope. For now, though, Rebecca has a few more physical therapy appointments and at least one final neurologist appointment." He started in on a piece of pie, apple. The freshly made ice cream was turning into a puddle of creamy vanilla, but it didn't matter to him.

"That's *gut*, *gut* to hear." The bishop nodded and tasted his own bite of pie, his long beard bobbing up and down has he chewed.

He appreciated the bishop's concern for the family's economic well-being. The security of his Order had been one of the many reasons he stayed. They had helped immensely with Rebecca's medical bills. But Jacob could have never voiced his doubts and questions as he had to Henry in Florida. His faith had been shaken, yet still remained. He wished he could find better answers to more questions.

Before leaving for Florida, he thought he had an answer to the most pressing question in his life. Well, an obvious answer. But as time passed, the answer seemed to elude him again.

The remainders of the meal were soon cleared away, and chatter among the younger people was about a singing tonight.

"Are you going to the singing, Jacob?" Jonah Yoder, Betsy's younger brother, asked.

In his periphery, he saw the new girl take notice of Jonah's questioning. Brown eyes looked at him.

"I doubt it," he said aloud. "I'm too old to go to a young people's singing and the *kinner* need me."

"All right. Well, see you around." Jonah tromped back toward his friends. The new young woman still stared at him. He might as well acknowledge her with a nod, which he did.

Her face bloomed red and she whirled around to face the women's table and pick up an empty plate.

There. It was done. Let the speculations begin, or not.

Daed wasn't the same since they had returned to Ohio. Rebecca was used to his sadness after *Mamm* died, but this was something different. She missed her *mamm*, but didn't cry like she used to.

She sat between her *Aenti* Katie and her grandmother at the women's table. They kept asking her if her leg hurt, but she was fine.

Then someone started talking about Betsy Yoder and *Daed.* Rebecca wasn't so sure she wanted Betsy to be her new *mamm.* Not that she had a choice. Once, before the accident, she was sure she could help take care of her *Daed* and the house and finish eighth grade someday, without a *mamm's* help. Now, she knew it. They didn't need anybody.

"So, Rebecca, what is your favorite game?" a young woman across the table from her asked. They had moved to Ohio only a few weeks before Rebecca and her family had come from Florida.

"Jump rope," Rebecca replied. "I once jumped over two hundred times in a row without stopping."

The woman's brown hair reminded Rebecca of Natalie, but her voice was all Amish. The varying accents in Florida had sounded funny to Rebecca at first, but the longer she was away from Ohio, she didn't have to listen as hard to understand.

English was much easier for her now, and even Zeke was ahead of his class in his English skills, now back in Ohio.

"My name is Anne," the young woman said.

Rebecca knew that already. She hadn't missed the nudges Anne's *mamm* had given her in their direction. Anne must be old enough to get married.

Then someone started talking about Betsy and *Daed*. Rebecca ate her last bite of roll—her grandmother always made the best ones—and heard the conversation down the table. Then when *Aenti* Katie spoke up, Rebecca wanted to clap her hands and cheer like at the circus.

Yes, they were doing fine without anyone.

As the meal ended, Rebecca stood up from the long bench, careful not to wrench her hip. Someone walked up to her *daed* and asked him about going to a singing.

A singing? But it wouldn't be like the ones in Florida. She missed the park and all its goings-on, especially the music on some nights with the happy banjo, and what they called bluegrass music. It made her want to hop and skip and clap her hands.

Anne's gaze drifted in *Daed's* direction to where he sat with the men. She'd seen the look before, when she would bring chicken feed out to the hens and they saw she had a pan in her hand.

Daed refused the man's invitation and Anne looked disappointed. She blushed, red as a berry, and turned to pick up a plate from the table. Then, she squared her shoulders and whirled back around. She glanced at Rebecca, then marched over to where *Daed* stood.

Rebecca did the only thing she knew to do at the moment. She grabbed her forehead and sank to the ground, screaming.

Natalie found the green fields of Ohio a beautiful sight, but she missed her palm trees. The GPS chimed more directions, taking her deeper into Amish country. Her destination had seemed to confuse the unit at first.

Destination: Her Amish family, in Ohio. The GPS at least located the road, if not the exact mailbox.

Once she had cleared her schedule with Grace, she had written her *mammi* a letter, saying she would be in Ohio in mid-April, and would be coming by the house on the second Saturday of the month. She received a short reply, saying she would be home and expecting her visit.

Natalie pulled off the main highway. *Breathe, breathe.* According to the now not-confused GPS, she would arrive at the farm in approximately five minutes.

She had dozens of questions, especially about her mother, but no idea if her grandmother would be willing to answer them.

Lord, help me. I have no idea how this journey will end, but please, let it be a beginning. She gripped the steering wheel tighter to keep her hands from shaking.

Family, real family. Not that Dad wasn't. Of course, he was and always would be family.

But maybe this family wouldn't have room for her, much as her father's new family didn't have room either. She'd taken Grace's suggestion and talked to Dad in a roundabout way about a trip to California. Dad had talked about how busy they all were. So that was her answer.

"Destination ahead."

Indeed. The next driveway had a simple sign at the edge: "Fresh vegetables; honey; soaps; fried pies." The mailbox said Yoder.

Natalie turned and negotiated the driveway, with fences on both sides. On one, a pair of horses raised their heads to study the vehicle, then dipped their heads to the ground for more grass. On the other side, young corn stalks waved in the breeze.

After the driveway, came an open yard area with several buggies parked beside a barn. Beyond this drive, it extended and Natalie glimpsed at least one more house farther along. Anna, or JoAnna, Yoder had said that her house was the first one.

A cat streaked across the farmyard and shot into the barn. Nope, probably not many motorized vehicles traveled this yard, not counting tourists who came through during the summertime to purchase goods.

Natalie killed the engine, then smoothed her hair.

Here goes . . .

She remembered the first—and last—time she'd tried trapeze. She was four. Dad had insisted; Mom had begged. All Natalie understood was the sensation of her stomach dropping into her feet as the world turned upside down and she reached for her father's hands to catch her, but felt only air.

Dear Lord, please catch me with this one.

She ambled up to the main door, trying to pretend she was merely calling on Rachel Miller, or seeking out Imogene's house, although she'd never seen it.

Anna Yoder answered after only one knock. "Please, come in."

Natalie stepped into the main room, lined with chairs. The chairs were all occupied by more Amish. Only two chairs remained vacant.

"Let me look at you." Anna clasped Natalie's hand, and squinted. "My eyesight's not what it used to be, but, yes, I see her in your eyes, your mouth. Pretty hair like her, too."

"Thank you for letting me come." Natalie found her voice and tried not to study the others in the room. She couldn't see approval or disapproval, not with the quick glances she was giving them.

Maybe she should have worn the cape dress.

Maybe she should remember to breathe.

"Please, come, sit down." Anna moved to the pair of vacant chairs and patted the one she didn't sit on. "We have many things to talk about. You must have questions."

"Yes, yes, I do." Natalie took the seat beside her grandmother, her *mammi*, that's what the Millers called their grandmother. "I . . . I only learned right before Christmastime about my mother's, uh, past. She only said she'd grown up in Ohio and—well, we always visited my father's side of the family. He was an only child, and had a few cousins." Now, she was blabbing. She closed her mouth.

Natalie glanced around the room and counted. Four couples.

Anna nodded. "These are my children and their spouses."

Her aunts and uncles. Natalie tried not to stammer the obvious, and only nodded. "I'm Natalie Bennett. I—I wish my mother had told me about you a long time ago."

The oldest man spoke. "I am your Uncle Isaac, and this is my wife Emma. We have four children, one about your age, and two grandchildren."

"Your children, my cousins. Cousins? I have cousins." Natalie struggled to suck in more air. She sounded like a babbling fool.

"Between all of us," said Emma Yoder, "you have seventeen."

"Oh." Her heart swelled. These were her people. Strangers, yes, but they shared the same bloodline. *Oh, Mom, why'd you do it?*

The answer was simple. Mom would never be satisfied with an existence like this in Ohio.

"And, your mother, how is she?" asked Anna.

"She . . . she passed away last July." Natalie's throat cracked. "I wish I could have brought better news."

When Anna and the others in the room said nothing, Natalie continued.

"She had cancer, and didn't suffer for too long. She fought it for a year, or more. We were very close." Glancing around the room, she realized another person who should be present, wasn't. "And, my grandfather? My *daadi*?" She'd guessed the answer all along by what Anna hadn't said in her brief letters.

"He died two years ago. He had a full life before he left this one," was all Anna said.

"I'm glad he had a full life. My mother did, too. I know her life wasn't one you'd approve of—"

"She could have come back anytime she wanted to," said the youngest-appearing of the men. "Right, *Mamm*?"

"You're right," Anna said. "My door was always open to the repentant soul."

Natalie nodded. "I—I found you through help, with friends of mine in Pinecraft, in Sarasota. They were the ones who suggested putting an ad in *The Budget*."

"Pinecraft, eh?" said the youngest son. "We were there this winter, with our children. Right before Christmas. Visited some friends and distant cousins for a week."

They'd been in Pinecraft, and what timing. Natalie nodded.

"So, why seek me out now, Natalie Bennett?" Anna's eyes probed Natalie's face, but she didn't flinch.

"Like I said, I didn't find out until right before Christmas that my mother had grown up Amish." She explained about the quilt top and the dress and prayer covering, and the paper torn from a Bible page. "My parents divorced about five years ago. Dad's on the West Coast, remarried, and has another little family. And me . . ." She shrugged.

"Are you married?" asked Uncle Isaac.

"Not married." She couldn't explain about Jacob, not in front of all of them, still nameless except for three. "I grew up in the circus and was an aerial silks performer, had ankle trouble and needed several surgeries, so I had to retire from that. Now, I teach at a circus school in Sarasota. I'm a Christian and I go to a good church. Since I found out about my mother, I've been spending a lot of time in Pinecraft. Or, I did."

"*Ach*, I see," said Aunt Emma. She glanced at Uncle Isaac. "Well?"

He coughed. "*Ach*, the reason we're all here with our mother is, well, we wanted to make sure of your motives. It's been more than twenty years since we've seen, uh, Katie, and we had no way of knowing anything about you."

"I understand." Natalie nodded. No, she didn't blame them, having her appear before them. "I'm . . . I'm not asking anything from you, but all I want is to get to know you."

"Well, the rest of you, introduce yourselves." Anna waved at the others in the room, brushing her hands as if swatting away flies. "Natalie is our family. Isaac is my oldest, married to Emma."

"Next is me, Joseph, and this is my wife Clara." Clara followed up her husband' introduction with a nod and a smile.

"I'm Dora, and my husband is Henry." More nods. "Our last name is Byler."

"I'm Reuben, the youngest, and this is my wife Mercy."

"I can't tell you how happy I am to meet all of you. Just knowing you're here, you're all here, and I have seventeen cousins?" Natalie laughed, but tears filled her eyes. She tried to blink them away, but one ran down her cheek. "I might not be Amish, but it's good to know who my family is. Very *gut*, as you would say."

She looked down to see one of Anna's wrinkled hands clutching her own.

"Stay for the day, stay for supper," Anna said. "All of you; bring supper here tonight. If any of the children can come, send word for them to do so as well." Her aunts and uncles stood, and the tension in the room dropped immediately.

It was probably the closest anyone would come to killing the fatted calf for Katie Yoder.

"Thank you, Anna." She'd have to call the hotel—in Millersburg, ironically—and let them know she would be checking in late, but that was no problem. "If you don't mind, I do have some things from Florida I brought for you." Good thing she'd planned ahead and brought bags of grapefruit, lemons, and oranges. She knew she'd likely have a good-size family, but to see and hear it confirmed . . .

"Of course, then come back inside. We still have much to talk about."

Natalie nodded, and smiled at the others as they all filed out. Three uncles, one aunt. Seventeen cousins.

She left the house and scurried out to her vehicle, popping the trunk. The bags of grapefruit, oranges, and lemons waited, as did another bag. She wrangled everything from the trunk.

"Here, let me help you," said a male voice. Uncle Reuben. "Was it a long drive?" He took two bags from her grip.

"Two days, and I stopped one night. Do you take the bus or hire a driver when you go to Florida?"

"A driver. It's easier that way. We can stop when we want, especially with the five kids all needing something or other, to eat or to use facilities." He had the same little squinty look around his eyes as Mom, but his singsong accented voice sounded different to her ears.

"I almost can't believe it, you were there before Christmas. So close. But then I didn't go to Pinecraft until after Christmas."

"*Ach*, Pinecraft, the Las Vegas for we Amish. Yes, we enjoy taking the children. My *mamm* and *daed* would take us when we were children, too."

"Do you know the Millers, Isaiah and Rachel? They're probably a little older than your parents." *Her grandparents.* But she was still getting used to the idea.

"I think we might." He led her to the door. "*Mamm* would know for certain. She's good with names and such."

"Uncle Reuben." Natalie plucked up her courage as she followed him into the house.

"Yes?"

"Trying the sound of your name. I have an Uncle Reuben. So, what do you do? Are you a farmer?"

"Ah, no. I run a restaurant in Millersburg, Yoder's Amish Fare. I have a business partner who's Mennonite and we get along fine."

That explained her uncle's open demeanor. He was used to negotiating in the *Englisch* world. Talking to her was likely no more different than addressing one of his business colleagues.

"Oh, fresh fruit," said Anna as they lugged the fruit into the kitchen. "I'd say this calls for some lemon meringue pie to go with supper."

"I'll be glad to help." Natalie stood, holding her purse and the tote bag she'd retrieved from the trunk.

"Please, you can put those in the living room. I'd much rather talk in the kitchen, if you don't mind."

"What time will supper be, *Mamm*?" Reuben asked.

"Five o'clock."

Reuben nodded before he left the kitchen. "We will be back then. Mercy has made shepherd's pie. We'll bring that."

And then, they were alone.

"So." Anna lit the gas stove with a match and set the kettle on top. "I know enough to know you're not just in the neighborhood by chance."

"No, I'm not." Natalie took a seat at the end of the farm table. "I wanted to meet you all. I've felt so, alone, since Mom died. Dad has his own family. And there's—there's just me now." She shrugged.

"Ah, but how did you come to Pinecraft and your friends there?"

The story tumbled out, about meeting the Millers and then following them to Pinecraft to return Rebecca's doll. She tried to leave out the parts about Jacob, but even now, the memories tasted sweet on her tongue even after the bitterness of goodbye.

"So, there is no young man in your life? No, dating, as you *Englisch* call it? How old are you?"

"I'm twenty-eight." Natalie shook her head. "And no, not dating."

"But this Jacob Miller and his family. He sounds special to you." The teakettle whistled and Anna poured them both a hot cup of tea.

"Jacob said our worlds are too different, and it wouldn't work." Natalie held back a sigh at the admission. The sting still hurt and she performed the ritual of ignoring it as best she could.

"He's probably right, you know." Anna slid a container of honey toward Natalie.

Natalie nodded, and swirled a dollop of honey into her tea. Maybe this sweetness would help wash down the truth of Anna's words. But it felt as if a scab had been ripped open anew. This fresh sting was harder to ignore.

"I've heard of some who join the Amish, or Mennonites." Natalie said the words aloud. "But I'm not sure that's for me.

I'm not very, um, Plain." She recalled the sensation of wearing her performance costume in front of her Amish and Mennonite friends. The women's fresh modesty clashed with the circus getup which wasn't particularly concerned with freshness or modesty.

"It's wise when you consider what you must say no to, in order to be Plain." Anna took a generous sip of tea. "Some people think it is downsizing, like Reuben would say, turning off technology, wearing different clothes, and a new hairstyle. But it's more than that."

"I tried on my mother's dress and her *kapp* a while back."

"You have her clothes?"

"Just one dress and a *kapp*."

"What was that like for you, seeing yourself in the mirror?"

"Different." Natalie paused to take her own sip of tea. "Yes, different. I didn't *dis*like it. I don't know if it's for me or not."

"It's a matter of the heart." Anna placed her cup on the table. "You are the one who must pray and decide where you belong. Here, we work hard. We're up early. I have a garden to tend to. Not long, I know, and they'll be sending me to the *Mammi haus* when the next grandchild marries and moves into here. But I like to keep busy. You're of the age, though, you would marry, have children, keep house. Do you cook or sew? What skills have you?"

"I—I've learned some quilting this spring from Rachel Miller, but I'm nowhere near professional. I'm a so-so cook." Natalie sat up straighter. "But I'm good with children. I can teach. Not that circus skills are in demand among the Amish or Mennonites."

Anna stood. "Have you ever made a piecrust?"

"No. I've just unrolled premade dough from a package," Natalie admitted.

Anna frowned. "Your mother was never one for cooking, either. Well, it is easy enough to learn. Come to the work table and I'll show you before I start rolling out dumplings for the chicken."

Natalie joined Anna at a rectangular island in the center of the kitchen, and tried to take mental notes as Anna added shortening to flour, along with salt and water. She used a hand tool to break up the mixture into bits, quietly explaining the importance of *not* mixing the dough too much or it would turn out rubbery and not flaky.

When she was finished, a ball of dough waited on the table. Anna sliced it in half. "We only need half a crust for the lemon meringue pie. Now, if you could roll this piece into a circle while I fetch some fresh eggs." She handed Natalie a wooden rolling pin before sweeping through the kitchen and out the back screen door. "Be sure you flour the board and your rolling pin," she called in through the screen.

Natalie held the weathered wooden cylinder in her hands. Her mother had likely and very reluctantly touched the same utensil, here in this same room, trying to learn the same lesson. She floured the counter and the rolling pin, then started to roll the ball of dough into a circle. It reminded her of the Play-Doh she'd loved as a child. She rolled the dough into what resembled something of a circlish oval, after it wrapped itself around the rolling pin a few times.

This was why she always picked up premade crusts at the store. A lot less waste of ingredients, time, and aggravation. But she made the most of this opportunity.

Here came Anna with an apron full of brown eggs in varying tones. "We'll need some to whip up the meringue. Ah, that looks passable. We can use your crust." She set the eggs on the countertop.

"It's not quite a circle," Natalie observed.

"No, not quite. But it'll do." Anna nudged Natalie to the side. "Fold it like this, then pull it onto the plate, like this. Then unfold." Her callused fingers maneuvered the piecrust dough in swift movements.

Maybe, with practice, she could do the same someday. But who would she make pie for? She shrugged off the thought. "I suppose next we'll need lemon juice?"

"That's right. I'll pop this crust into the oven first." Anna covered the crust with what looked like little ceramic marbles. "Pie weights."

"Ah." Natalie watched Anna place the crust in the oven. "Is that a wood stove?"

"Propane." Anna whipped out a pair of bowls, then a plastic storage container. The mix of modern and old wasn't as vivid as in Pinecraft. "Now we make the lemon filling, quite simple, on the stove top"

A knock sounded on the back door. "*Mammi*, we're here," a young female voice rang out.

"We're here to help with supper," said another voice. "*Mamm* said we should come meet our cousin."

Cousins!

"Come in, come in," Anna said.

A quartet of young women, wearing dark cape dresses and black aprons entered the kitchen. They smiled at Natalie, before looking down at their shoes.

"My four youngest granddaughters."

"I'm Natalie." She returned the smile. "I'm very happy to meet you."

"I've never had an *Englisch* cousin before," said the youngest.

"Well, I've never had Amish cousins before," Natalie returned, laughing.

Anna shook her head, waving her hands at them. "Let's get busy. We have a big supper tonight."

24

An MRI scan followed by an EEG confirmed Rebecca likely hadn't had another seizure, although it wouldn't be a surprise if she suffered from headaches regularly. By Tuesday afternoon, the hospital released her after more tests, saying there was "nothing acutely wrong" with the child.

Nothing acutely wrong. Jacob frowned as they loaded her into the van to go home. Acute meant urgent, some fresh bad news.

Then why had Rebecca collapsed into a shrieking heap in the middle of the yard on Sunday?

All she would say was her head hurt and offered no other explanation. However, the last thing Jacob remembered before Rebecca had her "event," was the new young woman approaching him, saying something about the singing, and wouldn't he change his mind about coming? Coincidence, Rebecca had collapsed then? Maybe. Maybe not.

They arrived home right before supper with Ephraim, Katie, and the children. Zeke was already with his cousins, playing at their house, when the van stopped at Jacob's home.

Rebecca looked guileless as she studied the picket fence surrounding the house. "It's good to be home."

"Yes, *dochder*, it is." He carried her small bag, and she left the van without assistance.

"Thank you," he said to the driver, giving him the agreed-upon cash fare back from the hospital.

So much like her mother, and so much unlike, Rebecca opened the door. Jacob followed her into the quiet house.

"Oh, *Daed*, I'm sorry to worry everyone." Rebecca's head hung down.

"I know. But if you had a headache, there was no need to scream about it." He set down her bag and crossed his arms across his chest.

"My head did hurt."

"Rebecca Miller."

"I didn't want you to go, not with *her*."

"I don't even know *her*."

Rebecca surveyed the front room, with its simple Plain furniture, the handwoven oval rug, and one of two wood stoves to help warm the house in winter. "I miss Florida. I want to go back."

"We talked about that. We'll go visit *Mammi* when it's winter again."

"I miss my school at Sunnyside, and *Mammi* Rachel, and Miss Natalie, and the beach, and Big Olaf's. And fishing." The last word came out as half a sob.

"I do, too." Of course, he missed Natalie. To deny that would be a lie. But here, things were better for him. The familiar was around once again. And now, maybe, life would somehow go on, just like it was for everyone else.

"Here, it's just not the same as it was before."

"No, it's not. It hasn't been the same since . . ." He didn't want to be having this conversation with his little Rebecca. When had she learned to talk like this, to see things like this? She was but a child.

Yet, Rebecca had had to grow up fast in some ways. Before Pinecraft, he'd been proud of her for learning grown-up ways without her mother around, mending, cooking, helping keep the house straight, tending the garden, and keeping up with her schoolwork. He was the one to blame for this, despite him letting Katie help with the children on occasion.

"It won't be the same, ever."

"No, it won't."

"I don't want you to see her."

"Now, Rebecca, it's not your decision." He squatted to get on her eye level. "It's mine, and mine alone. We're making do, you, your brother, me."

"If I get another *mamm*, I know who I want."

He nearly asked who, but then decided against it. Speaking a name between them—it didn't matter.

"That's not your decision either." Besides, with Natalie, he'd already been down that road in his mind. It couldn't work, wouldn't work.

Rebecca frowned. "May I please lie down before supper?"

"*Yah*, you may." He watched as she picked up her bag, containing the dress she'd worn on Sunday, and clomped upstairs to her room.

Soon, Rebecca would turn eight, on the first of May. Not five more years and she'd be finished with school. Then, she'd begin her training in earnest, of what it meant to run a home, to be a mother, to care for children. Perhaps she'd discover a special skill or trade, like quilting or being a seamstress.

His hands were full now, but what then? *Gotte* would provide. He believed it to the core of his soul. So far, *Gotte* had, in spite of their present unorthodox life.

Hopefully, Rebecca would be in a better mood when she awoke. Despite her spirited nature, she had always been a respectful child. *Gotte*, help him be a *gut daed* to the young ones.

A rap sounded at the open front door. "I heard the van." It was Ephraim. "How's Rebecca?"

"She's fine. She's upstairs resting before supper."

Ephraim pulled the door open and entered the front room. "We had a phone message. I didn't know if you heard."

"What's that? Is it *Mammi* Rachel? Is she all right?"

His brother shook his head. "Natalie Bennett called."

He hadn't even allowed himself to murmur her name, but left the very idea of her back in Sarasota. "Why did she call?"

"She called to speak to Katie. She's in Ohio right now."

"Here?" So close . . . he couldn't imagine his bishop seeing the capris, the uncovered hair, nor could he imagine himself keeping his eyes and heart from wandering in her direction.

"Visiting her mother's family."

"So she found them. Very *gut*." Maybe it would help her feel more like she belonged. Or maybe it would only heighten the difference between her world and the Plain life.

"Katie invited her to come for a visit, with her being so nearby. She's in Millersburg."

Less than two hours away. "She's coming here?"

Ephraim nodded. "Sometime tomorrow, it's likely."

He would see her tomorrow. "Ah, well, of course, she should stop for a visit. The children will be happy to see her. Rebecca, especially." Although it might cause more problems than help any of them. Zeke still looked sad at certain moments, and missing Natalie was the only explanation Jacob could find.

"So how will you be?"

"I'll be fine." He tried to make his tone sound reassuring. "Natalie is someone we met in Florida. She helped us through one of the most difficult times of our lives and I'll always be thankful for that."

"*Ach*." Ephraim scratched his chin. "I know there was something there, with the two of you."

"It was never a good idea," Jacob forced himself to say. But how many times had he turned the same thought over in his mind? Of course, it was a horrible idea.

"She's not Amish, she's not Plain at all. She may be a Christian, but I don't see how her beliefs will match ours. She might say she's willing to leave what she knows, but look at what her mother did." Ephraim frowned.

"*Yah*. There *is* that." His brother made a valid point. If Natalie's mother had left the Amish, who's to say the same wanderlust wouldn't rise up in Natalie? And then, where would they be?

"*Gut*. I'm glad we're in agreement then." Ephraim nodded. "The bishop came to me—not *daed*—and wanted to know what had happened to you in Florida, as you seem different."

That bit of information rankled Jacob. "How could I not be different? You know what we went through—you were there for some of it. I had to stay there for months on end, in a strange city I didn't know."

"Calm down. Of course, you've seen a lot, staying in Florida as long as you have." Ephraim placed a firm hand on Jacob's shoulder. "But you're here now. I told him you were fine, you kept up your church attendance and worked hard while you were there. Other than that, he didn't care to hear about what Florida was like."

"Thank you." Why did he feel he had to explain himself? Of course, the source of his greatest temptation while in Pinecraft was arriving tomorrow, practically on his doorstep. It would involve a lot of explaining.

"Well, *gut*. I just wanted to prepare you for tomorrow."

Tomorrow. He'd see Natalie again tomorrow.

Natalie ended up staying three nights at Anna's, in her mother's old room. Natalie turned off her cell phone to conserve the battery. She'd received an email from Ringling Brothers, informing her that her application for an on-the-road trainer was under consideration, and they would be in touch with her soon.

"Thank you, thank you for letting me stay with you, Grandma. Or should I say *danke*, *Mammi*?" Natalie stood at the foot of the stairs.

"Either is fine. And I've been happy to have you here. Almost like having my Katie again. But you're quieter than she, more thoughtful, if no less energetic."

"I wish I'd met all of you much sooner than this."

"We still have time. And," Anna added, "were my husband still alive, he might not have appreciated your visit like I have."

"I see."

"He was so 'letter of the law,' I truly don't know if he would have even welcomed you into our home. Even though Katie hadn't been baptized yet—she left before that happened—he still would have been harsh with her if she'd returned."

"My mother—"

"She did a fine job raising you, even with you living like gypsies." Anna embraced her, and the pinpricks of tears poked the insides of Natalie's eyelids.

"Thanks. I promise I'll come back to visit when I can." She didn't think to mention the possibility of a circus job, being on the road again. These few days had been a start, at least.

"I'll wake you in the morning, so you can get a good start on the road."

"Thank you." Natalie hugged the older woman once more and headed up the stairs, their wooden boards creaking.

One thing she'd noticed that was different was the quiet out here on the farm. Sure there were other noises, one of her uncles out working his field, chickens in her grandma's yard, the whinny of a horse or the moo of a cow.

Once inside her mother's old room she'd shared with her sister, Natalie prepared for bed with the aid of a battery-operated lamp. She clicked it off, letting moonlight flood in through the window.

Her last night here. After that first night at supper, she'd been pulled into the bundle of energy of the Yoder cousins, had ridden in a covered buggy, helped milk the cows, tended the garden, and made another passable pie crust. Sang, laugh, and told stories of traveling with the circus.

Day in, day out—she wasn't sure if this would be enough for her. Although she supposed if this was all she knew, she wouldn't miss what she'd never had.

No wonder the Amish were urged to tread carefully where Pinecraft was concerned. She made her way across the bare floor, taking care not to stub her toes on the edge of the braided rug covering the middle of the floor, and took a seat at the window. She pulled the window up and let the cool night air drift into the room. It was perhaps only nine at night, but she could see her *mammi's* head drooping as they talked by lamplight earlier.

Now, since she'd come full circle after receiving the package from her father, she wasn't sure quite what to do. Especially since tomorrow, she'd be seeing Jacob Miller again, and the family.

She'd called Katie, on impulse, and left a message for her. Katie had called back the very same day, saying yes, please stop at the farm since she was in Ohio.

"The children will be happy to see you. It will be a nice surprise for them."

The call was brief enough so even now, she wondered at the wisdom of calling Katie. Yet, it would be a shame not to stop by. Also, Rachel had sent something for the family as well, the clothing they'd left behind.

The crunch of shoes on hard-packed earth made her look down toward the farmyard. Some dark shapes moved along the driveway, probably her uncles.

"*Daed* would have never stood for it," said one of them.

Another of the dark shapes muttered something in Dutch, but Katie caught the word *Englischer.*

"Doing business with the *Englisch* is one thing, letting them into our homes is another. She doesn't belong, no matter if Katie was her mother."

Natalie sighed at the last sentence. Of course, this wasn't her world. She wasn't trying to join the Amish. She squinted down at the figures, taking care she stood in the shadows by the window.

None of the voices belonged to Reuben. He likely would have stood up for her. He out of all of them seemed the most friendly, most approachable.

This was Ohio, not Pinecraft, where people looked the other way at things like cell phones and prodigals, too. Things were different here, with the bishop of the district overseeing the people, tending to the flock beneath him. She didn't think she could breathe in an atmosphere like this. Playing farmer and gardener and home baker was one thing. But this, no, she couldn't and wouldn't belong.

This was also Jacob Miller's world. Even if she wore her mother's *kapp* and cape dress, she could never be one of them.

25

Shreds of the conversation she'd overheard echoed in Natalie's ears the rest of the night, and she woke to a gray day along with Anna's soft rap on her door.

Seven a.m. That was sleeping in on the farm, she was fairly certain. Well, if she wanted to get a good start on the road, she might as well head out as soon as possible after breakfast. She had no idea how long she would be welcome at the Millers' home. A meal, perhaps, would be long enough to catch up, and then she would be on her way to Florida. Home.

The aroma of coffee and fried potatoes and ham drifted under the door. She'd probably roll halfway back to Florida, as much as Anna had fed her the past few days. She put on her most comfortable jeans, loafers, and a simple pullover T-shirt, and lugged her suitcase down the stairs, her tote bag slung over her shoulder.

"You're packed already," Anna said as she entered the kitchen.

"Yes, I am."

"Did you sleep well? Your eyes look shadowed."

"Well enough. But I'd love some coffee." Natalie stepped toward the shelf where the simple stoneware mugs were stored.

"The youngest ones will be over as quickly as they can after breakfast. The girls want to tell you good-bye."

"Well, I definitely want to tell them good-bye, too."

Anna loaded a plate with enough food to feed two farmers and set it at the place where Natalie usually sat. "Here, eat up. You need a good meal for the road." She grunted. "A young woman, driving halfway across country, alone."

"I have my cell phone and I plan to check in with my friends."

"Well, you must send word to me that you've arrived home safely. Call Reuben's restaurant in Millersburg and leave a message with his office."

"I will." Natalie sat at her place, the corner of the table closest to the front room.

As if on cue, the back screen door slammed and her young female cousins streamed into the kitchen. "We're here to say goodbye," said Miriam, the eldest. Her cheeks were flushed. "I almost wish I could ride with you."

"If you come to Florida sometime, any of you, let me know and I'll come to Pinecraft." Natalie dug into the fried potatoes on her plate. Starting tomorrow, she'd cut the carbs, but not in front of her grandmother.

"What's in that bag?" asked her youngest cousin, pointing at the tote bag tucked beside Natalie's oversize carry-on

"Mind your business, Esther," Miriam chided.

"No, it's quite all right." Natalie stood. "This is something for our *mammi* I brought from Florida. I thought she might like it."

She pulled out the quilt, the labor of love that she'd finished. At first, she figured she'd keep the quilt as a reminder, but truly, it belonged here.

"I haven't seen it in—I thought it was lost." Anna's voice caught. "It was the last thing she started to sew. Oh, we had some fights over the blocks. I almost told her the effort would be useless."

"No, it wasn't lost. My mother brought it with her, the blocks anyway." Natalie moved to the free end of the table and unfolded part of the quilt. The bright colors lit up the room, and Natalie's cousins ran their fingers over the stitches.

"You made this?" her grandmother asked.

"With help. Lots of help. Rachel Miller taught me how. I think she had to redo much of my stitching at first, but no, she made me work on it."

Anna clutched the corner of the quilt. "You did . . . you did a fine job."

"I want you to keep it," Natalie said. "My mother started it, and I finished it."

"But it's yours."

"No, it belongs here. Please, a gift from me." Natalie touched the fabric, recalling the needle pokes, missed stitches, and snarled threads it took to finish the quilt. Maybe someday she'd try another one. Right now, though, it seemed fitting to let this quilt come full circle, something Mom had probably never imagined.

"Thank you." The two words held all a mother's longing for her departed child. "You must come back sometime. Soon. Very soon."

"Oh, I will." Natalie took her seat again.

"Eat, eat," Anna said. "You have a long ride ahead of you."

Natalie nodded. Maybe she should have given her the quilt earlier, but the moment never seemed right, until now. "I'm going to stop by the Millers. Rachel sent some things for the family, so I told her I would."

"The Millers, huh?" Anna asked. "Do you think you'll see Jacob?"

She shrugged. "I probably will."

At that, the girls pounced, peppering her with questions about Jacob, the family, was she going to become Amish, and other such ideas.

"Girls," Anna waved her hands as if their questions were flies threatening to land on Natalie's breakfast. "Natalie is merely friends with the family. In fact, they helped her find us."

"But what if he loves her?" Miriam sank down onto the nearest chair, propping her chin on her hand.

"However we feel about each other, there's more to think about than what we want," Natalie admitted. "Our ways of life, our families, his children. It would change everything."

"There is much more to love than romance." Anna tapped Miriam on the shoulder. "Your cousin is right."

Your cousin. Natalie smiled. Even after a few days, it still felt strange, wearing this new title in her new family. No, she wasn't one of them, as last night's eavesdropped conversation confirmed.

"Someday, I want to meet my love." Miriam sighed, and smiled.

"How old are you again?" Natalie asked.

"Sixteen."

"You have plenty of time, for sure." Then she stopped herself. She'd been about to talk education and possibly a career, but realized Miriam's path was different.

Natalie polished off the last bit of her breakfast, including the mountain of fried potatoes. "This was delicious."

"When are you coming back?" Esther asked.

"I'm not sure. Maybe this fall, maybe Christmas?" She glanced at Anna.

"Oh, Christmas." The cousins clapped. "If our *daed* takes us to Pinecraft we'll come see you, too."

"I'd like that. I might not be in Sarasota full-time much longer, though."

"Why's that?" Anna collected Natalie's empty plate.

"I applied for a job, traveling with Ringling Brothers circus as an on-the-road trainer. I have an interview scheduled a few days after I get back to Florida. If I'm hired, I'll be joining the traveling show on the road within a month." Natalie took a final sip of coffee.

"But your home?" Miriam frowned. "Where will you live?"

"I only rent. My current boss said I can store my things with her and stay with her during the off-season."

Anna shook her head. "I don't understand. I thought you were happy, teaching the children at the circus school."

"I was. I am. But . . ." She didn't want to explain Jacob's leaving had done that to her. She wasn't satisfied where she was now.

After a round of good-byes, the little entourage helped Natalie load everything into her car. Anna sent some preserves with her, after Natalie whittled them down to a few jars of fruit and vegetables. If she was getting a new job, she didn't need to think about where to store things.

"You're sure about the quilt?" Anna asked one more time.

"I'm completely sure."

A pair of hugs from the youngest cousins, one of whom burst into tears. "I don't want you to go."

"I'll come back. Even if I'm on the road." She bent to hug the little one, about Rebecca's age.

"Promise?"

"I promise." Her throat caught.

"Well, we'll see you then," Anna said.

"See you, *Mammi*." She waved at them before driving off. As their figures shrank in her rearview mirror, Natalie let the tears flow at last. Family. So close, and yet so far. They accepted her as she was, but there was still *something* she didn't have.

"Ah, Lord, maybe it's me," she prayed. She set her GPS for the Millers. "Show me what to do. Maybe I'm not satisfied with me, but I can't change myself just to belong. Whether some of them like it or not, I do belong to them. Yet I feel like I don't fit."

Until she figured out what that missing piece was, she'd keep feeling like she was on the outside, looking in, again. She brushed away her tears. Now wasn't the time. Her heart skipped. She was going to see Rebecca and Zeke soon, very soon. They would likely be in school, but oh, what a surprise it would be for them to see her.

Jacob leaned on the hoe. What was once Hannah's garden had become Rebecca's responsibility, which meant while she was in school, he'd help tend the seedlings just finding their way out of the earth. They'd had a slow start planting, with arriving home from Sarasota much later than expected, but thanks to Troyer's Garden Center, they now had rows and rows of young plants to watch over. Katie had also started a few seedlings from her plantings.

Today was his "off" day from the cabinet shop, which had hired him back part-time. He'd prayed for a full-time position, but this was all they had for him, with the promise to give him the first full-time position that opened up. However, with Rebecca's doctor appointments, this was actually a better schedule for him.

Henry Hostetler had called and left a message for him, telling him hello and reminding him anytime Jacob wanted a job in Florida, he would have one with him. In fact, he was sorely missed.

Then a letter had come for all of them from *Mammi* Rachel. She was helping work a small garden in the neighborhood exchange for part of the produce. She had taken up shuffleboard. She had been out on a boat ride with some friends. Yet she still missed *Daadi*, of course.

"I will be sending some fresh preserves for all of you via a special courier," she'd said at the close of the letter. Special courier? Whatever that meant, he didn't completely understand. Ephraim didn't understand the cryptic statement either. Also, they had plenty of preserves.

Here came a crunch of tires on the gravel driveway. They had a sign posted at the edge of the driveway both families shared, advertising fried pies, soap, cheese, as well as vegetables in season. He wasn't sure what Katie had available, but certainly not vegetables. And, he wasn't in the mood to deal with *Englisch* tourists.

Every time he saw a slim young woman with long dark hair, he almost thought it was Natalie. If she was visiting family in Ohio, she had no real reason to visit the Millers. How long would it take for his eyes to stop tricking him? Or maybe it was his heart. He had nearly called Henry back the other night, asking if he knew a solution to help him and Natalie. But now, he knew for certain Natalie would be coming down the driveway, to his brother's *haus*.

Life had changed here for them forever and he was ready to go forward with life in Ohio. Even the idea of attending an event to see young Anne didn't seem so bad. Anne. That was also Natalie's middle name.

A silver car stopped at the edge of the picket fence framing Jacob's yard. He saw a swish of dark hair belonging to the driver behind the wheel.

But when the door opened, there stood Natalie, who now gaped at him, much like he was gaping at her. "Natalie—"

"Jacob." She shut the door behind her. "I figured you'd be at work."

"Off today."

"Ah, I see. Is Katie at the house?" The light breeze lifted the ends of her hair. The memory of touching the silken strands came back to him. Temptation now, even at his doorstep.

"I suppose she is." He wiped his brow. "The children are all at school."

"Right," she said. "It's Friday."

"Yes, it is." He wanted to scold himself. This was his friend. She knew things about him, and his family, most people didn't. But Amish males didn't have "friendships" with *Englisch* females.

"Well, I assume this is your house, so the other house must belong to Ephraim and Katie." She scanned its windows, the porch. Did she think it plain? But then, he shouldn't worry about what she thought about his house.

"You're very right." He wanted to begin a light banter with her, to see the wry grin light up her face, to feel his heart race as she tossed back a verbal response, tinged with her own wit. But he didn't.

"I, uh, I've actually brought some of Zeke and Rebecca's things." She gestured at the vehicle "Your *mammi* insisted that I bring them with me, so of course, I had to. And some orange preserves."

Mammi could have let whatever it was stay in Florida until next winter. Of course, she knew that. Natalie probably did too.

"That was kind of you."

"I've been visiting with my mother's family near Millersburg for a few days, and I've come by here on my way back to Florida."

"So, how was it for you, seeing the family?"

"It was good, very good. I plan to see them again, whether some of them come to Pinecraft or if I come to Ohio." She turned, pulling on her door handle. "Oh no."

"What's wrong?"

"I've . . . I've locked my keys in the car."

Jacob laid the hoe against the fence and joined Natalie on the other side of the gate. He pulled on the handle, then squinted through the window.

"I wonder if there's a way to put something through, like a hanger, and flip that switch." He stood close to her, nearly as close as the day on the deserted beach. She smelled like fresh soap, much like the kind Katie was so skilled at making. The scent of Amish soap on Natalie Bennett shouldn't make him want to kiss her.

Natalie seemed oblivious to his inner struggle. "I'm not sure. I could locate a lock service with my phone, and see if they can come out." Yet her voice quavered a little as she leaned beside him to look inside the driver's window.

He wanted to talk about anything besides her keys locked in her car. He wanted to tell her more than once he'd considered hiring a driver or hopping a bus back to Florida, to explore any possibilities they could be together. Yet, this was how forbidden fruit appeared—appealing.

"I'll see if I have a hanger to use," was what he said instead. "If not, you'll probably have to call someone."

"Thank you." She stood up straight, as did he. She blinked, but looked him straight in the eye. "Um, I'll go say hello to Katie while you get the hanger." Had she been about to say something else? She'd never seemed the quiet type, which was where any similarities between her and Hannah ended. Yet, it was one of the things which drew him to her.

Natalie scurried off across the driveway and farmyard in the direction of Ephraim and Katie's home, an exact replica of his home. Their parents' home lay farther down the lane, built over forty years ago.

Jacob wanted to scurry off as well, somewhere, anywhere but here. He wasn't quite sure of the time, but it had to be mid-morning. Undoubtedly, Katie would invite Natalie to stay, at least through supper to spend time with the children. Since their return from Florida and Rebecca's brief hospital stay, they'd taken to having the evening meal with Ephraim, Katie, and their brood.

But no, he couldn't run. What harm could a few hours' visit do? He could do this. First, though, he went for a wire hanger. He found one easily enough in the front closet and began untwisting it to form a tool to work to unlock the door. He'd never attempted something like this before, but had seen Henry unlock his ancient minivan in Florida.

He glanced toward Ephraim and Katie's house as he passed through the wooden gate. No signs of Katie or Natalie at the moment. His sister had developed a fond adoration of Natalie and had asked about her often. If she guessed at his feelings for Natalie, she never mentioned them.

Jacob stopped at the driver's door and looked through the window at the lock mechanism. He knew many vehicles had computers controlling them, but a lock was a lock, and something had to flip the switch inside the door panel.

He stuck the wire down between the window and the door, not sure what he was feeling for. Yet another skill he'd gleaned in Florida, never imagining it would be useful here in Ohio.

Ten minutes, he finagled the lock, trying to imagine what it was he needed to trigger inside the door. Another glance at the house across the way. Nothing yet.

Natalie Bennett. Here. He could do this. If he could get the lock popped, he could face the memories Natalie brought with her, with only a shimmer of hair and glance of her eyes.

"Help me, *Gotte*, with this door and with Natalie." He gritted his teeth as he murmured the words aloud. No one around could hear him. "I want Your will for me and I do know she is a distraction—" He twisted the hanger with a little more force than he'd intended "—and a temptation to worldliness I can't make room for in my life."

Another tug on the hanger and it was almost as good as an Amen. A click told him it had worked. The lock shot up, and he grinned.

A door banged, and Jacob looked across the yard. Here came Natalie, grinning.

"You did it."

"I did."

"Well, thank you. You helped save me some money here." Natalie glanced at the car. "Here, I can pop the trunk now and give you the children's things."

She moved around him and he followed. It was going to be a long, long day.

With the trunk open, she pulled out a pair of plastic bags emblazoned with the Yoder's restaurant "I love pies" logo. The memory of the Florida restaurant made Jacob smile in spite of the nerve endings that pinked and plunked at Natalie's nearness.

"I think it was some clothing. And the preserves." Natalie handed him the bags.

He shook his head. "She could have mailed these, or kept them until winter."

"But the kids would outgrow the clothes by then, I'm sure."

He hadn't thought of that. "*Ach*, you're right. As a father, I forget some things."

"You have done a wonderful job, Jacob Miller. Would that all fathers care for their children like you've done yours." Her voice was soft. She cleared her throat. "Anyway, Katie has asked me to stay for the day. I hear you are all having supper guests, a new family to the area?"

This was news to him. "I didn't know that. Well, we'll have a houseful then, I'm sure."

She nodded. "Katie and I are going to drive to town before the children get out of school and pick up a few extra things. Do you need anything?"

"No, can't say as I do."

"Thank you again, Jacob, for getting my door unlocked." She smiled at him, the open grin he'd missed since leaving Florida.

He tried to return the grin, but failed. Anne and her family would be at supper tonight.

Sometimes, a man just couldn't get a break.

26

Natalie didn't want to wake up from her dream. She was in Ohio, visiting her mother's family, and now spending time with the Millers. She'd seen Jacob right away, and after absent-mindedly locking her keys in the car, realized her feelings for him still flickered with a strong flame. Of course, they did. Sometimes it would be nice for feelings to come with an on-off switch.

"Is there anything else I can do?" she asked Katie, who bustled around the farmhouse kitchen. They'd already returned from a quick shopping trip to town via Natalie's vehicle.

"No, you've helped a lot. I had wanted a few extra potatoes for the mashed potatoes tonight, because I'm nearly out of what I canned from last year. You made going to market much faster today." Katie paused, then grabbed the ten-pound bag on the butcher block island. "Matter of fact, you can help. You can peel these. We have fourteen mouths to feed tonight."

"Yes, ma'am." Natalie marched over to the island and picked up the paring knife. "When will the children arrive home from school?"

"Close to four o'clock."

"I can't wait to see them." She opened the bag and pulled out a potato. "How have they been, since coming home from Florida?"

"They have done extremely well, although I think they miss some of the bustle of the city and all its novelties."

"I can imagine. But the quiet is nice—it's peaceful here." Natalie managed not to peel too much of the potato's flesh away with the skin. "Plus, there's so much for children to do here, to stay active and outside."

Katie nodded. "There's always something to do, and they've been busy helping plant the gardens. I managed to get part of Jacob's garden planted before they arrived home."

"Your flower garden is beautiful. I saw it on the way in."

"*Danke.* Well, it's still getting started. You should see the vegetable garden in summertime, all the ripe fat tomatoes, rows of beans and sweet peas, ready for the picking." Her voice took on a wistful tone. "Right now it's not the prettiest, all the rain we've had."

"I did bring some preserves from Rachel. She wanted to be sure I brought something just from her."

"I miss her." Katie stopped working the bread dough for a moment. "She seems like she's doing well after losing *Daadi* Miller, from what I hear. Every winter, we'd go to Pinecraft, and I was used to seeing both of them. Even before I married Ephraim and I traveled with my family."

"I try to see her when I can. Now that the quilt's done, I don't have a built-in excuse to see her," Natalie admitted. She didn't want to add in the weeks the Millers had been gone, seeing Rachel and her surroundings only reminded her of Jacob and the children.

Katie's glance slid sideways, and Natalie kept her focus fixed on the potato she now held. "My *bruder*-in-law isn't there anymore either, nor are the children."

Natalie nodded. She wasn't sure what to say, how much to reveal to Katie. Did the woman think the idea of Natalie and Jacob together a good thing? Or did she see their differences loom between them?

"Well, I know all of them miss you, even Jacob, who's stubborn and won't admit it." Katie rolled the dough into a bowl, then covered it with a clean towel.

"But . . ."

"Yes, there is that but." Katie frowned. "I've seen women try to join the Amish, not many, but a few. It's a hard way of life. It's all I've known, so I don't think it's so bad. The Lord gives me joy in my journey. But most women start pining for their pretty clothes and jewelry, they tire of the head covering and our simple dresses. For them, the chores become endless. I wouldn't want Jacob to be left alone again, nor the children."

"I understand, believe me." Natalie set down her paring knife. "I've thought about it, too. It would be cruel to all of them. They deserve someone who's able to love them without having to make such a difficult decision."

"There is a family coming for supper tonight, a new family to our district. They have a daughter who's of marriageable age. I thought you should know, especially since you are a good friend to our family." Katie pulled a tall stockpot from a shelf. "It's no secret people like to make matches around here. It can be a good thing, or a bad thing, or awkward, depending on the situation."

"So, is that what you're doing, matchmaking?" Natalie fought to get the words around the lump in her throat. So Jacob hadn't chosen Betsy Yoder. Betsy was still in sunny Florida, but here was another prospect coming to his doorstep.

"No, not really. We decided to be neighborly, since they purchased the farm down the lane from us." Katie motioned for Natalie to join her by the sink. "Bring the potatoes, and we can get them on the stove next."

"Well, I won't say your brother-in-law hasn't been on my mind," Natalie ventured to say. "But I've thought of the same reasons you have. Part of me wishes we could find some kind of compromise."

"There is no compromise to entice Jacob to leave his home, his family, everything he knows behind, only for the sake of love. It is very difficult in the world for the ex-Amish. My—my little brother left and he has more than paid the price for his decision." A flush of red sprang up in Katie's cheeks.

"Here, I'll put the pot on the stove." Natalie picked up the pot while Katie lit the burner. "Gas stove?"

Katie nodded. "So much easier to use than wood fire stove. Ephraim's parents believe propane is a bit of compromise."

"But, your brother. What happened to him?"

"He left, right before he was baptized. He started partying with alcohol and drugs, then got an *Englisch* woman with child. They 'broke up,' as the *Englisch* say, and now he has a son he never gets to see."

"Oh, Katie, how terrible. I'm so sorry." Now she understood a bit better why any hint of compromise was a sign worldliness was at the door, ready to pounce on them like a rabid dog.

"And his pride, his wicked pride—well, it keeps him from coming back to us. He drowns his sorrows in alcohol, and sometimes says he doesn't care if he's bound for hell." Katie rubbed her eyes. "He could come back to the district at any time, but for his stubbornness."

"If he only knew how much he was loved, how much God loves him." Natalie frowned. "He could have even started a good life, without the drugs and alcohol and partying lifestyle."

Katie shrugged. "He was done with the rules."

Natalie wanted to explain compromise on Jacob's part needn't mean compromising his faith, but even she wasn't sure what would be considered leaving the church. There were Amish who lived outside the district year-round, like in Florida.

The conversation switched to the supper menu, plus Natalie's consideration of looking for a new job—"Imagine, getting to travel again, to so many different places," Katie had said.

"I'm not sure if it'll work out, but I was looking for a change," Natalie explained. "It's time."

Slowly the hands of the battery-operated clock on the wall slipped closer to the 4 o'clock hour. The children would be home soon. Natalie smiled at the thought of their faces when they saw her at their aunt's supper table.

Soon the chatter of children's voices coming up the driveway filtered through the open kitchen window.

"Here they are, full of energy. I wish I could find a way to harvest some of it," Katie said, going to the kitchen door. Her trio bounded inside, then skidded to a stop when they saw Natalie.

The stair-stepped children turned from all talk and laughter to a more solemn outlook.

"Children, this is Natalie, who became Rebecca and Zeke's friend when Rebecca was in the hospital in Florida."

They bobbed their heads, whispering in Pennsylvania Dutch and carrying their lunch coolers to the counter.

Katie kissed each of them on the head in turn, then gave a flurry of instructions as her brood scampered away. "It's easier to use our language. I told them to wash their hands and start homework before supper, because we're having company and might have some singing or games."

Natalie nodded. Of course, Rebecca and Zeke would see their father first after school. She imagined they had the same reception once they skipped through the wooden gate and up the front porch steps.

"She's here, she's here!" a little voice called from outside. "I knew she'd come visit us one day."

Zeke pelted through the screen door like it was of no consequence. "Natalie, you're here." He threw his arms around her neck and hopped into her lap.

She would have tumbled over in the wooden chair, had she not been bracing herself. "Oh, my Zeke, how I've missed you." Only he wasn't hers, nor was Rebecca. She regretted the use of "my" as soon as the two-letter word slipped from her mouth.

Rebecca soon followed, limping as she crossed the threshold. "You *are* here." She limped the rest of the way across the kitchen and joined in the embrace. "I thought Zeke was being silly."

"No, not today." Natalie blinked. She couldn't and wouldn't cry, but Katie gave her a knowing look and a slim smile. "How are you feeling? How is your leg?"

"It is better and better every day. I can walk to school, most days."

"And your schoolwork is going well?"

"Yes, we kept right up with everything in Florida, too."

Then they pestered her with questions about Rachel, if she'd been fishing since they'd been gone, if she was still working for the circus school. No, she wouldn't tell them she was thinking of leaving the school. The news wouldn't matter so much to them.

Would it matter to Jacob? Her whole world changed since they'd been gone, and maybe distance and more change would help her miss them less, help her forget what was likely a foolish dream, even now taunting her at the sight of these precious children.

Jacob saw the Troyers' horse and buggy pass the house and continue until it reached Ephraim's farmyard. He ought to stop working, wash his hands, and prepare for supper. The children hadn't returned since he'd told them that Natalie was at the house with Katie and their cousins.

Should he change his shirt? He had another shirt in the closet, not his Sunday shirt, but an extra one was not so work-worn. However, Anne might get the wrong idea, as if perhaps he was dressing for her. But then, he didn't want to show up to supper with the dirt from the work day on his clothing.

It would mean extra laundry, but he changed his trousers, too. He should have seen if the children's clothing was passable after their day at school, but he hadn't thought about it at the time. Every second with their Natalie was precious to them, and he didn't see the point in calling them home only to change clothes.

Let them enjoy time with her; time which likely wouldn't come again. As far as tonight went for him, he would try to keep an open mind.

When Jacob crossed the yard, he found the other men engaged in talk about Ephraim's newest horse, ready for training to the buggy.

"Here's Jacob, at last," said Ephraim as he approached. "He's still getting used to holding the reins of a buggy once again, aren't you, my brother?"

He nodded. "Biscuit has only tried to run off once, though."

"Saw the car in front of your house," said Mr. Troyer. "*Englisch* friends? Or Mennonite?"

"*Englisch* friend, from near Pinecraft, in Florida, who was visiting family near Millersburg."

"Ah, not far from where we used to live." Mr. Troyer nodded. "Who is her family?"

"The name's Yoder, I don't recall her grandparents' first names," Jacob replied. He'd wanted to keep conversation from drifting toward Natalie, and hadn't thought about the car parked in front of his house.

"Supper's ready," called Katie from the back door steps.

"Smells mighty good, Ephraim," Mr. Troyer said as they flocked like a line of birds toward the house.

"I think she cooked a roast for the main dish. I'm sure it will melt in our mouths." Ephraim nodded at Jacob.

They were greeted by the swarm of Ephraim's children, along with jubilant faces of Zeke and Rebecca, who sat on either side of Natalie.

"*Daed*, *look*!" Zeke beamed, and patted Natalie's shoulder. "She came to see us, all the way from Florida."

"I know; she came while you were at school today."

"I want her to stay with us," said Rebecca.

Good thing he hadn't started to eat the meal spread on the long table that ran the length of the kitchen. He'd have choked on the bite.

"Oh, I was planning to drive into Sugarcreek and rent a room," said Natalie.

"You can have the girls' room here," said Katie. "They can pile in with their brother on the floor for one night. No need to go to the expense of a room."

"All right then." Natalie glanced at one child on each side of her. "I'll stay the night and head out first thing in the morning."

After they'd settled into their seats under Katie's direction, and after Ephraim asked the blessing, introductions were made all around the table.

Jacob didn't miss the similarities between Anne and Natalie, the same tone of dark brown hair, the same slim, yet strong build, the determined chin, and brown eyes that laughed when either woman spoke. Natalie's face held a little more maturity than Anne's rounded cheeks of youth. She glanced his way as she took a bite of mashed potatoes.

He had yet to address her again since talking to her about her locked car. Two seats away from Natalie sat Anne, who kept glancing from her plate to Jacob.

"So, Anne, have you enjoyed any time with the other young people in our district?" Jacob heard Katie ask.

"Yes, Mrs. Miller, I have. They are a good group, always something happening." Her brown-eye focus shifted to Jacob. "However, sometimes they seem rather childish to me."

"Anne Troyer," her mother said.

"I think of myself as a grownup. I might only be nineteen, but I feel that I'm ready to assume more adult responsibilities. I was thinking of becoming a teacher. I love children."

The hint wasn't lost on Jacob. She was letting him know in front of everyone she didn't mind their age difference, that she was ready to marry and head into adult life, and she was more than willing to take over the role of mother, should he choose her.

Or maybe he was assuming. No, he wasn't. She smiled at him when no one seemed to be watching, while her younger brother was speaking of an escapade with some frogs at the creek.

After the meal, the ladies began clearing the dishes, with the Troyer women helping despite Katie's protests. She didn't protest about Natalie helping, Jacob noticed.

"There's still enough daylight left to play some corn hole," Ephraim said, after they'd seen to the animals.

"We can stay for that." Mr. Troyer looked at Jacob. "So how's your throwing arm? We could be on a team, with Anne's brother making a team with your brother."

Anne's brother. Not calling the young man Eli, but Anne's brother. Yes, he realized Anne was here tonight. Jacob didn't want to keep reading more from people's words than was there, but he couldn't help it. His shirt collar constricted around his neck. He tugged to rid himself of the sensation.

"So, you work at the cabinet shop?" Mr. Troyer asked as they stood beside the corn hole box.

Jacob squeezed the beanbag, trying to gauge the distance from the hole and how hard to throw. "Yes." He threw. The bag flew to the opposite end of the yard where Ephraim and Eli stood beside their box.

His beanbag hit the wooden surface and slid toward the hole. It stopped mere inches from the hole. Jacob grunted, then let Mr. Troyer take his turn.

"So what's your job there?"

"Right now I'm a cutter. I cut out the pieces for each cabinet according to specifications. My old job, I was an assembler, putting them together. What I'd really like to do is work up to a quality control position." The salary would be even better for him and the children. Part of him, though, missed working with Henry in Florida. It was hard work, but he realized he liked not having to punch a time card. But that was there, and not here.

"It sounds like you have some fine plans, there." Mr. Troyer frowned when his own beanbag didn't even reach the corn hole box.

"*Gotte* willing, it will work out. What about you?"

"Besides working the farm, I build yard furniture from logs. Chairs for the porch, swings, benches," he said. "You should come see it sometime. I'd like a fellow craftsman's opinion on my work."

"I'd be glad to." Again, that tightening around the neck feeling.

"Anne will make her specialty, chicken potpie."

He didn't recall agreeing to come to supper.

He hoped they'd end the game before his supply of air ran out.

27

Natalie missed Florida, but on her last night in Ohio, she realized she'd miss the quiet here, too. She turned down the covers of the bed, and listened to the giggles in the hallway of the children settling in for bed.

"Time to be tucked in," she heard Ephraim say. "Now, I want no complaining when you wake up in the morning."

A chorus of no's was the response as they pounded down the stairs. Zeke and Rebecca had begged to stay with a solemn promise they, too, would behave and not complain. For the entire evening, they'd stuck to Natalie and she hadn't minded in the least.

Come morning, they'd say goodbye once again, but this time it would be with promises to see each other in the winter. Upon saying goodnight, Rebecca had frowned.

"It's a long, long time until winter," she'd said.

"You'll be busy with school and your garden and your friends." Natalie tried to sound bright and happy. "The time will pass quickly, believe me."

The little girl had looked doubtful.

Earlier in the evening, Natalie hadn't missed the matchmaking nudges from the Troyers to Anne and Jacob. They barely knew him; how could they possibly know he was a good match for their daughter? Of course, the first time she'd seen him, he'd had an effect on her as well, one she hadn't expected or looked for. She'd literally been minding her own business.

She turned out the lamp and once again looked out across a darkened yard at another house, just as she had the night before at her grandmother's home. He hadn't said good evening, or good-bye to her, either. But what should she expect? He'd made it clear before he left Florida it was her fault. She was the temptress, luring him away from his beliefs and causing him to compromise. She'd never felt that way—well, maybe after the circus performance, which she'd looked at through different eyes since.

Her cell phone warbled, a Florida area code and number seemed familiar but wasn't in her contact list.

"Hello?"

"Natalie, this is Jacob Miller." His voice sounded different over the phone.

She sat bolt upright and looked out the window. "You're calling me. On the phone."

"Yes. I had your number in my phone."

"You still have your cell phone? Won't you get in trouble for having it here?"

"I kept it. I just don't show it around to people." The words were tight.

He certainly wasn't used to talking on the phone. It made her smile. "You do know we're right across the yard from each other?"

"Yes, but it's nighttime. I couldn't come across to tell you goodnight without . . . without . . . people talking."

She chuckled. It was as if they were a couple of teenagers. At least he wasn't texting her.

"You're laughing at me."

"I just never expected my phone to ring and for it to be you." There was so much she wanted to tell him, to ask him, but it wasn't right for a phone call, and probably wouldn't work in a face-to-face conversation. She'd opened her heart to him in Florida, and he'd laid it splintered on the sand and walked away.

"I'm not planning to tell anyone around here about the phone."

"Okay, it's probably a good idea."

"I, er, so what do you think about Anne Troyer? Her father has invited me to their home for supper one night."

"Oh, Jacob . . . why are you asking me this?" The chuckles had vanished, replaced by the pang of a sore heart.

"Because I don't know what to do, and I know my family and Order will tell me exactly what to do, because they think they know what's best for me."

"It's not fair, though, to ask me." She swallowed hard. "My . . . my feelings haven't changed. You're asking me, the source of your temptation, for advice?" Ouch, she sounded harsh. But it was the truth.

"I—I saw tonight, you with the children. Maybe I was wrong about some things. I still count you as . . . a friend."

"I'm glad you feel that way. But I can't tell you what to do about Anne, or anything, or anyone else in your life. In the end, Jacob, we're held responsible for our own choices. Not our friends, or our family, or our church. Their opinion and input can only help so much. Or not. We don't answer to them; we answer to God."

The line fell silent, and for a moment, she thought the call was lost.

"I can see you in the window."

She nearly darted back away from the window, but realized she was dressed modestly enough in her button-down shirt and cotton pants. She looked again at the house across the yard. A dark shape was framed by a faint light in one of the upstairs windows.

"I can see you, too. Sort of."

"You're leaving in the morning."

"Yes. I need to be on the road. I—I might have a job interview when I get back."

"You're leaving the circus school?"

"I applied for a traveling trainer position with the circus. I'd be in Sarasota during the winter, but gone the rest of the year."

"But you love teaching. And your students love you."

"I, well, it's time for a change. I'm praying—God's will be done. Who knows? Anyway, I might not get the job." She wanted to tell him there wasn't much left in Sarasota for her, about the gap created when they left, and she didn't know how to fill it, nor did she know if she wanted to fill it with anyone or anything else.

"I see."

"Well, tomorrow comes early. I should go now." Why'd he call her? Now she knew sleep would try to elude her after she turned out the light.

"Good night, then. If I don't see you in the morning, see you in the winter, maybe?"

"Maybe. Good night." She ended the call and turned off the light.

The tree outside the window made shadows on the wall and ceiling as it moved in the breeze. Stillness fell over the house again, but Natalie imagined the children whispering to each other in the dark. The cousins seemed close. She thought of her own cousins, not so far away. She hadn't had those times with them, but she intended to keep in touch via letters, or a rare phone call, now she knew her uncle had the restaurant.

She lay there, thinking about her brief conversation with Jacob. On the phone, of all things. He had to feel something for her, to call her and talk as he did. But if he wasn't 100 percent sure they should pursue a life together, then she wasn't going to push, or ask.

"Lord, I don't know what to do. Is this just a season of my life, ending? I feel as though a season was beginning, searching for my grandparents, getting to know the Millers, learning from the people in Pinecraft. But now, I'm not so sure." She whispered the words in the dark. "Being with Jacob would mean big changes for me. Honestly, Lord, I'm not ready to be Amish. I—I can't. I'm afraid I would start to resent not having conveniences, because I don't think they're evil and a distraction in themselves. He won't change, and I can't. Please, show me where to go and what to do."

She lay there, listening to the silence, until her eyelids grew heavy.

A click of the door made her eyes open. Had she slept? It felt later. She checked her phone in the dim light. 3:05.

"Natalie," came a small voice. Rebecca.

"What is it?"

"I can't sleep."

"Well, come on up for a few minutes." She patted the bed beside her.

Rebecca padded on bare feet, with a hint of a limp, across the wooden floor. "I tried and tried to keep my eyes closed."

"It happens to me sometimes, too."

Rebecca piled onto the bed, pulling the covers off Natalie and tugging the blankets up to her own chin. "I like your night clothes. They're pretty." Natalie wore pink cotton pajamas, a shirt covered with tiny daisies, with pants to match. "The flowers look like flowers I see in the field on the way to school."

"Thank you."

"Sometimes I don't like to be Plain. I like pretty things like that."

"I understand. But your gown looks comfortable."

"My *mamm* made it. She was a good sewer."

"I heard she was good at a lot of things." Natalie shifted from her side to a sitting position.

"Yes. She could sew and garden and cook. She could sing, too." Rebecca yawned, and paused before continuing. "I don't want Betsy Yoder, or that Anne Troyer, to be my new *mamm*."

"Well, I know it's up to your father to decide. I think you should pray he chooses the right person." Natalie was waiting for the little girl to drop off again.

Rebecca remained quiet, then yawned once more. "I should pray for *Gotte's wille*."

"Yes, for God's will. That would be best."

"Sometimes I wonder . . ." Her voice drifted off. Another yawn.

"What's that?"

"I wonder if *Gotte* minds us telling Him what we want to happen."

"I don't think we're supposed to tell Him what to do." Natalie smiled at the idea.

"No, I mean, I tell my *daed* I'd like to make ice cream after supper, and sometimes he lets me. That's what I mean." Rebecca sighed. "I miss Big Olaf's."

"You're right. I don't think parents mind, or God minds, hearing us talk about what we want, as long as we have a right attitude about it."

"Yes, a right, attitude." Rebecca worked over the word, which made Natalie smile.

Another yawn came from Rebecca, which Natalie couldn't help but echo.

"Natalie?" Rebecca finally murmured.

"What is it?"

"If I am going to have another *mamm*, I'm going to tell God I'd pick you."

Jacob looked at the phone on the chest of drawers as he paced the room. He shouldn't have called her. No, he should have left the phone in Florida, with *Mammi* Rachel. She could use it if she needed it, although she probably wouldn't.

He couldn't help it, though. All evening long, he'd been keenly aware of Natalie. How could he not? Yes, Anne Troyer was a pretty young woman who seemed to have had a good upbringing, but she was no Natalie.

Then they'd all parted ways and he left without so much as a good night or good-bye to Natalie.

Letting the children stay at Ephraim and Katie's on a school night had probably not been the best idea. They would probably laugh and play all evening, despite his brother and sister-in-law's chiding to settle down and sleep. Tomorrow's day would probably begin with a pile of young bear cubs, grouchy from lack of rest.

That, and tonight left him rattling around in the farmhouse like a solitary pea in a pod. His thoughts rattled in his mind as well.

Tomorrow, he reminded himself. Tomorrow morning Natalie would head off down the driveway and not be a regular part of their lives anymore. A friend, someone they knew in Florida.

What had surprised him most was her admission she was seeking another job, this one a traveling job. She was prepared to reenter the life of a nomad. He couldn't imagine how people did that, sleeping every few nights in a different city, driving for days on end in a traveling show. The Pioneer Trails bus trip to Florida was plenty of travel for him.

He couldn't imagine her, either, not teaching. He still recalled the faces of her students as they greeted her after that show. Even in his haze, at the height of his temptation at seeing her in pink froth, he'd recognized she was a good teacher.

And she'd be alone, still.

It's your fault, too.

She'd begged him to figure out a way for them to be together, back in Florida, and he'd dismissed it without even trying. He closed his eyes, remembering the early evening on the nearly deserted beach, when he'd broken a dozen or more of his own rules by yielding to temptation, and let himself kiss Natalie.

"Is there a way, *Gotte*?" he asked aloud. He would not leave his Order, but he could not ask her to convert, to become Amish, for him.

He thought about the dream he'd had about Hannah, and he was right. He hadn't dreamed of her again. What had she said—he would have more children one day? Only *Gotte* knew the future. Maybe it was just his wishful thinking, or the consequences of him being distracted had made him have that dream.

Jacob made his way downstairs, not bothering to turn on a light. What would he do with the house, were he to live in Florida? Maybe one of his cousins would live in it. Likely his father would decide.

He already knew his father's advice. He needed to remember who he was, where he belonged. His life was here, in Ohio, raising his children and working at the factory. *Gotte* had already set his lot in life, and it was his duty to follow. Briefly, he'd thought of Betsy Yoder, then negated that idea. Then there was the distraction of Natalie and all that happened in Florida.

Now, he'd been introduced to a suitable young Amish woman in Anne Troyer. She was young, yes, but she'd made it clear she was willing to become an instant mother.

He paced the kitchen, wondering about what his future held here in Ohio. Could he follow the adage, *What happens in Pinecraft, stays in Pinecraft*? He'd heard the saying before, which mimicked the *Englisch* saying about the city of Las Vegas, nicknamed by the *Englisch* themselves as "sin city." Had he sinned, where Natalie was concerned?

He tried to imagine if instead of what had promised to bloom with Natalie, if it had been Betsy. Would he have been so hard on himself, kissing Betsy and then mentally flogging himself for it? No, Betsy was Amish, nor was she a former circus star who'd led him into temptation. But then, was it a sin to remember what it was like to be married?

No, the simple fact was: Natalie Bennett wasn't Amish. Then why wasn't that simple fact easily overcome?

If he could overcome it somehow, what was stopping him? The opinion of his family, his bishop, his Order. Some might never accept Natalie, even if she were to go through a time of proving before being baptized. She was a city girl, too. She'd never last here, without her modern conveniences and her car. She would have so much to learn, and might always feel as though she were on the outside looking in at a world she was never born into.

Sometimes, Jacob Miller, you think too much.

What he'd like right now was to talk to Henry Hostetler. He remembered their conversations, their debates on this or that, but always friendly, always full of grace. Henry might not be Amish, but he was a true friend, and in some ways, a counselor as if he were Jacob's bishop or father.

He thought of the cell phone upstairs.

One phone call to Henry could help still some of this. Henry wouldn't judge, wouldn't tell him what to think, but could help him discover the answer he sought.

Even if that answer wasn't one he truly wanted.

28

When Rebecca woke, she didn't remember where she was at first. Then she remembered tiptoeing upstairs to the room where Natalie was staying, and talking to her until she fell asleep.

There was the dresser, the chair by the window, the row of different size cape dresses hanging from hooks, but no suitcase and no cell phone. The room was empty of anything not—Amish. Natalie was gone.

Rebecca pushed back the covers and hurried downstairs, not caring if her bad leg ached with her quick movements. She stumbled into the kitchen.

"Natalie?" She glanced around. Her *aenti* Katie was cooking at the stove, the other children waking up in the front room where they'd slept on piles of blankets and quilts on the floor, so Natalie could have the bed.

"She's loading her car now," her aunt said. "She has a very long drive ahead of her."

With that, the door opened and Natalie entered, carrying a plastic travel mug with a lid. "Thank you, Katie. I apologize for eating and leaving in a hurry this morning."

"You are very welcome, and no apology necessary. Here, let me fill your coffee cup before you leave." Aunt Katie reached toward Natalie and took her plastic cup.

"I thought you were gone," Rebecca said.

"Not yet. I wouldn't go without telling you and your brother good-bye." Natalie held out her arms. "Where's Zeke?"

"In the front room." Rebecca buried her face in Natalie's shoulder and inhaled. She would do her best to remember the smell of Natalie's perfume. It smelled like spices and flowers. She would miss Natalie's hugs, too. "I wish you didn't have to go."

"Winter will be here again, before we know it. We'll see each other again."

Zeke bounded into the room like a little goat and joined the hug. "Bye."

She kissed them both on the tops of their heads. "You be good, work hard in school, and I'll see you in the winter if I can."

"We will." Rebecca couldn't say anymore. *Aenti* Katie returned the plastic cup to Natalie.

"Thank you, thank you again, Katie. Your family means a great deal to me." Natalie's voice sounded like she had a bite of dry bread caught in her throat.

"You, as well, Natalie. You were a blessing from God during some very dark times. Travel safely." *Aenti* Katie blinked.

"I'll do my best."

Rebecca followed Natalie out the door and into the yard, watched Natalie get into the driver's seat of her car, then Rebecca waved until she couldn't see the silver car anymore.

She looked up at the clear blue sky from where she stood in the empty yard. "*Gotte*, I'm not telling you what I want, with a bad attitude. But if you have another *mamm* for me, I sure want her to be Natalie, please. She's not Plain, but I love her anyway."

❧

The trip to Florida dragged on, mile after mile ticking along, and by the time Natalie reached Sarasota, she was ready to sleep for a week. She couldn't bear the thought of stopping for the night and sleeping in an empty hotel room. Instead, she caught a few hours' sleep at a rest stop.

"I still say, you could have flown," Grace told her when Natalie called to share her progress home. No, she couldn't have. Not if she wanted transportation throughout Amish country.

"It was easier this way, even though it takes longer. I needed some time, on my own, to think and pray."

Grace had begged her to stop by her house as soon as she arrived home.

She pulled up in the Montgomerys' driveway, knowing she wouldn't hear the end of it, if she bypassed Grace's place. She rang the doorbell, her eyelids drooping.

"You're back, you're back!" Grace's voice rang out as she opened the door. "It feels like it's been forever." She enveloped Natalie in a hug. "You must have a million stories to tell, about your mother's family, and seeing Jacob." Grace pulled her into the house.

"Yes, it feels like I have a million stories to tell."

"Well, I can't wait to hear about you meeting your mother's family. Go, relax on the lanai while I get a tray of refreshments. Just don't conk out before I get there. Iced tea on the lanai and scones sound good?" Grace bustled around the kitchen, with her dogs scampering back and forth from Grace, to Natalie, whose eyelids begged for the mercy of sleep.

"Yes." Natalie had to smile. She'd missed the sun, the palm trees, the fact that people had lanais, and the mercury stayed at a balmy level most of the time.

Once settled in the screened porch facing a canal, Grace let Natalie tell the whole story. To her credit, she didn't interrupt or offer her opinion.

"And so, I left after giving the kids hugs and kisses." Natalie sighed, then took a bite of scone. Chocolate chip. Made with real butter. She wondered if Rachel Miller had ever baked scones before.

"So lovely. And so difficult for you. But now, you know where you have family. Besides your dad."

"Yes, I fell in love with them. And despite what my mother had done, rejecting that faith—rejecting them, too—they didn't hold that against me. Even though I'm not Plain like them."

"Ha. I can't picture you getting up at four a.m. to milk the cows."

"Ha, yourself. I might just become a passable cook one day. My grandmother, or *mammi*, I should say, even taught me how to make a pie crust." Natalie's heart swelled at the recollection. She should have asked for the recipe. However, she had their phone shanty number and address, and could contact them as often as she liked.

"So, to deal with the elephant on the lanai, are you sure you still plan to leave the school? I know I can find someone to take the next set of classes, somehow. But . . ."

It hurt her to leave the school, but leaving Sarasota, at least for part of the year, would help her not miss the Millers as much. On the road, she'd be busy, training and overseeing some of the performers, she'd be working 18-hour days. But she didn't say any of this aloud.

Instead, Natalie said, "I'm sure. I'm sorry, Grace."

"But of course, I did give a glowing reference for you to the circus HR department." Grace gave her own sigh.

"Well, thank you for the reference, and I'm happy you'll be able to find another teacher."

"So, after all this, there's no chance for your *verboten* love? Are you sure?"

"No, I can't live in Ohio. Meeting my mom's family for the first time is something I'll never forget. I'm looking forward to visiting them again, but I'm realistic enough to know I couldn't convert to Old Order, not like that." She was tired of the round, and round, and round. "Jacob likely wouldn't think of moving to Florida permanently, either, especially if being with me means leaving his Order."

"Hmm . . ." Grace stared out at the water. "So, did you ever think about becoming Mennonite?"

"Well, no, I haven't." She hadn't explored that option, didn't think it was one. "I . . ." Joining the Mennonite church wouldn't be forsaking her faith, her whole way of life. The more conservative Mennonites she'd seen in Pinecraft still had cars, electricity, and used technology, although some didn't have televisions. Giving up television altogether wouldn't be such a bad thing, and of course Jacob wouldn't want it in the house.

She thought of her mother's dress and the prayer covering, not so different than what she'd seen the conservative Mennonites wear. The men wore their beards long, like Henry Hostetler did.

"I can see the wheels spinning in your head so fast, there's smoke pouring from your ears." Grace chuckled. "So, what do you think?"

"I think . . . I think after I've had a nice long nap, I should call Mr. Henry Hostetler and see if he can put me in touch with someone from his church." A faint hope bloomed in her heart.

It might not be possible, but she had to investigate the possibilities, at the very least. Then once she had all the information together, maybe, just maybe, someone like Henry Hostetler could talk to Jacob.

Three days ago, Jacob had had a very interesting conversation with Henry Hostetler. Afterward, he felt as if he were standing at the edge of a cliff and someone had just offered him wings, telling him he could fly.

Men weren't made to fly. They weren't birds. Neither were they made to race like the wind in vehicles made of steel. Yet, they did so anyway.

He sat in the break room at Stoltzfus Cabinetry, eating the lunch Rebecca had carefully packed in his insulated cooler. A simple sandwich with beef from last night's supper, some fresh fruit, and a small glass container of milk.

After today, he was off for four days straight. He didn't like the fact his paycheck would just cover expenses for their little household. The bulletin board section listing current job openings at the factory was empty. No hope of a promotion or raise anytime soon.

Yes, despite his efforts, he still had his pride of not taking good enough care of his family. Talking with Henry had reminded him of an opportunity in Florida; and something else he had never considered as a possibility.

The time clock clicked, one minute closer to him having to clock back in for the rest of his shift.

Here came Stan Stoltzfus, his supervisor, and part-owner of the factory. "I saw your note on my desk, Jacob."

"Is that all right? I hope it doesn't put you in a bad position."

"No, not at all, not at all. I appreciate you letting me know." Stan looked thoughtful for a moment. "Just, keep me in informed if anything changes."

"Yes, I definitely will." He nodded.

The rest of the afternoon dragged, just like he knew it would. "Spring fever," some called it. The restlessness he felt surprised even him. Usually he was the one chiding the children to be patient. Now, he was schooling himself in the same discipline. Patience, a fruit of the Spirit. Patience everything would unfold as it should, Lord willing. Some might call him foolish, but then some might call him full of faith.

He remembered what Natalie had told him, echoed three days ago by Henry—he would answer to *Gotte*, and not to man. After he clocked out, during the van ride home he prayed for *Gotte's wille* will to be done.

The children came running to the end of the lane to meet him after work, as they usually did if they weren't seeing to their studies or running around the yard with their cousins.

"You're home," Zeke nearly leapt into his arms. Did he imagine it, or did Zeke cling a little tighter? Jacob had never grown up with hugs like this from his parents, nor had he or Hannah ever hugged them very often. However, since their time in Pinecraft, somehow the hugs and demonstrations of affection had grown more frequent between the three of them. He didn't mind.

"I missed you, *Daed*," Zeke whispered as Jacob leaned over to return the hug. Of course, Jacob had to work, the children had their duties at school. The same had happened in Florida, once Rebecca had recovered from the worst of her injuries.

"I missed you, too." He stood straight, then ruffled Zeke's hair. With his other hand, he touched Rebecca's *kapp*. "How were your days?"

"Rebecca got in trouble for talking too much during class." Zeke released his father.

"Ezekiel Miller, *I* was going to tell him." Rebecca stomped her foot before they continued along the driveway together. "I . . . I was punished, and I apologized."

"We'll talk about it after supper, and a few other things." They ambled along the driveway. Jacob took in the sight of his snug farmhouse, the white picket fence separating it from the rest of the yard—built after Hannah had caught the cows eating the laundry not long after they'd wed.

Some sad memories here, but yes, some happy ones too. The children chattered as they walked along, but Jacob heard the whispering of breezes through the rows of young corn. A cow bellowed out in the pasture somewhere.

He had talked to Ephraim last night about his decision, reached after much prayer and counsel. His brother was still in disbelief. Katie had cried, and Jacob wasn't sure if the tears were joyful or not. *Women*.

Once inside the house, he let the children run ahead of him. Rebecca bragged about learning how to make soap from her Aunt Katie, and Zeke chattered about the frog he'd almost caught in the garden.

"Rebecca and Ezekiel, I have something to tell you." He motioned to the chairs in the front room, one on each side of the fireplace.

They both complied. Rebecca opened her mouth as if to say something, but Jacob waved his pointer finger and she closed her mouth.

"Tonight, you are going to stay with your aunt and uncle for a few days, because I won't be home. I'm going to make a trip."

"You're going away?"

Jacob didn't miss the quaver in Zeke's voice.

29

"Thank you, thank you very much." Natalie ended the phone call. She wasn't sure she'd made the right decision and wanted to apologize to Grace for causing her even a few moments of worry.

She looked around her apartment. On her budget, a good apartment in a decent neighborhood was hard to come by, and this place had served her well. Natalie sucked in a deep breath at the thought of the changes that lay ahead for her. Good changes. Necessary changes.

Her breath shuddered. She needed to get some air. The world's most beautiful beach was minutes away by car. Siesta Key and the waters of the Gulf of Mexico would soothe her. She hadn't been there since the last day, when Jacob met her before he ran away back to Ohio.

Natalie had sent the children a letter. She didn't want to make it any more painful for them than it already seemed when she left Ohio. But kids were resilient. She knew it first-hand, growing up as she had.

She stopped by Rachel's in Pinecraft, paying no mind to the curious looks the neighbors gave her as she left her car and strode to the front door. Yes, she was still Natalie.

When Rachel opened the door, she did a double-take. "Well, look at you. My, my."

Natalie touched her hair, caught up into a bun and pinned, covered with the same *kapp* her mother had once wore. Women owned more than one. She supposed there must be a store, somewhere, although she'd never seen a *kapp* store in Sarasota. Rachel would know, and would help. And Imogene, once she knew.

She tugged at the waist of the Plain dress. "I . . . I thought I would try this on. I think it could use a little taking in? But then, you already know about my sewing skills. I'm not dressing up, you know. This . . . this isn't a costume, to me."

Rachel nodded. "Henry has filled me in about everything."

Natalie continued. "I've talked to his bishop at the Mennonite church, and they've welcomed me. Not as a member yet."

"No, not yet. But I think you'll find the Mennonite church more to your liking. And, the services are in English, so you'll follow along just fine."

"I'm not planning to stay long today, I just thought I'd stop by to say hello on my way to Siesta Key Beach."

"Well, hello then. They're having a haystack supper Saturday night at the park, in case you didn't know."

"No, I didn't."

"It might take a while before some don't question your motives." Rachel studied the dress. "Yes, it's a mite big on you. But that's easily fixed."

"*Mammi* Rachel, the best motive in the world is what's moving me to do this."

"I pray you find clear direction, then." The older woman smiled at her.

"Thank you." She almost hugged Rachel, then reconsidered.

With that, Natalie got back into her car and continued on her way until she reached the sparkling waters of the Gulf of

Mexico. So much water reminded her of how small she was in the scheme of things. Did it matter what she wore? Yes, and no.

She pulled off her flats and walked barefooted onto the sand, warm from the day's heat. This was another reason she wouldn't live in Ohio. Maybe, when the time was right, she'd tell Jacob and the children of her decision. Maybe, if it wasn't too late for her and Jacob, but she didn't linger on that thought.

She couldn't make a change like this, just for Jacob. She'd told the Mennonite bishop that to her, joining the church felt like coming home again. Her parents had done the best they could while raising her.

Dad, now, she hadn't called him to tell him of her decision. Openminded though he was, she had a few reservations about his reaction. However, Dad being Dad, would fill her in on all the details of his new family. She didn't begrudge him his happiness. Not anymore.

She wanted the same second chance for Jacob, if not with her, then someone else. Although Jacob hadn't sounded very enthusiastic at the prospect of Anne Troyer, who she'd heard was very much available in Ohio. If he stayed there, which he likely would, his world would remain undisturbed. Life would go on. Hers had.

Natalie wiggled her toes in the sand and inhaled the air. She had the beach virtually to herself, with a few beach-combers down by the water. People were at work, children in school. No one paid her any mind, her wearing her mother's cape dress. She walked to the water's edge to see if any shells worth collecting had washed ashore. Much as she used to enjoy swimming in the ocean, she wondered if the Mennonites swam. Wasn't there some super-modest swimwear available? She imagined there was.

She'd attended several services at the Mennonite Church and found warmth of new friends. She enjoyed the simple yet profound Bible teaching, the earnest testimony and prayers. The bishop and his wife weren't too much older than her and had a gaggle of children whose energy reminded her of Zeke and Rebecca. Yes, there were a few single men at the church, but she paid them no mind.

Maybe she couldn't be Amish, but she could meet her family halfway. In this new fellowship, she felt like part of her had come home, the part that had always longed for a circle of family. If only Jacob—

Her phone warbled, the mysterious Sarasota number that had once turned out to be Jacob's. Her heart leapt.

"Hello?"

"Hello, Natalie." *Jacob!* He continued to speak, his voice cutting in and out because of the breeze whipping the phone's mouthpiece.

She had to hold the phone completely against her ear to make out what his words. "I can't quite hear you, Jacob?"

"I said, did you find any shells?" a familiar voice sounded behind her, plus echoed in her ear.

"What?" She turned. It couldn't be him. Not here. "You—you're *here*."

Jacob had hopped the next bus to Siesta Key, as soon as *Mammi* had told him where Natalie was headed. He easily found her car, its Pathway to the Stars Circus School decal on the back window, in the parking lot. However, scanning the beach at first, he didn't see her.

Then he saw a lone figure wearing a cape dress and *kapp*, at the water's edge. Surely not—

So he'd found her number in his phone and pushed the button, glad he hadn't erased it.

The look on her face made him smile now.

"Yes, I'm here. Two days on a bus, and I'm here." He almost reached out to touch her cheek. "Natalie . . ."

"But the children? Did they come, too?"

"They're in Ohio. I came—I came to set things right between us. I've been talking to Henry . . ."

"You have?" He couldn't discern the expression on her face, but he was still pondering the idea of seeing her wear a cape dress. He had a flashback of the curves he knew existed underneath, and swallowed hard. *Easy, man. She isn't your wife.*

Natalie nodded. "Me too. I'm . . . I'm going to the Mennonite church now. Um, it'll be quite a while before I'm eligible to be baptized as a member, but I like it. The bishop and his wife are kind, the others as well. I feel at home there." Her cheeks shot with pink. "The Mennonite school needs a teacher's helper, so I'm going to work there instead of the circus school. I think that's a good compromise. I'm downsizing, too. Grace and her husband are going to rent me a room. Until I can find something closer, in the village."

"I spoke to the Mennonite bishop by phone." This time, Jacob took her hand in both of his. "He talked with my Ohio bishop. It seems, uh, there are special cases sometimes where an Amish from Ohio can attend the Mennonite church here in Sarasota, and it's not considered leaving the Order."

"I would have never, ever asked you to do that. All I ever wanted was a compromise, but I didn't know how." Her voice trembled.

"And I didn't believe it was possible, either." Jacob frowned. "I wasted precious time . . ."

"Stop, Jacob. You needed time, as did I. So, does that mean . . . ?"

"The children and I will be moving to Florida as soon as school is over this spring. Henry needs me here, and I can make more money than I did in Ohio to support us." *Us*. He liked the sound of that.

"You're moving, here? To Sarasota, and Pinecraft?"

"Yes, that's exactly what I said."

The wide smile he loved spread across Natalie's face. She threw her arms around him. "Oh, Jacob!" He held her close, breathing in the scent of her hair. Whatever shampoo or soap it was, he hoped she wouldn't stop using it.

"We likely can't marry until our proving time is over," he murmured in her ear.

"I can wait . . . I think." She clung to him. "Not that it'll be easy."

"No, it won't. I think" He allowed himself to kiss her. "But the wait will be worth it."

"I'm sure it will." She gave him a saucy look of her own. "I'm ready, Jacob. This is what I know is meant for me. I have no doubt."

The church would have questions for them, to be sure, during their proving time. Were they both sincere? They would go through their proving, for them to join the Mennonite church. He gave her a long look after the kiss.

He held her close once more, not trusting his voice. He never imagined the tragedy of nearly six months ago would have led them to now, but he knew he would thank God every day for the remarkable gift who had shown up in a hospital room at Christmas time.

He finally found his voice again. "I loved you fancy, Natalie Bennett, and I love you Plain."

"Jacob Miller, I love you, too."

THE END

AUTHOR'S NOTE

The village of Pinecraft in Sarasota, Florida, is indeed a real place where thousands of Amish and Mennonites from across the country like to spend time during the winter. Yoder's Restaurant, Big Olaf's Creamery, and Emma's Village Pizza are very real places. The Haiti Benefit Auction is a winter highlight annually.

However, the characters in this book are fictional except for the mention of a man named Henry, an Old Order Amish man who makes a fabulous cowboy stew. The character of Imogene Brubaker is loosely based on a Pinecraft resident who is an avid photographer and blogger.

My research was thorough during my visits to Pinecraft; however, any inaccuracies in the Amish and Mennonite lifestyles portrayed in this book are completely due to fictional license, and Pinecraft is unlike most other Amish-Mennonite communities.

Glossary

Ach—oh

Aenti—aunt

Boppli—baby

Bruder—brother

Daadi—grandfather

Daed—father

Danke—thank you

Dietsch—Pennsylvania Dutch

Dochder—daughter

Englisch—non-Amish

Gotte's wille—God's will

Gut—good

Kaffi—coffee

Kapp—prayer covering

Kind—child

Kinner—children

Mamm—mom

Mammi—grandma

Mudder—mother

Naerfich—nervous

Nein—no

Onkel—uncle

Ordnung—set of rules for Amish living

Rumspringa—running around; time before an Amish young person has officially joined the church, provides a bridge between childhood and adulthood

Verboten—forbidden

Ya—yes

Discussion Questions

1. Who was your favorite character in the village of Pinecraft?

2. Illness and other troubles don't take holidays, as the Miller family knows. What are some ways to celebrate holidays during a time of illness and other personal stress?

3. Jacob struggles with what he believes are worldly compromises while living in Pinecraft. How do you decide what's harmless and what's compromise?

4. What is your favorite theme in A Season of Change?

5. Natalie deals with a blended family. What advice would you give her about maintaining a relationship with her father, stepmother, and much younger half-sibling?

6. Betsy Yoder decides to stay in Pinecraft in the hopes that Jacob will notice her. How would you counsel a young woman wanting to make such a potentially life-altering decision?

7. Natalie has never quilted before, but she learns how to quilt from Rachel Miller. What new skill have you learned that you've never tried before?

8. What is the most surprising thing you learned about the Amish in this book?

9. Rebecca Yoder is a rather precocious, adventurous child. What kind of things did you get into when you were a youngster?

10. The Haiti Benefit Auction has a wide variety of food made by the Amish. What's your favorite Amish meal or dessert?

Want to learn more about Lynette Sowell
And check out other great fiction from
Abingdon Press?

Check out our website at
www.AbingdonPress.com
to read interviews with your favorite authors,
find tips for starting a reading group,
and stay posted on what new titles
are on the horizon.

Be sure to visit Lynette online!

https://www.facebook.com/lynettesowellauthor